T0195996

Also by Gin Jones

Garlic Farm Mysteries
Six Cloves Under
Rhubarb Pie Before You Die

Helen Binney Mysteries
A Dose of Death
A Denial of Death
A Draw of Death
"A (Gingerbread) Diorama of Death" (short story in *Cozy Christmas Shorts*)
A Dawn of Death
A Darling of Death
A Display of Death

Danger Cove Quilting Mysteries
Four Patch of Trouble
Tree of Life and Death
Robbing Peter to Kill Paul
Deadly Thanksgiving Sampler
"Not-So-Bright Hopes" (short story in *Pushing Up Daisies*)

Danger Cove Farmers' Market Mysteries
"A Killing in the Market" (short story in *Killer Beach Reads*)
A Death in the Flower Garden
A Slaying in the Orchard
A Secret in the Pumpkin Patch
Two Sleuths Are Better Than One

Laid Out in Lavender

A Garlic Farm Mystery

Gin Jones

LYRICAL UNDERGROUND
Kensington Publishing Corp.
www.kensingtonbooks.com

LYRICAL UNDERGROUND BOOKS are published by
Kensington Publishing Corp.
119 West 40th Street
New York, NY 10018

All Kensington titles, imprints, and distributed lines are available at special quantity discounts for bulk purchases for sales promotion, premiums, fund-raising, educational, or institutional use.

Special book excerpts or customized printings can also be created to fit specific needs. For details, write or phone the office of the Kensington Sales Manager: Kensington Publishing Corp., 119 West 40th Street, New York, NY 10018. Attn. Sales Department. Phone: 1-800-221-2647.

Lyrical Underground and Lyrical Underground logo Reg. US Pat. & TM Off.

First Electronic Edition: April 2021
ISBN-13: 978-1-5161-0960-0 (ebook)
ISBN-10: 1-5161-0960-0 (ebook)

First Print Edition: April 2021
ISBN-13: 978-1-5161-0963-0
ISBN-10: 1-5161-0963-5

Printed in the United States of America

CHAPTER ONE

"I'm going to kill that woman," Emily Colter announced as she burst through the Skinner Farm's kitchen door and made a beeline for the harvest-gold refrigerator. Emily had traded in her usual white painter's overalls for a caterer's outfit consisting of a white apron over a black shirt and pants. She was in her mid-twenties, and looked like the tall, blond trophy wife she had been until about two months earlier. "Unless she kills me first by suffocating me with the gallons of lavender perfume she's wearing."

"I'd really rather no one died." Mabel Skinner closed the laptop in front of her at the kitchen table. "We've had enough death here already."

Emily's face fell. "I'm so sorry. I didn't mean any disrespect to your aunt."

"I know." Mabel glanced at the laptop that held her notes about a promising candidate for the job of farm manager. If he was as good as his résumé suggested, hiring him would let her go back to her usual work as an app developer. She'd been trying to fill the position for the past eight months with no qualified candidates applying until now. Unfortunately, Richard Wetzel had only been available for an in-person visit today, which was less than ideal timing. The farm was hosting a wedding for the first time, with the rehearsal and related photography sessions underway already out in the lavender field and the ceremony scheduled for the next afternoon. Emily had been setting up the buffet for the wedding party on the patio outside the kitchen before she'd come inside to announce her homicidal intentions.

Mabel pushed aside her laptop. She was desperate to hire a manager for the farm, or she would never have agreed to schedule the interview at the same time as the wedding events. Wetzel had all the necessary qualifications, according to all the books she'd consulted, and she was as prepared for the interview as she'd ever be, so until he arrived, she had to focus on making sure the wedding events went smoothly.

It had sounded so simple when Emily first suggested the project as something that could benefit them both, but Emily's usual serenity had been shaken recently. This was her first major contract as a caterer, and she needed to make a success of it in order to grow her new business. Mabel needed it to go well, too, since, according to Aunt Peggy's records, the income from renting out the lavender fields as a backdrop for pictures had gone a long way to keeping the farm financially stable. Mabel had hoped to expand the service from just a setting for pictures to hosting the entire wedding weekend on the farm, for a significantly larger fee. If today was a success and the property could be rented out regularly at a time when not much else was going on in the fields, then it could help keep the farm sustainable, regardless of what Mother Nature might do to the crops.

"Who's the woman annoying you?" Mabel asked.

The planner, Paige Middleton." Emily had retrieved the pitcher of Mabel's iced tea from the refrigerator and was pouring herself a large glass. "You know how brides have a reputation for turning into lunatics over their weddings, making extra work for their planners? Well, Donna Markos is the most laid-back person I've ever met, and instead it's her planner who's the crazy one. Do you know what she just asked me?"

"No." Mabel went over to the sink to fill the kettle for a new batch of iced tea. It sounded like they were both going to need it to get through the day.

"She wants me to change the lavender-flavored wedding cake and make it lemon instead, because she just found out the bride is allergic to lavender." Emily took a long swig of iced tea and set the glass down with an emphatic thump. "Can you believe she thinks I can produce a whole new wedding cake with only twenty-four hours left before the wedding? I don't have time to make another one myself, and it's the peak of wedding season, so it's not like I can get someone else to make it for me. Bakers are booked to capacity and beyond. I'm just glad I decided not to add lavender to today's cheesecake bars, and I have extras for tomorrow, so there will be at least one dessert the bride can eat."

Mabel wrinkled her nose. "I'm glad too. I don't like lavender any more than my aunt did, and those bars are fabulous without it."

Emily brushed away a tear of frustration. "I wish I could just tell Paige to stuff it, but I really need this job to go well, and I need her to give me a good reference. Catering is the only way I'll be able to earn enough to keep my goats."

Emily's estranged husband had recently given her an ultimatum along with the divorce papers—if she couldn't earn enough money on her own within six months to prove she could cover all the expenses of keeping her goats at what had been their marital home, then it would have to be sold as part of the court proceedings. Emily was convinced she'd also have to sell the goats in that case, since she wouldn't be able to afford another farm for them to live on, and it would break her heart if she had to let them go. The goats were working animals, producing milk for the artisanal cheese she sold at the farmers' market, but she also loved them like pets.

"I'm sure the bride will give you a good reference, even if the planner won't," Mabel said. "And unlike the planner, the bride is local and probably knows more people around here who could use your catering services."

"It's like the planner is trying to ruin both the wedding and me," Emily said as if she hadn't heard Mabel's reassurances. Her usually sweet face turned dark. "I bet my not-soon-enough-ex-husband-to-be paid her to sabotage everything. He's determined to hurt me any way he can, and he knows it would kill me to have to sell my goats. I can't let him get away with it, and catering is the only skill I have that would earn me enough to cover the farm's expenses."

"You've still got four months left. And you've got Rory on your side." Rory Hansen was a mutual friend, the wife of a local police officer, and the moving force behind the local Community Supported Agriculture group. She knew everyone in town, and most people tended to do whatever she asked them to, although sometimes they had to be dragged into doing the right thing. Mabel herself had found herself doing things she'd had reservations about, simply because Rory insisted. "She's been promoting your new catering business to everyone in town."

Emily wasn't willing to be mollified. "Having Rory on my side would be enough in most circumstances, but my husband doesn't fight fair. If he did, he never would have carried on with a colleague behind my back for months and then had divorce papers served on me with no warning."

He had been unnecessarily cruel, but there was nothing Mabel could think of to make her friend feel better, so she settled for saying, "I'm sorry."

"He's such a jerk," Emily said before launching into a rant about how, after he'd been sure the papers had already been served, he'd called from his new girlfriend's house to explain that he'd had enough of his wife's "artsy-fartsy, new-agey ways" and she needed to learn to live in the real world.

Mabel went about brewing the tea while her friend vented. She tuned out a bit, since she'd heard it before. The water had boiled, the leaves had steeped and been removed, and ice cubes had been added to the pitcher before Emily wound down.

"I'll show him a real world he never imagined," Emily said with quiet determination. "I'm going to be the most successful caterer in West Slocum, maybe even all of western Massachusetts, and then I'll buy *more* goats, and he won't be able to stop me."

That was better, Mabel thought. Emily wasn't her usual sunny self, but at least she wasn't giving up either. After today's wedding reception, when everyone told her how wonderful her food was, she might even lose a bit of the anxiety that had dogged her for the last two months.

"Is there anything I can do to help so you'll be ready for the rehearsal dinner?"

"Thanks, but I can handle it, and you've got a lot to do today already," Emily said. "That reminds me, how did it go with the candidate for the farm manager position?"

"I haven't finished interviewing Richard Wetzel yet," Mabel said. "We'd barely introduced ourselves after he arrived, and he insisted on viewing the property before we talked in depth, to make sure it was something he thought was worth his time. Apparently he's been looking for just the right farm for the last two years, and nothing has quite lived up to his expectations. He was particularly impressed when I told him we had our own water source, so he headed out in the direction of the creek to inspect that first."

Unfortunately, Mabel didn't think he'd approve of it. She'd briefly described the main features of the farm before he'd headed out on his own, and even without viewing them closely, he'd made it clear that he considered them inferior to what was on the farm he'd grown up on. She half-expected him to report back that water didn't flow downhill on his family's farm, so the creek was clearly doing it wrong and would have to be fixed if he took the job.

Emily had enough to worry about at the moment, so Mabel didn't share her less-than-optimistic expectation for hiring Wetzel. "He should be back soon, but until he returns I can help with the buffet if you want. As long as I don't have to cook anything."

Emily laughed. "I'd love to sic you on the wedding planner, but you'd probably find her even more annoying than I do. Perhaps you could keep an eye on the patio while I go out to the lavender field to try to talk some sense into her. The best man, Thad Dalton, keeps sneaking back here to sample the food, or worse, to light up a cigarette while he's snacking instead of using the smoking stations away from the patio. It's like he thinks no one can see him as long as he's on the other side of the buffet table, where it's supposed to be staff only. Keeping the guests where they belong is the planner's job, but of course she isn't doing it. I wouldn't mind so much if he just sneaked some tidbits discreetly—there's way more than enough food for everyone—but he dives into everything practically headfirst, and leaves the dishes looking like wild animals got at them. And then he throws his cigarette butts all over the ground nearby, stinking up the place so no one can even appreciate the food."

"I can definitely guard the buffet for you while you talk to Paige. If Wetzel comes back while you're gone, I can still keep an eye on the best man while I do the interview."

"Thanks. After the last mess Thad made, I filled a couple plates with a ton of food and put a little flag in each of them with his name. They're on the back side of the buffet table, so if he shows up, you can just grab them and offer them to him. I should be done with the planner and back here before he can finish both plates. I hope. It's hard to believe a guy who's as skinny as he is could eat that much." Emily glanced out the window and squeaked. "Never mind. He's here again. I'll go give him the first plate before I go find Paige."

* * * *

Mabel followed Emily outside, both to keep an eye on Thad Dalton and to watch for Wetzel's return from checking out the farm. The patio, designed for Aunt Peggy's parties, attended by half of West Slocum's residents and almost as many more from farther away, ran the entire length of the farmhouse's back wall and about thirty feet deep. To Mabel's left, near the far end of the patio, a pair of buffet tables were set up across its width, separating the serving area from the dining area, which held five widely spaced six-person round tables for the rehearsal dinner. Additional tables were stored behind the buffet table for the wedding reception's larger crowd on Saturday.

She'd been counting on Emily and the other contractors to take care of everything without Mabel having to do much more than make a few quick appearances to greet the bride and groom, and maybe check back with them later to make sure everything had gone smoothly. Then she could have spent most of the day in her home office, doing her real work as an app developer, with just a brief break to interview the candidate for the manager position. She wasn't going to be able to do that if the wedding planner was as flaky as Emily said, and there was no reason to doubt her, since she always seemed to see the best in everyone, except perhaps for her soon-to-be-ex-husband. Emily would be too busy with food service to oversee the planner as well, so if Mabel wanted the wedding to be a success, she was going to have to be the one who smoothed over any problems.

Heaven help them all.

Smoothing over personal problems had never been Mabel's strong point. She could fix a buggy app with ease, but when it came to dealing with misbehaving people instead of code, she was more likely to cause problems than solve them. Fortunately, she didn't have to actually talk to Thad yet, since Emily had lured him over to the table farthest away from the buffet. He seemed content enough there, alternately studying the contents of the plate she'd given him and pouring a visible layer of salt on anything that wasn't sweet. Mabel settled at a table near the buffet, so she could allow him some privacy while also being well-situated to guard the beautifully displayed food from his pillaging.

Since Thad appeared fully occupied, Mabel took advantage of what she expected to be a brief bit of calm to appreciate her surroundings. Even for someone more comfortable indoors, all alone in her room and hunched over a computer, it was far from a hardship to sit outside on an idyllic June day. Everything on the farm was green with potential, and there wasn't any pressing work to be done in the fields over the next few weeks. She and her workers had recently finished seeding the squash in May, and the harvesting of the fall-planted garlic wouldn't happen until July. June was mostly for maintenance, which her employees could handle on their own, probably better than she could herself.

Over the past eleven months, she had come to understand—in her heart, not just in her head—why Aunt Peggy had loved the farm so much. The beauty and serenity almost made Mabel want to stay on the place even after she hired a manager, but there were too many distractions on the farm that kept her from concentrating on her real work as an app developer. And nothing could ever make her appreciate getting up with the literal early birds as she'd done during the planting season and then again today to make sure everything was as perfect as possible for the wedding rehearsal. This event could make or break both her farm's bottom line and Emily's. And until Mabel had handed off responsibility for the farm to a manager, she would do whatever was necessary to keep her aunt's legacy sustainable. Even if it meant getting up at dawn. And mingling with strangers.

Mabel shuddered. The sooner she hired a manager, the better.

She glanced out toward the fields to see if she could spot the manager candidate wandering around out there. He wasn't on any of the tractor paths that ran through the farm and divided the fields, or with the guests out near the lavender crop, or in any of the areas where garlic was growing in neat rows, rapidly approaching its maximum height. From this distance, she couldn't see the inter-planted squash seedlings that had only sprouted in the last ten days but would completely fill in the beds after the garlic was harvested. Her part-time field hand, Terry Earley, was wielding a hoe around the garlic in the field nearest the lavender one that served as a backdrop for photographs of the wedding party. A wheelbarrow overflowing with mulch—purchased straw this time, not grass clippings acquired in a midnight raid—was parked in a path near Terry for use in covering any bare spots.

Mabel's reverie was interrupted by the sound of Pixie yowling—the cat's standard announcement of a vehicle turning into the driveway—loud enough to be heard easily through the kitchen's screen door. She'd been shut in Aunt Peggy's office, so there would be no chance of someone letting her out in the chaos of the rehearsal dinner, but the inner closed door had done little to muffle her piercing screech. Given how many visitors had arrived already, it was surprising Pixie hadn't given herself laryngitis, but if anything, her warning cries seemed to have grown louder as the day progressed and the total number of visitors increased.

Mabel confirmed that Thad still had a huge amount of food to eat, so he wouldn't be likely to raid the buffet again any time soon, before heading over to the driveway to see whose arrival Pixie had been announcing. As far as Mabel knew, the entire wedding party had already arrived and gone out to the lavender field, but perhaps someone was late and would need to be escorted out to where the pictures were being taken.

An older-model compact car came to a stop in the middle of the driveway and idled there, its owner apparently not sure where to park. Mabel had moved her own Mini Cooper into the front yard, and then asked Terry to move the farm's truck out of its usual spot in front of the barn, leaving the parking spaces there for the two dozen or so people attending the rehearsal. The guests had filled the area in front of the barn and even double-parked a couple of vehicles, leaving nowhere obvious for the newcomer to park.

Mabel gestured for the driver to put his vehicle next to her Mini Cooper on the front lawn and followed to greet him.

A middle-aged man climbed out of the car and went around to the passenger-side door. His clothes didn't give any indication of why he was there. He was dressed casually, for the most part, in khaki pants, a dark polo shirt, and a rumpled tweed sports jacket. The only note of formality was the gray fedora with a black band, which made Mabel think of 1920s gangsters. The hat had a bright yellow piece of laminated paper stuck into the band with the word *press* on it.

Now she knew who he was, and she was already having second thoughts about having invited him. She'd been counting on giving him her full attention for the brief time he was on the farm, but she didn't even have that much time to spare for him.

The man bent to grab a tablet and a Nikon camera from the passenger seat before slamming the door shut and heading for Mabel. He draped the strap of the camera around his neck as he walked, the weight of its massive professional lens tipping him forward to lean at an uncomfortable angle as he walked.

"Do you know where I can find the farm's owner?" He straightened when he came to a stop in front of Mabel. "I'm Andrew Rainey with the *Times*."

The pride and gravitas in his tone made it sound like he worked for the *New York Times*, but Mabel knew he was actually affiliated with a small regional paper here in western Massachusetts. It featured a lot of local sports and town politics, along with fluff pieces and syndicated columns, nothing that would count as investigative journalism or even serious news. Still, she couldn't complain, since she was hoping he'd do a fluff piece on the farm to get it some free publicity for the expanded services offered for weddings.

"You found her. I'm Mabel Skinner."

He pointed toward the lavender field. "And that's where the wedding rehearsal is happening, right? For the soon-to-be Mr. and Mrs. Bellingham?"

"It is."

"I was hoping to get a few pictures of the rehearsal. I'm not just an award-winning reporter, but an acclaimed photographer too. I used to do my own prints to get them just the way I wanted them, although nowadays, with digital technology, I can make the adjustments on the computer instead."

"Then turn your camera on the farm," Mabel said. "You're here to write about the sustainability of small farms, not weddings." At least that was what he'd claimed when he'd gotten her permission to visit the farm on the day of the wedding.

"You said that having additional streams of income is part of sustainability, so the wedding is part of my story. Besides, a good journalist can spin facts any number of ways and is ready to jump on any opportunity that presents itself. This is the social event of the century for West Slocum.

Did you know that Bellingham was born and raised right here by a single mother, and then went on to become one of the richest people in the state?"

She hadn't known that, but presumably, if true, the groom's upbringing and wealth were well-known by people who cared about such things. "That's not news. Neither is his wedding or his upcoming retirement. They were announced months ago, so there's nothing happening here that's worth writing about."

"I'm the one who decides what's worth writing about." Rainey pointed to his chest as he spoke, only to get his hand tangled in the strap of the camera.

"You can ask Mr. Bellingham if he's willing to be interviewed, but only after the rehearsal is over," Mabel said, ushering him past Thad and over to the table she'd vacated on the patio. He could interview her there while she also kept an eye on the best man. At least Thad was still where she'd left him, working his way through the plate Emily had filled for him, instead of raiding the buffet table or smoking near the food.

Once they were seated, Rainey said, "I'll need to talk to Bellingham's business partner too. Rumor has it, being best man is all part of the price for buying the company. Bellingham couldn't find anyone else to stand with him at the altar, so he put in their contract that the sale won't go through until the marriage happens. It's a great story—money can't buy you friends, but it can buy you a best man. I just need confirmation from someone with firsthand knowledge before I can write it."

Mabel forced herself not to look in Thad's direction, since apparently Rainey hadn't recognized him. "You need to wait until the rehearsal is over to talk to anyone involved with the wedding, and even then, I expect you to be discreet about it."

Rainey shrugged. "Discreet doesn't get the story."

"Then you'll have to leave right now," Mabel said. "I won't have my guests disturbed."

"What about the story on your little farm? If I leave, I can't write it."

Mabel couldn't afford to alienate Rainey completely. She needed the publicity about the use of the farm for weddings to get more bookings. And Emily needed some good press to get her catering business launched.

Perhaps she could guide him toward the topic he was supposed to be writing about. "We might as well talk now before the rehearsal is over. What do you need to know about why I rent out the farm to weddings, or the other things I do to ensure the sustainability of my aunt's farm?"

Rainey glanced around him at what even her biased eyes could see was an ordinary little farmhouse with an average-looking little barn, surrounded by only about ten acres of land. It didn't look like much in objective terms, but she knew how much effort had gone into creating all the fields of garlic and the one of lavender. She'd had just a small taste of the work recently while planting a previously unused section of the farm with a few hundred rhubarb roots.

"To be honest," Rainey said, "There's not much of a story here. You've got a basic little hobby farm."

He said the last two words with extreme disdain, confirming that he had definitely lied when he'd claimed to be interested in the extraordinary efforts small farmers had to take to stay afloat these days. Mabel had never heard the "hobby farm" term before moving to West Slocum, but she'd since learned that it was often used as an insult, a put-down meant to distinguish the property from a "real" farm, which apparently had to consist of hundreds, if not thousands, of acres, and produce enough food that it had to be transported thousands of miles to find a market. Some farmers were trying to reclaim the "hobby farm" label as a badge of honor, but Rainey clearly hadn't meant it that way.

"Not everyone wants to feed the world," Mabel said, trying not to sound defensive. "My aunt was satisfied with feeding her neighbors, but it's hard to do that and still turn a profit. That's why I'm trying to expand on her work by diversifying the streams of income with things like adding niche crops and hosting weddings."

"Good luck with that," Rainey said, not bothering to hide his insincerity. "So, when will the rehearsal be over?"

Mabel was distracted by the sight of Thad getting to his feet. His first plate was still about a third full, but he seemed to have decided that he needed seconds on something that had been particularly tasty before attacking the rest of what was already in front of him.

"Sorry," she told Rainey as she jumped to her feet. "I need to take care of something. I don't know when the rehearsal will end exactly, so you can ask for an interview, although it should be at least another hour or so, since the buffet isn't scheduled to open until then. While you're waiting, you can go talk to my employee, Terry, if you'd like." She pointed to where he was working. "Maybe he can convince you that the farm is worth writing about."

Rainey started to object, so Mabel added, "And if you're not interested in talking to Terry about the farm, then you need to leave right now."

CHAPTER TWO

As soon as Rainey started to get to his feet to head out into the garlic field, however reluctantly, Mabel raced over to intercept Thad before he could ravage Emily's beautiful buffet again.

"Shouldn't you be out with the wedding party?" Mabel asked Thad, maneuvering past him to stand between him and the buffet table.

Thad's face was as round as the rest of him was lean, and the softness of his features made him look like he was about twenty-five rather than the mid-forties he had to be. According to Emily, he'd worked for the groom for more than fifteen years, straight out of business school, and then had been his own boss as junior partner for the next five.

In keeping with Thad's role as best man, he wore a lightweight business suit for the rehearsal, but his behavior hadn't shown any respect for the event. At the moment, he had a linen napkin tucked into his collar to cover his shirt and tie so he could continue to eat while the rehearsal went on without him. Of course, from what Mabel had seen, the groom wasn't being all that much more attentive, since every time she'd caught sight of him, he'd been apart from the wedding party, doing something on his phone. Mostly reading or texting, as opposed to disruptively carrying on a conversation, but definitely not paying much attention to the rehearsal.

Thad waved a hand dismissively. "They don't need me for the pictures. I'm not particularly close to anyone involved. Stan only asked me to stand with him because he doesn't have any actual friends. He's brilliant, but terrible with people."

That was exactly how Mabel herself was often described, especially by her boss. *She's brilliant, but don't ever, ever let her talk directly to clients.* She had a sudden burst of sympathy for the groom, who'd originally struck her as distant and snobbish, but it sounded like his standoffish behavior was due to social awkwardness rather than a feeling that he was too good or too important to interact with mere staff. He was probably used to delegating all the socializing to someone else, like his bride or his business partner, and was as awkward as she herself was when she had to make small talk.

"Stan's lucky to have you as his business partner."

"He is, isn't he?" Thad reached around Mabel to grab a roll, knocking several others off the neatly stacked pyramid and onto the table. "For the past ten years, I've had to do all the socializing for the company. Today is just more of the same, as far as I'm concerned. A business obligation. I don't feel the need to stick around and watch when I'm not actually part of the proceedings. Especially when the food is so much better than at most business events I attend."

Mabel picked up the rolls that fortunately hadn't continued across the linen tablecloth to land on the ground and returned them to the pyramid as best she could. At least Thad hadn't decided to cut into one of the goats'-milk quiches. Yet.

"I hope you'll tell everyone how good the catering is," Mabel said as she steered Thad back toward his original plate of food. "It's by Emily Colter, and her name and contact information will be in the wedding program if you ever need a caterer."

"Sure," he said, stopping and refusing to return to his plate. He looked over his shoulder at the buffet table. "The only thing missing is something to drink."

Mabel refrained from telling him that was because the buffet wasn't open yet. "I could get you some water. Or iced tea. I make excellent iced tea."

"Nah. What I really want is a nice glass of wine to quench my thirst and complement the food. They must have some behind the table, keeping it out of sight until the guests arrive."

"The beverages haven't been unpacked yet," Mabel said, although she didn't know if that was true. She just needed to keep him from doing any more damage to Emily's work.

Undaunted, Thad stepped to the side to go around her. "I'll just have some more of the fruit salad then. It will keep me hydrated until the wine is available."

Mabel hurried to block him again. "Why don't I get it for you?" She'd prefer to give him the second plate Emily had prepared, but it would look odd if she gave him a variety of foods instead of just the requested fruit salad. Still, she could serve him what he wanted more neatly than if Thad helped himself. At least she'd try, while he wouldn't bother to be inconspicuous about his inroads into the dishes. "You're a guest, after all. Go on back to your seat, and I'll serve you."

Thad frowned slightly. "Who are you, anyway?"

"Mabel Skinner, the owner of the farm." Pride welled up unexpectedly. She still tended to think of the farm as her aunt's, but between the grueling work of last fall's garlic planting and then the addition of the rhubarb field this spring, she was starting to feel like she deserved to claim at least some ownership.

"Ah," he said. "In that case, I would like some fruit salad. And not just a tiny spoonful, but a man-sized serving." He didn't wait for her agreement before heading back to the table, where his plate and saltshaker were waiting for him.

Mabel went over to the buffet, where a huge bowl of fruit salad was on display at one end, along with what she recognized as the cheesecake bars that thankfully were not flavored with lavender. She grabbed a dessert plate to fill for Thad, but was reluctant to dig into the fruit salad that had been topped with a layer of strawberries cut to look like roses, with edible mint leaves replacing the original flavorless ones. She remembered seeing more of the salad, all mixed together in a gallon-sized glass jar in her refrigerator but without the pretty toppings, for use in refilling the serving bowl.

"I'll be right back," she told Thad as she headed for her kitchen. "You'll want the fruit salad from indoors, where it's perfectly chilled."

He grunted in apparent acceptance without pausing in his attack on the remaining mound of food on his plate, except to shake on more salt.

Inside, Mabel spooned out some fruit salad, considered how quickly Thad would go through the already super-sized serving, and topped it off with another large scoop. She added a big dollop of whipped cream made out of goats' milk and raced out to deliver it before Thad could get restless again.

* * * *

Mabel was in the midst of plunking the fruit salad on Thad's table with less than proper food-service cheerfulness when she heard her name called.

She looked over to where the patio opened onto the driveway to see the wedding photographer, Ken Linden, escorting the bride in Mabel's direction. Donna Markos was wearing a fitted sleeveless lilac-colored sheath that fell to just below her knees. If Mabel hadn't been introduced to everyone earlier, she'd have assumed the couple were the bride and groom. They were around the same age, in their late fifties, and he was as formally dressed as she was in an impeccable linen suit, while the actual husband-to-be was still out near the lavender field in his shirtsleeves, having set aside the jacket of his ill-fitting suit. Ken didn't have the camera with him that would have marked him as a contractor instead of the groom, and he hovered over the bride like a solicitous lover, while she gripped his arm tightly as if requiring support, both emotional and physical, to walk along the dirt tractor path. Mabel glanced down at the woman's feet, but she was wearing sensible flats that shouldn't have posed a problem for walking on the packed dirt.

Mabel looked past them to see if the rehearsal had ended early. It didn't seem to have, since the rest of the wedding party, plus Emily and the planner, were all still out in the lavender field. So, why was the bride leaving her own rehearsal? Unlike the best man, who could slip away unnoticed with impunity, the bride was the centerpiece of the wedding, and couldn't leave without the whole event falling apart.

As Donna approached, it became obvious why she needed a break from the rehearsal and photographs. Her oval face was puffy, her eyes and nose were red, and tears had melted her mascara so that it soaked into the lines around her eyes, making her appear older than her actual age. Not the sort of look anyone wanted in their wedding pictures.

"May we use the bathroom in the farmhouse?" Ken asked. "The lighting in the barn facilities is a little too primitive for fixing makeup."

Aunt Peggy had installed a half-bath in the front left corner of the barn years ago. It was designed for the use of daily laborers, not guests for a dress-up event, so the facilities were, as Ken said, primitive.

Mabel hadn't anticipated the possibility of strangers invading her home as part of the wedding activities, and if it had been anyone other than the bride who wanted to go inside, she'd have been inclined to insist that they make do with the barn's facilities. But poor Donna looked like what was supposed to be the happiest weekend of her life was turning into the worst time of it.

"Come on in. It's in the hallway just past the kitchen. I'll show you the way." Mabel ushered the bride and photographer inside and down the hallway.

Donna sniffled before saying, "Thank you so much. I didn't expect my allergies to be quite this bad. I just need a moment to freshen up, and then we can get back to work." She glanced at Ken, waving the little quilted clutch that matched her dress. "I'll let you know if I need help with the makeup."

"I'll be right here," he said. "Like always."

Donna smiled through her puffiness. "I know. I can always count on you." She slipped inside the bathroom and closed the door. It opened a moment later. "I'm sorry to bother you, Mabel, but would you happen to have some makeup remover and a cotton pad? I'm going to have to start over with my mascara, and I don't want to ruin your towels trying to wash it off."

Mabel had to stop and think, because one of the perks of working from home was not needing to wear makeup. "I've got something you can use, but it's upstairs. Just give me a minute to get it." She turned to Ken. "You can wait in the kitchen, if you'd like."

"Thank you. I do need a bit of a break. Brides have adrenaline to get through the day, but for me it's just another day of work, so I don't have those extra energy reserves. I suppose it's a little different for me today, because Donna and I are such close friends, so I'm personally happy for her and that's energizing. But it's still a demanding job, and I'm not as young as when I first started doing weddings."

He went in one direction while Mabel went in the other to run upstairs to find her aunt's jar of Noxzema cleansing cream and the pads she'd used with it. Finding them took longer than she'd expected, because while she remembered her aunt using them, Mabel had tucked them away and forgotten where, so she had to ransack the upstairs bathroom's closet and cabinets.

When Mabel finally found the supplies, she hurried downstairs to knock on the first floor's bathroom door. Donna opened it just enough to reach through it to accept the supplies before offering her thanks and disappearing again behind the closing door.

Mabel went to wait with Ken. He was pacing between the windows and the long kitchen table that could seat a dozen people. It dominated the space her aunt had added to the old kitchen a few years earlier in order to have room for large dinner parties.

Mabel sat on the other side, where she'd abandoned her laptop earlier to go outside and defend the buffet table from Thad. She could still see the patio, and was somewhat surprised to see that Thad had abandoned his not-quite-empty plates while she'd been inside with the bride and groom. Maybe he'd decided to have a smoke and, somewhat against character, had been considerate enough not to do it too close to the food. From where she was sitting, she could watch for his return, as well as make sure that Rainey, possibly having used his reporter's skills to identify Thad as the best man, didn't double back to harass him.

As soon as she settled at the table, Ken stopped pacing and sat across from her, putting away the handkerchief he'd been twisting nervously. "I hope we're not being too much of an imposition."

Mabel gave the polite response—"Of course not"—even though she wished she could insist he leave her home. It wasn't just her natural preference to be alone in her home, but something about the photographer's mere existence set her teeth on edge. He was elegantly good-looking, he said all the right things, and he was as considerate of others as Thad was rude, but she didn't want to have to be in the same room with him. Her reaction to him was completely irrational, and the only explanation she could think of was that she was still annoyed that the wedding planner had rejected Mabel's recommendation of a local photographer, and instead had brought in someone who was based in Boston, as if that automatically made him better than the professionals in a small town. There were at least three excellent photographers within a ten-mile radius of the farm, and they all had the advantage of having used the lavender field as a backdrop in the past, so they already knew the best angles and where the light came from. Besides, Mabel had become a convert to buying and hiring local, ever since moving to West Slocum. In fact, she couldn't think of any item or service she hadn't found a local source for in recent months, other than the premium leaves she used for her iced tea, which simply couldn't be matched by anything available in West Slocum.

It wasn't really Ken's fault that the planner had rejected Mabel's advice, and it was time for her to get over her annoyance. In a sense, there was no local option for the photography of this particular wedding, since Ken had unique qualifications as a longtime friend of the bride. He would have better insights into what Donna wanted and would be able to capture the bride's experience in pictures better than a stranger could, since she would feel more relaxed and comfortable in front of his camera than anyone else's.

To make up for her previous coldness, Mabel tried for some small talk. "Have you known the bride for long?"

"Pretty much forever." Ken's voice was warm and confiding, as if he either hadn't noticed Mabel's coldness when they'd met earlier in the day or hadn't been offended by it. "Stan, too, and he's a great guy, but I only met him when they started dating, maybe ten or fifteen years ago. I've known Donna since elementary school, which is as far back as I can remember anything, so I've never known a world without her."

"Then you must know about her allergies. Is there anything I can do to lessen them?"

Ken snorted. "Not unless you want to dig up your whole lavender field and throw it away. She never should have agreed to have the wedding here. She's ferocious when it comes to protecting the people she loves, but a total doormat when it comes to taking care of herself, so she didn't say anything when Paige announced she'd reserved this place for the wedding. Donna thought an extra dose or two of her allergy meds would take care of it, and they probably would have if we were just talking about a few sachets, but not when it's a whole field in peak bloom. I didn't know about any of it until it was too late to change the venue."

Selfishly, Mabel began to worry that the next day's wedding ceremony and reception might still be relocated now that everyone knew just how badly the lavender was affecting the bride. Then the farm would lose the good publicity she'd been hoping to get. Worse, Emily might lose the larger part of the catering contract if the new site for the wedding wouldn't give her access to the kitchens. Many venues placed restrictions on who could cater there, preferring to work with contractors they were familiar with and had a track record for cleaning up after themselves and not damaging anything.

"We could relocate the wedding stage and chairs away from the flowers and out to the front of the farmhouse for tomorrow." A small platform with a simple arch that went over the bride, groom, and officiant had been placed at an angle in the tractor path in front of the corner of the lavender field so the flowers would serve as a natural backdrop for the eighty or so guests. It could be moved without too much trouble. "The farmhouse isn't as pretty a backdrop, but setting things up out front would at least put some distance between the bride and the lavender."

The bathroom door had opened while Mabel was speaking, and Donna answered. "Thank you, but that's not necessary. I'll be fine with the original setup."

Donna had washed her face and reapplied her makeup, but she hadn't been able to erase the redness of her eyes or the puffiness around them. If something didn't change before the actual wedding tomorrow, the bride would look like she was crying throughout the entire ceremony.

Mabel moved over so the bride could take the chair closest to the end of the table, directly across from Ken. Relieved that the disaster had been averted so easily, Mabel still felt obliged to ask, "Are you sure we shouldn't rearrange everything so the ceremony happens at least a little bit away from the lavender?"

"I'm sure." Donna took the vacated seat. "I wouldn't want you to go to all that trouble. It's not your fault that I'm having an allergic reaction. It's not anyone's fault."

"It's Paige's fault," Ken said, taking the little quilted clutch from the bride's hand and scrounging around inside it. "She should have asked if you had any allergies, if only to make sure your bouquet didn't send you into anaphylactic shock. I've done enough weddings to know that's become standard practice for any competent planner. They always warn me if the bride's allergic to anything I might want to use as a prop in a photograph."

"Paige is young and inexperienced, but I know she's doing her best and she only wants the best for me," Donna said. "She's right that the photographs will be amazing against the lavender background, and the guests will all enjoy the setting tomorrow. I'll just take some extra meds tonight, and it will be fine."

"It won't be fine if all the photographs capture what looks like a crying bride." Ken pulled a little bottle of liquid foundation out of the quilted clutch. "I'll do my best to clean up the images digitally, but there's a limit to what I can do before you start to look like a mannequin instead of a human being."

Donna patted Ken's hand as he turned her face from side to side so he could touch up the makeup. "You always make me look better than I really am."

Mabel was increasingly glad that Donna had brought her own photographer, even if there were still some tendrils of residual resentment against him for taking a job that she'd wanted to go to a local resident. Donna clearly trusted Ken, and the current situation would have been so much worse with a photographer she'd just met. In fact, the bride might well have decided to move the rest of the wedding to another venue by now if it weren't for her confidence in the photographer's skills. Mabel should feel grateful to him, not irritated, but the uncomfortable feeling just wouldn't go away.

Maybe her discomfort wasn't actually directed at Ken specifically, but was more generalized, simply due to all the strangers around her. She was used to working alone or with maybe a few other people she knew well, like Emily and Rory and the field workers. She wouldn't have minded the group of bridesmaids and ushers, or the reporter, or the manager candidate if each one had been the only challenge today, but all together, they were starting to overwhelm her.

Mabel glanced out the window to see that Thad had returned to the patio and was pushing back his now-empty plate that had been heaped with fruit salad. As she watched, he turned to stare longingly at the buffet table. She was about to excuse herself to go get him the second plate Emily had prepared and marked with his name, when he picked up his phone and started trying—unsuccessfully, judging by his expression—to get a signal on his phone. She'd had the same problem when she'd first moved to West Slocum. She'd had to switch carriers to the one and only telecommunications company that could reliably provide service in this corner of Massachusetts. As a result, the only person in the wedding party with a reliably working phone was the groom, since he was a local resident with the right carrier. The bride, too, probably, but she was too busy to use her phone. Mabel might have to provide wifi for future weddings, or perhaps she could advertise the lack of connectivity as a feature instead of a bug, guaranteeing that guests would be focused entirely on the wedding and not on their phones.

Thad gave up in frustration and peered at the distant buffet table, now that there was nothing to distract him from his appetite. How on earth could someone that skinny eat so much and still be hungry?

"If you'll excuse me," Mabel said, jumping up, "I need to check on something. You two can use the kitchen as long as you need it."

CHAPTER THREE

The bride and photographer followed Mabel out of the farmhouse after insisting they didn't need to impose on her hospitality any longer.

Mabel was trying to figure out how to distract Thad from the buffet table when Ken called out to him. "Hey, Thad. Come join us out in the field. I'm going to need you for the next set of pictures."

After one last longing look toward the buffet table, Thad nodded and let Ken pull off the napkin that had been serving as a bib. The three of them headed for the lavender field, passing the manager candidate, Richard Wetzel, who was coming from the opposite direction on his way back to the patio, apparently having completed his review of the property.

Please, please, please, let the farm have passed. Or at least have done well enough to tempt Wetzel to take on the job.

Wetzel looked much more like a farmer than Mabel ever would. Even more than her aunt had, despite having thrown herself into the role with gusto. Wetzel didn't have a piece of straw dangling from his mouth or anything quite that bucolic, but he wore a rugged jacket despite the pleasant June weather, along with well-worn loose jeans and scuffed construction boots. Covering most of his stringy brown hair was a baseball cap with a tractor company's logo. His hands were in his pockets at the moment, but when he'd arrived earlier in the day, she'd checked to make sure his skin had the appropriate amount of scarring and calluses consistent with the heavy physical labor of farming ever since he was a child, some twenty-five or thirty years earlier. Those signs of hard work had been missing from a man falsely claiming to be a farmer in order to buy Skinner Farm last fall. She wasn't going to be fooled by another imposter, although she couldn't quite imagine why anyone would pretend to have the necessary skills to manage a farm if he wasn't actually a farmer. It was a hard lifestyle and not one that was likely to lead to the sort of wealth that might tempt someone to lie in order to attain it.

Now that the buffet table was safe from Thad, at least temporarily, Mabel didn't need to stay out on the patio to keep an eye on him while she interviewed Wetzel and could instead enjoy a little more privacy in the kitchen. She ushered him inside and over to the huge farm table, where her closed laptop held her notes for the interview, including several incisive questions to ask candidates. Until she could retrieve them, she led with a polite, "How was your inspection of the property?"

"It wasn't an inspection," Wetzel corrected irritably. He didn't wait for her to sit, but instead took the seat she'd been using before, in front of her laptop. "That would take a week or more to do properly. I just skimmed the surface, so to speak. To do it right, I'd need to take soil samples and observe when and for how long the sun hits various locations."

"Then what did you think of the surface?" Mabel reluctantly took the seat across from him with her back to the patio. Surely Thad wouldn't return immediately, and she could spend a few minutes focusing completely on this interview instead of keeping half an eye on the patio. She reached for the laptop and turned it around to face her so she could check her notes on what to ask the manager candidates, since her attempt at small talk hadn't worked.

Wetzel pulled his cap off and set it on the table between them. "To be honest, this place is a mess. The fields aren't oriented ideally for either sun exposure or maximizing the land under cultivation, and the water source is unlikely to be of any use during a drought, which is the main time you'd actually need it."

Mabel resisted the urge to sigh. It might be possible to reorient the fields after the next harvest, but there wasn't anything she could do about the creek. She wasn't even sure Wetzel was right about its uselessness. Yes, it dried up in late summer, but by then, the garlic had already been harvested, the lavender thrived in dry soil, and the deep mulch around the butternut squashes and rhubarb minimized the amount of manual watering required. The water table was high, and a combination of wells and rainwater collection had provided ample water for both human and agricultural consumption for as long as Aunt Peggy had owned the farm, and probably for much longer than that.

"Is there anything about the farm that's being done right?" Mabel asked, hoping he'd at least appreciate her aunt's attempts to diversify her income streams, with the lavender field and the companion planting of butternut squashes added to the main garlic crop.

"Not really." Wetzel picked up his cap and tapped it on the table to emphasize each item in his list of grievances. "Having the squash in with the garlic reduces the quantity of your main crop and adds to the labor needed to maintain the field. I saw you've started a rhubarb field where you could have added something with a better return on investment. Not much demand for rhubarb. And your farmhand doesn't know what he's doing. Not in real, practical terms. He's just a kid who thinks he knows everything because he went after an advanced degree when he could have been learning from the land itself."

Mabel was the first to admit she wasn't an expert in agriculture, either the actual growing or the economics of it. That was why she was hiring a manager, after all. But everything Wetzel was saying felt wrong to her. She didn't particularly mind his criticism of her rhubarb field. The decision to plant it hadn't been particularly rational, other than believing in diversification, and she hadn't done any research into which crops paid the most per acre. She'd chosen rhubarb because she'd developed an emotional attachment to the plants that had once been owned by another local farmer.

Even if Wetzel was right about the financial considerations, his attitude still rubbed her wrong. Especially his criticism of both Terry and, by implication, her aunt, who'd made most of the choices about crops and the siting of the fields. Aunt Peggy had known a great deal about small farms and had been a very organized and logical person. Her decisions about the use of the land had been based on research and experience, not whims. Perhaps Wetzel was right that Aunt Peggy hadn't squeezed every ounce of harvest out of the available land, but she was good enough with numbers and balance sheets that if she'd wanted to be more efficient and productive, she would have been. The fact that she hadn't put every inch of arable land into cultivation suggested that she had other criteria for her decisions. Her journal had mentioned her concern for the aesthetics of the farm, plus the continued health of the soil, and the benefits of not being dependent on just one crop, even if it limited her ability to sell to the larger buyers.

If Mabel was going to delegate the management of the farm, she needed the person to be on the same general wavelength as her aunt had been when it came to priorities. Clearly, Wetzel was only interested in dollars and productivity without consideration of less tangible factors. Mabel wanted to ensure that the farm could produce enough money to cover its expenses, with a little profit left over, just as her aunt had done, but making more money than that wasn't the top priority. Or even the lowest priority. All Mabel cared about was sustaining her aunt's legacy.

Unfortunately, Wetzel was the only candidate she'd found who was even remotely qualified, despite almost eight months of advertising. Mabel opened her laptop to glance at the document with the questions she'd intended to ask him. The first one was a review of the candidate's education, experience, and specialty training, but she was already satisfied with his bachelor's degree from the local university's agriculture program—the same program that Terry would soon have the maligned graduate degree from—plus his lifetime of working on his family's farm. She didn't need to cross-examine him on any of that. She needed to know more about his agricultural philosophy, which wasn't addressed in any of her prepared questions.

Mabel looked at her laptop screen as if what she was about to ask him had been planned in advance. In fact, she was just buying herself some time to think of the right words to get at what she needed to know about Wetzel. She'd never been any good at spontaneous conversations, especially with strangers, and she'd always prepared in advance for big talks so she would know exactly what to say. She was going to have to wing it this time, and she wasn't even sure about all the right terminology, which made her doubly nervous, since Wetzel would undoubtedly pounce on any mistakes.

She thought of the other small farmers she knew—her neighbor, Emily Colter; and the farmer who'd introduced her to growing rhubarb, Graham Winthrop—and what made them so good at what they did. She thought it boiled down to their passion for their work. Farming was their lives, not just a job, not just dollars and cents. Money wasn't all that mattered to them, even now, when Emily needed to earn enough to keep her goats. She wouldn't stint on the animals' care, just to make it easier to prove her husband wrong about her ability to provide for them. The good of the farm came first.

Mabel needed to know that Wetzel felt the same passion for the land he would manage.

"You obviously know a lot about agriculture and its economics," she said at last. "But what is it about farming that you're most passionate about? Besides productivity and profit."

Wetzel blinked. "What kind of question is that? I could manage this farm in my sleep. What more do you want?"

"I want passion." Mabel closed the laptop and stood, signaling an end to the interview. "I'm sorry, but I won't be offering you the job. There's no point in continuing this interview. Thank you for coming, and I hope you find a position that's better suited to you."

For a long moment, Wetzel seemed frozen to his seat, unable to believe he'd been rejected. When the reality finally sank in, he swiped up his hat from the table and jumped to his feet. "I can't believe I wasted my time coming all the way out here to meet you. I should have known you'd be this stupid. Thinking a celebrity wedding could save your farm. The lavender field is a total amateur move, just like all the other crazy fads that hobby farmers try, when you should be focusing on maximizing your return on investment with efficient crop choices."

As far as Mabel could tell, the net return on investment for the established and low-maintenance lavender field was already higher, per square foot, than any other part of the farm. The income was likely to increase over time, especially if she could get some good publicity out of today's wedding and increase the number of events using the flowers as a backdrop.

It wasn't worth arguing the matter with Wetzel, though. His little temper tantrum had confirmed she'd made the right decision in rejecting his application, even if he was the only qualified candidate she'd found in eight months.

"I'm satisfied with the return on investment," Mabel said calmly as she opened the kitchen door for him to leave. "But it obviously wouldn't be enough for you. It's best we realize that now, rather than later. I wouldn't want to waste any more of your time."

Wetzel stomped through the doorway. "You're going to be sorry. No one treats me like this."

Yeah, yeah. Mabel had heard that sort of thing before, generally from people who were actually treated badly on a daily basis, but whose egos refused to acknowledge it.

She meant to escort him to his car to make sure he left without venting his anger anywhere near the wedding party, but just then, Pixie yowled from the office at the other end of the house to announce a new arrival. Mabel wasn't expecting any more visitors, and in fact, would have been happier with several fewer people on the farm, starting with Wetzel, along with both the reporter and the best man.

* * * *

After Wetzel slammed the kitchen door behind him, Mabel quickly checked on Pixie, who had already settled back into her favorite spot on the chair behind the desk. As Mabel left, she closed the office door behind her securely to keep Pixie safe, then headed for the patio to see who the new arrival was. Whoever it was had parked somewhere out of view from the kitchen, probably near her own car and the reporter's out in front of the house, since the parking area in front of the barn was full.

Once on the patio, she was relieved to see that Thad hadn't skipped out on the photographs to come back and raid the buffet again while she'd been busy with Wetzel. The table where he'd been eating was unoccupied. Thad had apparently taken the little flag with his name on it as a souvenir, but the empty plate was still on the table where he'd left it for someone else to clear away instead of placing it on one of the nearby busing trays.

Her relief turned to dismay when the sound of a utensil scraping on a serving dish caught her attention and she saw that now Wetzel was the one raiding the buffet, presumably as compensation for his "wasted" time. She didn't begrudge him the food, but worried that he'd take out his anger on Emily's work, digging into the beautifully laid-out offerings like Thad had, rather than taking a discreet serving from an inconspicuous spot. He was already turning away from the buffet to carry his heaping plate to the nearest table, so it was too late to prevent whatever damage he'd done. She decided she might as well leave him to his ill-gotten gains for a couple of minutes while she checked on the new arrival announced by Pixie. Then she could double back and fix whatever mess Wetzel had made at the buffet table. She had plenty of time, with another half hour or so to work on it before the bridal party arrived.

Mabel continued across the patio to the edge of the driveway, where she could see that the new arrival was Charlie Durbin. He was leaning over the tailgate of the pickup he'd parked just off the driveway in the grass of the front yard. Charlie was tall and solid, his muscles the result of his background in construction before he'd become a real estate developer. He still worked with his crew occasionally, both to help out and to stay fit. Usually, he wore jeans and a blazer, but today he'd swapped the blazer for a sweatshirt emblazoned with the name of his company, just like his workers wore.

When he turned away from the truck, he had a carpenter's belt full of tools in his hand. He wrapped it around his lean waist as he walked over to the edge of the patio where she waited to keep an eye on Wetzel.

Something was finally going right today.

Mabel was always glad to see Charlie, or at least she had been ever since their initial meeting, when she'd assumed he was a developer trying to buy her aunt's land to turn it into a subdivision. Once they'd worked out that misunderstanding, they'd become friends and then, for the last few months, had been dating casually.

"What's up?" she asked him.

"Do I need a reason to come see you?" Charlie pulled her into a hug and leaned down for a kiss.

She'd have liked to keep kissing him, but she was distracted by thoughts of Thad returning and teaming up with Wetzel to completely destroy the buffet table. She pulled away and said, "Today is by appointment only. You know how important this wedding is for both me and Emily. Especially Emily. I can't let her down. She's been so helpful to me since I got here, and now I can finally do something for her."

"So, pencil me in for a date tomorrow," he said. "Meanwhile, I'm actually here on business. I want to take a final look at the stage to be sure it's what I'd envisioned. I didn't get a chance to inspect it after the crew told me they finished it yesterday."

"Don't you trust them?" Mabel asked, thinking that if she had to double-check everything her eventual farm manager did, it was going to make it difficult to return to her home in Maine by the end of the fall harvest, as she'd been planning to do.

"For the most part, I trust them," Charlie said. "It's just that this time they were working from my rough sketch instead of professional blueprints, so there was some room for interpretation. It should be fine, but I want to be sure they used their discretion well."

"The rehearsal is still happening at the moment," Mabel said. "I expect them to be done in another fifteen minutes or so."

"I don't mind waiting," he said. "Especially if you've got some iced tea in the fridge. I'm parched. I meant to come over here earlier, but I had to put in a full day at a site, filling in for a worker who called in sick."

"You can help yourself to a drink," she said. "The kitchen door's unlocked and the tea is in the fridge."

"I was hoping you'd come inside with me," he said. "Then we could finish that kiss in private, since there's no rush for me to get to work."

If only she could. "I'll join you in a minute. I need to take care of something else first." She nodded in the direction of Wetzel. "He's the farm manager candidate who came out for an interview today. It didn't work out, and he's not taking rejection very well."

"Most people don't," Charlie said. "I, of course, am above such pettiness."

"You are, indeed." Mabel laughed. She had rejected him any number of times, even accusing him of wanting to steal the farm and turn it into condos. And yet, he never seemed to take offense. At first, she'd thought that his persistence in the face of her hostility was part of some long-term strategy to scoop up the land when she failed to keep the farm going, but instead it had just been his naturally laid-back and patient personality. He'd seemed content to wait for her to decide whether he was a good guy and someone she'd like to spend more time with. They'd become friends and had even dated casually for the last few months, with both of them aware that Mabel wasn't planning to stay in West Slocum for much longer than whatever it took to hire and train a farm manager. Which was turning out to be longer than she'd planned, but she still hoped it would only be another few months before she could return to her home in Maine.

Charlie said, "You could make it up to me by inviting me to the wedding tomorrow."

"You're already invited." He'd built the house that the bride and groom had lived in for the past five years, and had maintained a friendship with them after the construction was completed.

"I'd rather you were the one who invited me to the wedding," he said. "As your plus-one."

"I don't get a plus-one," Mabel said. "I'm here as staff, not as a guest."

"You can be my plus-one, then."

"You're a glutton for punishment," she said lightly. She didn't like rejecting him yet again, but it was for the best that he not get the wrong idea about any long-term relationship. There was something so committed about going to a wedding with someone.

She glanced away so she wouldn't have to see Charlie's disappointed expression. He never complained, but he couldn't as easily suppress the sadness in his eyes. Avoiding looking at him, she noticed that out in the lavender field, only the bride, groom, and the mayor, who would be officiating the ceremony, were on the stage, and everyone else was starting to head toward the patio.

"I'm sorry, but you'll have to get your own tea now," she said. "I need to go fix the buffet table before the wedding party shows up. The rehearsal seems to have ended, and everyone will be hungry. I don't want them to blame Emily if Wetzel made a mess of things."

"Do you need any help?"

She'd rejected Charlie enough for one day, she decided, and she might need some backup for dealing with Wetzel. He'd left his table and was heading for the far side of the buffet table, where only the staff belonged, as if he might have missed either some special food or an opportunity to make a mess, and once he was behind there, with the table in the way, it would be harder to evict him.

"Sure," she said. "Do you want to be the one strong-arming Wetzel out of here or the one fixing the food displays?"

Before he could respond, Wetzel uttered a high-pitched scream, and then a plate shattered on the patio's bricks.

That couldn't be good, Mabel thought, cautiously heading for the buffet table, with Charlie at her side. Had one of the barn cats startled Wetzel? Or perhaps a spider? She wouldn't have expected someone who'd grown up on a farm to react so badly to natural things, but then again, Wetzel didn't seem to appreciate nature except as something to be used. He probably hated to see evidence of creatures he couldn't control.

Whatever the reason for Wetzel's scream, it had elicited a response from the people returning from the lavender field. The mayor and the members of the wedding party were all frozen in place, but the reporter, Rainey, was racing toward the patio, one hand on his camera to keep it from bouncing against his chest, where it would likely leave bruises.

Wetzel ran out from behind the table. He paused when he reached Mabel and Charlie. "This place is worse than I thought. You can't keep anything alive here."

He hurried off before Mabel could ask him what he meant, so she continued over to the buffet table. Charlie ran on ahead while she slowed to check the food display at the front of the table. To her relief, it was mostly intact, with Wetzel having courteously taken his servings from inconspicuous spots. Nothing frightening there.

She started to follow Charlie around to the back. He held up one hand. "Don't come any closer. And call the police."

"Why?" She kept walking, and as she reached the back corner of the linen-draped table, she traced Charlie's gaze to the ground about a yard behind the buffet.

There was a body there. The best man's. Apparently the wedding photographer hadn't been able to keep Thad out in the lavender field after all. He must have returned for another raid on the food while Mabel was interviewing Wetzel with her back to the patio, and he was now sprawled on the patio's bricks. An empty plate—the second one that Emily had filled and left for Thad—was in pieces on the ground beside him, along with the little flag with his name on it. The remnants of one of Emily's cheesecake bars were smeared down the front of his shirt.

And he didn't appear to be breathing.

CHAPTER FOUR

Thad wasn't dead, as it turned out, just unconscious, and unable to be awakened by the EMTs. It didn't help that the reporter insisted on joining them in the relatively tight space behind the buffet table and taking pictures of both Thad and the two men working on him.

Rainey had refused to leave, claiming the public had a right to know what had happened, and he was acting on their behalf. Eventually one of the paramedics informed him they were going to have criminal charges filed against him for interfering with their work if he didn't get to the other side of the buffet table in the next three seconds. Rainey withdrew, but only the very minimum distance they'd specified, and then pushed aside anything on the buffet table that might obscure his view of the scene.

A squeak of dismay announced Emily's arrival. Mabel tried to intercept her—the pretty display was a lost cause now, and if anyone made a fuss, they'd only get into trouble with the EMTs—but Emily got to Rainey first and shouted, "You're worse than Thad. Look at the mess you've made."

Mabel had never seen her friend that angry before. Emily definitely believed in turning the other cheek and walking a mile in the other person's shoes before getting upset. Except when it came to her ex-husband, at least. And now was not a good time for letting anger get the better of her. Emily would regret it as soon as she realized why the EMTs had been called.

"Forget about the buffet," Mabel said, taking Emily's arm and dragging her away from the table. "There's a bigger problem now."

Emily turned her anger on Mabel. "What could possibly be bigger than someone ruining all the hours of work I put into this buffet?"

"Thad Dalton is sick," Mabel said. "Unconscious."

Emily blinked, then looked past Mabel toward where the EMTs' heads could be seen bent over something—someone—on the ground. "Thad? But he was just..." She waved vaguely toward the lavender field. "I mean, I saw Ken bring him back out there for a set of pictures, so I thought the buffet was safe from him while I finished dealing with Paige, even if you had other things to do."

"I didn't see him come back either," Mabel said. "But he obviously did."

Emily sighed. "If I didn't know better, I'd swear my almost-ex caused all of this. He'd do anything to force me to give up the farm."

"I don't think this had anything to do with him," Mabel said. "And it may not be as bad as it seems. Thad couldn't have been unconscious for long before the EMTs arrived, and they know what they're doing. We should get everyone out of the way, though, and let them work."

"We can send the guests back to the lavender field," Emily said. "The sooner they're out of sight of this mess, the better."

She and Mabel herded the wedding party away from the patio, with the mayor's soothing assistance. Charlie retrieved a case of water from where Emily had stored extra supplies in the barn and carried it out to the field so there was no risk that someone would get dehydrated and add to the day's casualty count.

The bride took a seat on the edge of the stage and covered her face with her hands. She might have only looked like she'd been crying earlier, but Mabel thought it was more than allergy symptoms now. Donna was quickly joined by a young woman on one side and a young man on the other. They gently pulled her hands away from her face and linked their arms with her. They both turned toward Donna, forming a barrier around her, as if they were determined to protect her from any further upsets. With the three of them grouped together that way, the similarities in their facial structure made it clear they were related. Mother and children, Mabel supposed. She vaguely recalled having been told that the bride had two children and the groom had one.

Speaking of the groom, where was he? Shouldn't he be making sure his bride-to-be wasn't unduly upset by the latest crisis? He wasn't anywhere near the stage, or even mingling with the other guests.

And where was the wedding planner? She wasn't anywhere in sight either. It was her job to placate brides, after all, and Donna had every reason to need a little reassurance. No bride wanted EMTs and the police—Mabel could hear the approaching sirens—crashing her wedding rehearsal.

Mabel eventually caught sight of the groom, Stan Bellingham, across the tractor path from the lavender field, half-hidden under some trees near the creek where he was talking on his phone. She'd seen him hunched over his phone earlier whenever he wasn't needed for pictures, and assumed he was a workaholic, given his career as a consultant. She had to wonder how he'd been as successful as she'd heard, since he always seemed to look like he was trying to duck away from anyone's attention. He was short, with a slight stature, and he kept himself apart from the wedding party, presumably people he knew and liked, not strangers whom he might have had a good reason to avoid. Even his hairline had crept away from his face as if to escape notice. In the shade, Stan almost looked like a ghost, with his extremely pale skin, faded brown hair, and pale gray suit.

While Mabel debated going over and encouraging Stan to return and sit with his obviously upset bride, she saw him finish one call and start another immediately. A moment later, the town's mayor, who was officiating the wedding in his other capacity as justice of the peace, crossed the path to talk to the groom but was waved off irritably. If the mayor—a big bear of a guy with a quietly persuasive demeanor—couldn't get Bellingham to do the right thing, Mabel certainly wouldn't be able to.

By then, Emily had disappeared, too, probably huddled with the planner, wherever she was, and the sound of the ambulance leaving meant that it was safe for Mabel and Charlie to go back to the patio to check in with the police. They would undoubtedly want to talk to the people who had first found Thad unconscious, in order to find out what had happened to him. Wetzel was the one they really should talk to, but she wasn't sure where Wetzel had disappeared to. The police would have to settle for her and Charlie initially. With luck, that would also put an end to her involvement, and she could concentrate on what would happen next for the wedding party.

Joe Hansen—the husband of Mabel's friend, Rory—had been the first officer on the scene. Joe was solidly built with a slightly bulging waistline from the cookies he always had at hand as part of his weaponry, claiming that sharing them was better at diffusing a tense situation than a gun could ever be. There weren't all that many tense situations in West Slocum, so he ended up eating a fair number of the cookies himself. Just so they wouldn't be wasted, he always said.

His cruiser was parked in the driveway next to the patio, and he was cordoning off the entire patio area, not just the small section at the far end where the body—the unconscious man, Mabel corrected herself—had been found. That seemed like an unnecessary precaution unless the EMTs had alerted him to something suspicious about Thad's unconsciousness before they left.

Joe took brief statements from Mabel and Charlie, then asked them to stay away from the patio, so they went over to sit on the tailgate of Mabel's truck, parked next to the path to Emily's farm. From there, they could keep an eye on the activity on the patio without being in anyone's way.

While they were getting settled, another cruiser arrived. A uniformed officer got out and took Joe's place guarding the patio while Joe jogged out to the lavender field. He had his notepad in one hand, and it looked like he was gathering names and contact information from everyone out there. That, too, suggested to Mabel that the police believed something more insidious had happened than a heart attack or some other standard medical crisis.

She considered asking Charlie what he thought might have happened to Thad, since he'd had a closer view, but she knew he would tell her she was worrying for nothing, and she should wait until she had more information to go on before she started to fret. He was probably right. Better not to speculate.

She aimed for a light tone and said, "I hope they're going to let me use the kitchen door sometime this evening so I can get into my house. I don't usually carry the key to the front door with me."

"Neither did Peggy," Charlie said. "I'd be surprised if she even had a key to it."

"She probably didn't," Mabel said. "Fortunately, my attorney in Maine did. He must have insisted on it when he learned that she'd written a will naming me her heir. He always did look out for my best interests."

"You've got friends to watch out for you now."

He scooted closer until they were just touching, more like friends than lovers, so she could feel his reassuring presence without it being overwhelming. Charlie always respected the wider-than-average boundaries she established for her personal space, which was one of the things she found so appealing about him. He didn't try to fix everything for her, but he made sure she knew he was there if she needed him. At the moment, she was trying to maintain a strong, in-control façade for the wedding guests, and Charlie seemed to be calibrating his friendly closeness so as not to take away from her strength, while still letting her know she wasn't alone. She wished she was as good as he was at fine-tuning social interactions like that, especially with him. Most of the time, Charlie didn't seem to mind that she wasn't as intuitive as he was when she was with him, but she knew she unintentionally tested his patience sometimes. The amazing thing was that he hadn't given up on her yet like past boyfriends had done.

Mabel's mind recoiled from the thought of Charlie eventually doing just that, and moving on to a new romantic partner. Even though she knew—they both knew, since she'd made it quite clear before agreeing to a first date—that she'd be leaving him behind when she went back to Maine, it still hurt to think of separating on the bad terms that could come of differing expectations from a relationship.

She forced herself not to think about it. Given how slowly the search for a farm manager was going, she had plenty of time before she had to leave Charlie behind. And at the moment, there were more time-sensitive matters to deal with. Once the wedding was over, though, she'd have to figure out what to do about her lack of a future with Charlie, and what that would mean for both of them. She wasn't entirely sure she'd made the right decision to date him, even casually, when she knew he was irrevocably tied to West Slocum and she'd be leaving before long. He'd agreed to a no-strings relationship, and she thoroughly enjoyed being with him, but it might not be fair to him. And it would be painful for her too.

A yowl came from inside the farmhouse. Pixie was probably announcing the arrival of more police, maybe even a detective if the situation was as serious as Joe's actions suggested.

"Did you see where Wetzel went?" Mabel asked. "The police might want to talk to him in case he knows something about what happened to Thad."

"Wetzel left," Charlie said. "Got into his car and sped out of here before the ambulance and police even arrived."

"I definitely made the right decision in not hiring him, then," Mabel said. "I don't need someone who will panic at the least little thing."

"An unconscious person isn't a little thing."

"Aren't farmers supposed to be tougher than that? I'm sure I read somewhere about the high rate of horrible, grisly accidents in agricultural work. Especially when using heavy equipment like tractors. Someone quietly and bloodlessly passing out shouldn't be all that shocking."

"The victim—" Charlie interrupted himself. "Who was he, anyway?"

"Thad Dalton. The best man, and the groom's business partner."

Charlie paused for a moment before saying, "I hate to say it, but I'm not sure Thad is going to be able to go back to work anytime soon. If ever. I've been around more accidents than I like to recall—it's a fact of life in construction, no matter how careful everyone is—and I've been on sites since I started helping my electrician brother when I was fourteen. I'm not a doctor, but Thad had the look of someone who was worse off than a little dehydration or overexertion. He looked like he was in shock. The kind that people die from."

"He got help quickly, though," Mabel said, a little desperately. "So he should be fine."

"Maybe," Charlie said. "The thing is, usually the EMTs will joke a bit as they work, as a way of coping with their stressful career, but they were completely serious today. And people in their profession tend to have the patience of saints, or at least they try to give that impression, but you saw how they snapped at Rainey. That tells me they thought Thad's condition was serious, too, and they couldn't afford to be nice to people."

"Thad looked like he collapsed suddenly." The image of his body lying there was etched in her brain. "A heart attack, perhaps?"

Charlie glanced past her, toward the lavender field, while he considered the possibility. Mabel followed his gaze, relieved that the guests had all stayed out there. The mayor was mingling with the members of the wedding party, who'd collected in small groups while waiting for Joe to interview them. The bride and her children were still in their huddle on the stage, the groom was talking on his phone over in the shade near the creek, and apparently Emily had dragged the wedding planner over to the gazebo in the middle of the lavender field, where their conversation wouldn't be overheard by the guests. Emily's nurturing instincts seemed to have reawakened with the crisis, since she seemed to be giving the drooping Paige a pep talk.

When Charlie turned in the other direction, Mabel did too. An unmarked SUV had just pulled up behind the two cruisers. A moment later, a short, thin, dark-haired man climbed out.

Mabel groaned. As if things weren't bad enough without Detective Frank O'Connor on the case.

Charlie seemed to understand how she felt about this latest development, since he said encouragingly, "You can handle him."

She'd met O'Connor the previous fall, when he'd been responsible for investigating the death of a rhubarb breeder whose body she'd found. O'Connor was about her age, young for being in charge of a homicide investigation, and without any obvious skills that would make up for his inexperience. In particular, he had a nervous giggle that gave away any bluff he tried to run. He also held on to a grudge with an iron grip. He really hadn't liked having an amateur like Mabel unmask the rhubarb breeder's killer while he'd been off on a completely wrong tangent, and to make it worse, he'd then blamed her for his own mistakes that had made him look like a fool in front of a superior officer. Mabel might not have handled that last situation as well as she should have, but she didn't regret getting involved in the search for the killer. If she hadn't figured it out, she'd have been the one in jail instead of the actual culprit.

Since then, things had been awkward between her and O'Connor. She thought he half-suspected that she'd somehow manufactured evidence in the case of the breeder's murder in order to frame someone for her own crime, so he was keeping an extra-careful eye on her, anticipating her downfall. West Slocum was a small town, so, despite Mabel's stay-at-home tendencies, it had been inevitable that she and O'Connor would run into each other from time to time when she ventured out to the grocery store, library, or local restaurants. Those chance meetings had been bad enough when they hadn't had to interact with each other beyond a little small talk, and now she was going to have to deal with him in a professional capacity again.

She forced herself to look away from O'Connor to tell Charlie, "I just hope that what happened to Thad is something straightforward and simple, so it's wrapped up quickly."

Charlie nodded. "Unfortunately, I don't think you'll be that lucky. At the very least, someone's bound to raise the possibility that Thad had a bad reaction to Emily's food. Hard not to, with the used plate lying next to him along with its name tag, and the crumbs all over his face and shirt."

Mabel groaned. "Emily really doesn't need that kind of bad press right now."

That reminded her—where was Rainey? She hadn't seen him since she'd helped Emily herd the wedding party back out to the lavender field. Had he continued to bother the EMTs and gotten himself arrested? Or had she not noticed when he went out with the wedding party? And if he was out there with them, was he trying to interview people who really didn't want to talk to the press?

She scanned the people out in the lavender field, grateful for the fedora that would have made Rainey stand out. He wasn't out there, though. Maybe he'd found a private spot to write up his notes.

"Do you know Andrew Rainey?" she asked Charlie.

"He's interviewed me a few times for pieces on local businesses."

"Have you seen him recently?"

"When I came out of the barn with the bottled water, he was talking to Joe Hansen at the edge of the patio, but I haven't seen him since then."

"He'd better not have gone inside the farmhouse," Mabel said, staring at the kitchen window as if she could actually see anything inside from this distance. She couldn't, of course, although she could see that Pixie had somehow gotten out of the office and was sitting on the windowsill.

"Don't worry. He's not inside." Charlie pointed down the driveway. "He just walked over to talk to O'Connor. Rainey must have been waiting on the front porch to pounce on newcomers."

The two men were standing between the back of Joe's cruiser and the front of O'Connor's SUV. Rainey had his notepad out, but he held it down at his side as if he didn't even know it was there. Mabel couldn't hear their words, just the alternating rumble of voices. Even so, two things about their conversation struck her as odd. First, that O'Connor would stop to speak to a reporter while on the way to a crime scene, and second, that she couldn't hear any giggles punctuating the detective's speech. She might have believed that O'Connor had finally overcome his nervous habit, but it was harder to understand why he'd be talking to a reporter before checking out the crime scene.

Maybe she was reading too much into the conversation because of her own distrust of the detective. The two men could be friends, sharing a few words before getting down to work. Or O'Connor could be telling the reporter that he had no comment yet, and Rainey wasn't accepting the brush-off.

"I should never have agreed to his being here." Mabel forced herself not to go over and intervene in the conversation. Neither man was likely to listen to her. "Rainey said he wanted to do a story on small farms and how raising crops isn't always enough for sustainability, so farmers add revenue sources like hosting events. I checked with the wedding planner, and she was supposed to ask the bride if it was okay for a reporter to be on-site during the rehearsal, but now that I've seen Paige in action, I'm not sure she actually got her client's permission before saying it was okay. In retrospect, Paige seemed overly excited about the prospect of press coverage. And now I'm thinking she was excited for herself, not so much for anyone else involved in the wedding."

"I don't think she's going to like the publicity she gets," Charlie said. "Police and ambulances may make for a good news story, but they're not the sort of things anyone wants at their wedding."

"She's not the only one who's going to get negative publicity. The farm will too," Mabel said. "And Emily, although I'll try to keep her name out of it if no one's spilled it already. I can weather the storm better than she can."

"I'm not so sure about that," Charlie said. "This is the second person who's been hurt on the farm in just a year. Not exactly good for your reputation."

"The farm hasn't done anything wrong," Mabel said. "What's happened is unfortunate, but not the fault of anyone here."

"Unless Thad had an allergic reaction to something. Anaphylactic shock can cause unconsciousness."

Mabel thought of the bride's red, puffy eyes. "It's possible, but it wouldn't be Emily's fault. The wedding planner should have found out if anyone had food allergies. And Thad himself could have mentioned it when Emily made a plate for him."

"What about food poisoning?" Charlie said.

"Not with Emily's cooking," she said automatically. Her emotional reaction wouldn't convince the detective if he asked her the same thing, so she needed facts. She considered the menu and whether it could have been mishandled, but it seemed unlikely. The casual, self-serve buffet consisted primarily of three different green salads, goats' milk quiches with a variety of fillings, veggie chips made locally, and then for dessert, cheesecake bars and fruit salad. She supposed the bars needed to be refrigerated for long-term storage, but they were intended to be served at room temperature, so they would be fine left out for several hours, especially in the mild weather they were experiencing. June could have hot spells, but the wedding party couldn't have asked for more perfect weather: sunny and warm, in the mid-seventies, with low humidity.

"No," Mabel said finally. "Food poisoning is just not possible. Emily knows what she's doing, and I'm sure she wouldn't take any chances with the food she serves."

"You're probably right," Charlie said. "Maybe he'd eaten something bad earlier today. I think it usually takes a few hours for symptoms of food poisoning to appear, so it couldn't have been the food on the plate next to him that made him sick."

"Definitely not that particular plate," Mabel agreed. "Unfortunately, ruling it out won't necessarily save Emily. Thad had eaten more than that one plate full of food. Emily told me he'd been following her around for hours, like a persistent cat begging for treats and helping himself to the food whenever her back was turned."

"Let's hope the cause of his unconsciousness turns out to be something else, then," Charlie said. "And that it's diagnosed quickly, because otherwise, I'm sure I'm not the only person who looks at spilled food and an unconscious victim and immediately thinks of food poisoning. Not the sort of thing any caterer wants associated with her work."

Speculation wasn't going to help anyone, so Mabel forced herself not to dwell on the situation. For now, there was still a chance that Thad would recover quickly and be able to tell the police what had happened to him, and that would clear Emily. Then, no further investigation would be needed, and no one except the wedding party would even remember what had happened during the first wedding held on Skinner Farm.

CHAPTER FIVE

Detective O'Connor broke away from the reporter and waved at Officer Joe Hansen, who was returning from the lavender field. Joe picked up his pace to jog the rest of the distance to where O'Connor waited next to the police tape cordoning off the patio.

O'Connor didn't make any effort to keep his voice low to avoid being overheard while he interrogated Joe about why the police had been called out to the farm. She couldn't hear everything O'Connor said, but the gist of it was clear, along the lines of Mabel thinking she was better than the police when it came to serious crime investigations, so perhaps they should just let her take care of the current situation on her own. She assumed he hadn't noticed her and Charlie in the back of her truck, since they were about seventy-five feet away from him and partially shaded by the nearby trees that separated her farm from Emily's.

Joe remained calm and respectful, although his tone was quieter and she couldn't make out any of his words. When he was finished, though, O'Connor seemed even more irritated than when he'd first arrived. "All right. I'll look into it. Where is she?"

Joe pointed at Mabel, and O'Connor glared at her before turning back to demand, "So, what did she do this time?"

Joe, who was famous for his patience, had apparently reached his limit. His tone was even, but loud enough now that Mabel could hear his words clearly, probably as he'd intended. "You mean, besides find the unconscious man and call for help?"

"How do you know she only found him and didn't cause him to be sick in the first place?"

"Because she said so," Joe said. "And even if I were inclined to distrust her, Charlie Durbin confirmed her statement. I've known him forever, and he wouldn't lie to me about something this serious."

O'Connor laughed, much more derisively than his usual light giggle. "Yeah, like no men ever do stupid things for a pretty face."

Mabel didn't consider herself a particularly pretty face. Not even on the rare occasions when she put in the effort with nice clothes and makeup. She was just average. Emily was the pretty one among her acquaintances. More than pretty, actually. Her looks had been an asset to her soon-to-be-ex-husband's business, while she'd mingled with potential clients at networking events while all glammed up. Emily was the kind of person men would lie for, not that she would ever ask them to, and not that she ever cared all that much what others thought of her appearance. All she wanted was to work with her goats, dressed in her overalls and boots, and her face covered with nothing but sunscreen.

Of course, the detective was right about the extent to which Charlie did find Mabel attractive, and men could definitely do silly things for a woman. Still, she and Charlie weren't in a serious relationship, not the sort that might give rise to the temptation to lie for the partner in a criminal investigation. Even if they were committed to each other, she didn't think Charlie would go that far to protect her. He had a reputation for honesty that was rare in the real estate development world, and he wouldn't risk it for anyone.

"Not Charlie Durbin," Joe insisted, echoing Mabel's thoughts.

"Yeah, yeah." O'Connor giggled, revealing the nervousness he hadn't shown until then. "So, what do you know so far?"

"The unconscious man is Thad Dalton. He's the business partner of the groom, Stan Bellingham. At least until tomorrow, after the wedding, when Thad will become the sole owner of their business."

O'Connor considered the information for a moment before asking, "Separating on good terms, are they?"

"It seems so." Joe nodded toward the dirt tractor path that ran from the lavender field to the barn, past where Terry Earley was working. "That's Stan coming in our direction now with his son. The groom's in the gray suit. You could ask him."

Mabel hadn't met Stan's son, since he'd arrived late, after the introductions, but she could see the family resemblance between the two men. They were almost identical, except in age, with extremely pale skin, slight stature, and receding hairlines. They dressed very differently, though, with the younger man in a much more fashionably current, well-tailored dark blue with a flashy lime green tie, while the groom wore an ill-fitting light gray suit that was so bland it wouldn't have looked out of place at any time in the past century.

While O'Connor waited for the men to come closer, he asked Joe, "You got preliminary statements from the EMTs?"

"Of course."

"What about from Skinner and Durbin?"

"Not officially. Just a quick rundown of what they'd seen. I wanted to be sure I got the contact information on the non-locals first in case they tried to leave."

"Good call. I'll talk to the guests after I view the scene. Skinner and Durbin can wait until everyone else has been interviewed."

Mabel didn't particularly care if O'Connor snubbed her by making her wait—she didn't want to spend time with him any more than he wanted to be around her—but she was annoyed on Charlie's behalf. He shouldn't have to stick around any longer than necessary, just because O'Connor was trying to mess with Mabel's head. He had to know that hurting her friends was the most effective way to hurt her. She wouldn't put it past the detective to start spreading sly innuendoes about how he'd had to detain Charlie for his role in a suspicious incident in which an unconscious man had been taken to the hospital. All to punish Mabel for having had the temerity to do his job when he hadn't.

"I'm sorry," she said to Charlie. "It isn't going to do your reputation any good to be associated with me. And I'm sure you've got better things to do than wait around for O'Connor to do his job."

Charlie shrugged. "I don't care what O'Connor thinks of me, and neither do the people I do business with. I'm much more interested in what you think of me."

"I think you're amazing," Mabel said.

"About time you admitted it," he said with a grin. "And now that you have, how can you resist being the plus-one of such an amazing person at the wedding?"

"I'm not sure there's even going to be a wedding tomorrow. Between the bride's allergies and now the best man's illness, they may decide to postpone it."

"The invitation stands, wherever the wedding happens."

"If it moves, I doubt they'd want me around as a reminder of what happened to their friend today."

"They probably won't even remember you," Charlie said. "In a different context, they'll just see you as my date, not the owner of the place where they held their wedding rehearsal."

Mabel wasn't so sure about that. "I'll think about it."

Stan and his son joined O'Connor and Joe. The detective pulled the groom aside to question him in relative privacy. The son started to follow until O'Connor made it clear that he wasn't interested in anyone except the groom. There was an angry expression on the son's face for a moment while he hesitated, clearly debating whether to ignore his dismissal, but apparently the nearby presence of a uniformed Joe Hansen made him decide not to push the matter. Instead, he looked around to see what his alternatives were. He quickly settled on Mabel, strutting across the tractor path to confront her.

"I'm Grant Bellingham, and I need to talk to the owner of this place. That's you, right?"

She nodded. "Mabel Skinner. And this is Charlie Durbin. He built the wedding stage, and he was with me when we found Thad."

"Good." He puffed himself up, although it didn't make much difference. Mabel, not particularly tall herself, had the advantage of sitting high on the truck's tailgate, so she was literally looking down at him, with his thin, receding hair the most visible thing in her line of sight.

Grant continued, "You should be able to answer my questions, then. I'm the son of the groom, and I want to be sure the police are doing their job properly here. It's an outrage what happened to Thad."

"Are you a friend of his?"

"More than a friend. He's like a cousin to me," Grant said. "And he was in perfect health before today, so don't try to tell me he passed out from some kind of natural cause. Something or someone here made him sick. I'm determined to get some answers, and I'm not convinced that kid detective talking with my father can get to the bottom of what happened. Is he better at his job than he looks?"

"Not really," Mabel said before she could stop herself. If she was going to continue in the wedding site business, she needed to get better at social lies.

Charlie intervened, bless him. "O'Connor is young and inexperienced, but he has the necessary training, a strong commitment to solving crimes, and a lot of local and state resources to call on for assistance. If there's evidence of wrongdoing, and he can't handle it by himself, he can get the necessary help."

"Are you sure he can handle it?" Grant looked over his shoulder at where the detective and his father were talking.

Mabel followed his gaze, but O'Connor seemed to have realized belatedly that he should keep his voice low, and she couldn't hear what he was asking the groom. Even more unfortunate, the detective hadn't equally muffled his increasingly piercing nervous giggles. Mabel couldn't get any insights into their conversation from Bellingham either. He seemed bored by the questions and impatient to get back to his phone. His answers were quiet and brief, just two or three words at most, and he ended each response by glancing down at his cell phone and swiping away a new notification.

"Your father doesn't seem worried about the investigation," Mabel said.

Grant turned back to give Mabel his full attention. "I'll give the kid a chance, then. But if it looks like he's not up to the job, I'll bring in my own investigator."

"That's fair," Mabel said. After all, that was essentially how she'd acted when the rhubarb farmer was killed. She'd given O'Connor a chance, and then when it had become clear that she'd end up in jail if she didn't find the real killer, she'd brought in her own investigator, who just happened to be herself. "Is there any chance the police will suspect your father of harming his partner?"

After the slightest of hesitations, Grant said, "Absolutely not." He glanced back at the detective before adding, "At least not if they're doing their job properly. I'm sure everyone who knew Father and Thad will confirm that they were the closest of friends, as well as business partners. Thad was treated like a second son. Why else would he have been asked to be the best man?"

"That does make it sound like they were close," Mabel said, although Stan didn't seem particularly worried about his partner. She also thought she might have heard a note of resentment in Grant's voice. Did he feel neglected by his father, who perhaps had spent more time with Thad than with his own son? After all, Thad had been the best man, not Grant. It was fairly common for a groom's son to serve in that role at a subsequent wedding, and instead a non-relative had been asked to do it. And it wasn't as if Grant was out of town or otherwise unable to take on the role.

"What about the arrangement for Thad to take over the business?" Mabel asked. "I heard that he was buying it from your father so he could retire. Could they have had a last-minute falling-out over it? Maybe one of them had buyer or seller regrets?"

Grant leaned forward in a manner that would have been aggressive if it weren't for the height disadvantage he had while Mabel was up on the tailgate. "Who told you about the business deal?"

Charlie tensed, but Mabel put a hand on his arm. She wanted to know why Grant was upset by a question so basic that even O'Connor had probably asked it. "I thought everyone knew about the deal and your father's retirement. The police were talking about it. It's not a secret, is it?"

Grant deflated. "No, I'm just a little sensitive on the topic. I was against the buyout from the beginning. Not because of Thad specifically, but more that I'm worried about how Father is going to like being retired. I mean, what's he going to do with his time? He lives for his work, just like I do. He doesn't have any hobbies and isn't interested in traveling or the usual retirement activities like golfing. The girlfriend doesn't care, though. She decided they should spend more time together, and she didn't think through what that would really mean. She extorted a promise out of Father that he'd retire, by saying she wouldn't marry him otherwise. And now he's going to go crazy with nothing to do at home. I mean, does she really think he'd be happy traipsing along after her while she goes to book club meetings and volunteers at the food pantry?"

"I'm sure he'll find a new interest," Mabel said. "I never thought I'd become a farmer, but look at me now."

"Just means you hadn't found your calling before," Grant said smugly. "That's something Father taught me. Never settle for a career that isn't also your life. Like they say, if you love your work, you'll never work a day in your life."

That was just silly, Mabel thought. She loved her app-development job, but it was still a job, something she wouldn't do if she weren't being paid. Aunt Peggy had loved farming, but it had still been hard work. Mabel didn't voice her doubts out loud, since now wasn't the time to get into a philosophical discussion with Grant about the nature of employment. She had to stay focused on the wedding and making sure nothing else went wrong.

"Assuming Thad is still in the hospital tomorrow, who's going to take his place at the wedding?"

"I have no idea," Grant said. "I suppose I could step in if necessary. It's not that hard of a job. Keep track of the rings and make a toast. Anyone could do that."

"Do you know where the rings are?" Mabel hadn't thought about that problem until now. "In case Thad isn't able to pass them along to his replacement."

"All I know is that they'd better not disappear," Grant said darkly. "Donna insisted on custom-made platinum pieces that must have cost a fortune, even considering Father's wealth."

"Maybe the wedding planner knows where they are." At the thought, Mabel scanned the area for the woman. "Have you seen Paige recently?"

He snorted. "I will never understand why Father allowed the girlfriend to hire that silly woman to plan the wedding. Paige is useless in a crisis.

She went into hysterics when she heard that Thad was unconscious. She kept saying the wedding was ruined now, and everyone would blame her."

Mabel understood how Paige might have taken the situation personally, because of its possible adverse effect on her work, but it seemed odd that she was more visibly upset by Thad's illness than the bride and groom were, when they'd reportedly considered him part of their family.

"I'll go check on her," Mabel said. "And I can ask her if she knows where the rings are."

"I'm not sure it matters in the short term," Grant said. "I mean, I'd be willing to be the best man if necessary, but I think it's more likely Father will postpone the wedding until Thad is able to work again. Someone's got to keep the business going, and it can't be done from the honeymoon cruise."

Mabel was starting to feel like indulging in her own self-centered hysterics like Paige had done. If the wedding was cancelled as a result of the best man's illness, and there was a rumor the cause was food-related, things wouldn't look good for either the farm or Emily. And with a reporter on the scene, the story was likely to reach everyone in town if not the entire state.

The farm could get along without doing weddings in the future, but Emily's fledgling catering business might not recover. Mabel wasn't ready to give up on anything quite yet, though. She needed to hear from the wedding planner herself that the wedding was cancelled before she warned Emily of the possibility. Perhaps there was still a way to salvage the situation.

CHAPTER SIX

Mabel was on the way to the gazebo in search of Paige when Terry Earley jogged over from where he'd been working on the nearby rows of garlic. Terry was British, tall, blond, and impossibly thin. His jeans and t-shirt were, as always, coated with a layer of the dirt he'd been digging in. He'd worked up a slight sweat, giving the skin on his arms a healthy sheen.

June was a relatively slow time on the farm, with nothing ready to plant or harvest, but there were always weeds and pests to try to stay ahead of. Terry had been in the field since dawn, since he was the cheerful type of morning person that Mabel found alien, and he liked to save his evenings for schoolwork. He was just a few months away from getting his master's degree in agriculture from the nearby university, and all through his education, he'd worked part-time on various farms, looking for hands-on experience to test his theoretical understanding of sustainability challenges faced by small-scale farmers. He'd worked for Mabel almost exclusively since the previous summer, and she'd grown to depend on him for his advice as much as for his manual labor.

"What's up?" Terry asked. "I heard the wedding is off because someone tried to kill the best man. I was thinking that if the lavender field won't be in use tomorrow after all, I'd harvest some of the flowers at the far end while they're at their peak for drying."

Mabel appreciated, more than ever, how unflappable Terry was. He wouldn't let a mere thing like an unconscious man scare him off.

"I'll have to get back to you on that. I don't know what happened to the best man, whether it was an accident or not, or whether the wedding's being postponed. I'll let you know when I have more information." Mabel thought of the people still milling around near the lavender field, with nothing to do but let their imaginations run wild. The wedding planner should be quashing the rumors, not hiding in the gazebo feeling sorry for herself. "Who said the wedding was off?"

"I think it was the bride's kids. They looked like siblings, a brother and sister, and they'd been hugging the bride right after you brought everyone back out here to wait for the cops. Anyway, whoever they are, they seemed awfully certain that the ceremony would be put on hold," Terry said. "They were really happy about it too. One of them said no one should be crying on her wedding day, but at least now they'd have more time to get the marriage called off completely."

"The bride wasn't crying," Mabel said. "She's allergic to lavender."

"Seriously?" Terry asked. "Then why is she getting married in a lavender field?"

"It was the wedding planner's idea, and apparently the bride can't say no to anyone."

"Is that why she agreed to marry the groom too? Her kids seem to think he was abusive, emotionally for sure, and maybe even physically."

It was hard to imagine the small, distant groom being abusive, but there was no way of knowing what went on in private. His son wasn't any more imposing of a person, and yet he'd been aggressive in demanding action on the investigation into what had happened to Thad.

"I have no idea how the bride and groom treat each other," Mabel said. "I'm just providing the setting for the wedding. At least, that's all I thought my role would be. I didn't think I was supposed to get to know everyone involved intimately so I could keep them from hurting each other. If that's part of the deal, and I need to socialize with the wedding party, then I'm not getting paid enough money to do this." She'd rather get up with the earliest of the early birds than mingle at parties.

"Don't give up on hosting weddings yet," Terry said. "Skinner Farm needs all the income it can get in order to be profitable. It's too small for most other sidelines, and you'd hate the ones that can be done on smaller acreage, like turning the farmhouse into a B-and-B or renting rooms to people who want to play farmer, like people play cowboy on dude ranches."

Mabel shuddered. "I'm absolutely not inviting people into my home. Poor Pixie would never get a minute's rest if people were always coming and going."

"Maybe your new manager will have some other ideas," Terry said. "How'd the interview go, anyway? I saw the guy out by the creek earlier, and he came over to talk to me on his way back to the farmhouse."

"He's not going to work out," Mabel said. "He had all the right credentials, but I'm not hiring someone who looks down his nose at everyone and everything around him. I'm definitely not turning Aunt Peggy's farm over to anyone who thinks she was stupid. Besides, it's clear that he couldn't handle emergencies. He panicked when he saw Thad lying unconscious on the ground."

"To be fair," Terry said. "I'd panic in that case too."

"Not the way he did," Mabel said. "I froze, too, at first, but only for a second, and I didn't run away screaming."

"That's true. You wouldn't run."

"You wouldn't either," Mabel said. "I'm sorry you've been affected by all of this. The cops probably won't let you leave today until they've taken a statement from you. If you're finished in the field and need to get some schoolwork done, you're welcome to use my office. Assuming we can find a way to get you inside without using the taped-off patio."

"That won't be necessary," Terry said. "There's always more weeding to do. And I wanted to get the rhubarb beds mulched soon, now that the plants are settled in and the ground is warm. I can start that today, and then take some time off next week for studying if I need it."

"Whatever you think best," Mabel said. "I'd better go see if the planner knows whether the wedding is still going to happen."

"You're heading the wrong way," Terry said. "Emily took her to the barn, probably so she could fix her makeup. You might not have noticed them, because you were talking to the stuck-up guy who beat up the reporter."

"Wait. What stuck-up guy, and when did he beat up the reporter?"

"The guy in the dark suit who left the lavender field with the groom."

"His son? Grant Bellingham?"

Terry shrugged. "Probably. We didn't get formally introduced, but they do look kind of alike, I suppose. When the groom got taken aside by O'Connor, the stuck-up guy went over to talk to you and Charlie. I would have joined you if you'd been alone, but I knew Charlie wouldn't let anything happen to you."

Mabel glanced back toward the farmhouse, where Joe Hansen and the other uniformed officer were pacing along the police line blocking off the patio. She could have the groom's son removed from the property or detained by the police for assault if she asked them, but doing that would probably hurt the bride more than Grant.

"Did he really get violent? In the middle of the wedding rehearsal?"

"Not during the rehearsal itself, but while some pictures were being taken, right after the photographer and the bride returned from their visit to the farmhouse, bringing the best man with them," Terry said. "It was definitely a physical alteration, but not like mixed-martial-arts fighting or anything. More like what the barn cats do sometimes to establish their dominance. A bunch of strutting and pushing, rather than landing hard punches."

That was bad enough. "What were they fighting over?"

"I didn't catch all of it, but I think the wedding guests were getting annoyed by the reporter's attempts to interview them. I heard the stuck-up guy—Grant, you said?—shouting, 'Leave us alone. We're not giving any statements.' And that's when I turned to see what was going on."

"Who won the fight?"

Terry laughed. "Kinda surprised me. It was Grant. I thought he was all hot air, and the reporter was tougher than that, but Rainey was the one who ended up on the ground, crying uncle. And red with embarrassment."

Mabel closed her eyes. Not just posturing, then, but physical contact. She was sure that was a crime. It was also the end of any lingering chance she'd had that the reporter would do a puff piece on the farm and its wedding services. Now she owed him an apology for what had happened to him on her property.

"Where's the reporter now?"

"He started to follow the wedding planner to the barn, but Emily told him off. Said he'd caused enough trouble already, like all men did, and she'd better not see him again while the cops were so conveniently nearby to arrest him." Terry added, "Emily really hasn't been her sunny, serene self since her husband filed for divorce, has she?"

"No, she hasn't." And things were likely to get worse for her before the day ended.

* * * *

Mabel followed the trail of overwhelming lavender scent to the bathroom in the front left corner of the barn. The woman she thought was the bride's daughter was pounding on the door and shouting, "Mom needs you. It's time to get over yourself."

Something too muffled to understand came through the door.

"If you don't come out right now, I swear, I'm going to tell everyone I know about how badly you messed up this wedding. And I know a *lot* of people. You'll never get hired again."

A miserable wail came from inside, but the door remained firmly closed, even when the woman outside gave it a frustrated tug. Like the bride, she had a round face and plump body, and starkly contrasting pale skin with dark hair.

Mabel stepped closer. "Perhaps I can help. I'm Mabel Skinner, the owner of the farm." It still felt weird to say it out loud, that she, not her aunt, owned the place.

"I hope Paige will listen to you, but I'm not optimistic." The woman tugged at the door again without any response from inside. She let go of it and stepped back. "I'm Beryl Markos, by the way. My brother, Harlan, and I have been trying to get Paige to do her job, with no luck. You'd think she'd respond to her client's daughter if she wanted to get a good recommendation later, but I'm not getting anywhere with her."

"Why don't you go check on your mother, and I'll take care of this."

Beryl eyed the closed door in front of her dubiously before saying, "Okay. But if she's not out in the lavender field apologizing to my mother in fifteen minutes, I'm coming back with my brother and we're breaking down the door. We'll make sure she reimburses you for the damage."

"I'm sure that kind of drastic step won't be necessary."

Beryl snorted and stomped out of the barn.

"She's gone," Mabel told Paige through the door. "It's time to come out now."

"Why?" Paige asked miserably. "So more people can yell at me?"

Mabel wanted to say that no one would yell at her, but she was pretty sure it would be a lie. The entire wedding party was probably lining up to take turns giving Paige a piece of their minds. "I won't yell at you."

"And you'll keep everyone else away?"

"You have to talk to them eventually. You really don't want to stay out here overnight. The barn isn't heated, and it will get cold when the sun goes down." There was no response, so Mabel tried, "And then the wildlife will come out."

"Wildlife?" It sounded like Paige had jumped to her feet in anticipation of an attack. "What kind of wildlife?"

As far as Mabel knew, the cats kept most of the four-legged critters out of the barn. That was their job, after all. That left birds as the wildlife, and most people weren't as annoyed by them as she was. But Mabel wouldn't mind making up some possibilities if it would motivate Paige to come out of her hiding place.

"Lots of critters. Raccoons and possums and..." Mabel paused to think. What else had she seen around the farm? And then she remembered something she'd been startled by the first time she saw them on the property. "Bats. They come out at dusk. Not too long from now."

"Bats?" A rustling suggested Paige had moved to hunker down with her arms over her head, protecting it from unseen creatures in the rafters.

"Bats," Mabel said definitively. "I don't want you to be attacked by bats, so if you don't come out voluntarily right now, I'll go get the key to this door and drag you out."

"All right, all right." The door opened, and Paige stood in the opening, not quite leaving her sanctuary.

Paige appeared to be in her early twenties, suggesting some of her incompetence might be due to inexperience with both her chosen career and life in general. She was tall and thin, with waist-length pale brown hair in a braid down her back. In an apparent attempt to fit in with the theme for the wedding, she wore lavender-colored leggings with an oversized dark purple vintage dress that hung on her like she was a child wearing her mother's clothes. More likely, it was part of a fashion trend that had completely passed by both Mabel and West Slocum.

"It's all so unfair," Paige said, finally emerging completely and letting the door close behind her. "This was supposed to be my big break, taking my bridal consulting work to a new level. Instead, everything keeps going wrong."

Paige's career had gone to a new level, all right, just not in the direction she'd been hoping for. Mabel made the soothing sound she'd been practicing on Emily whenever she was venting about her soon-to-be-ex-husband. "No one can blame you for what happened to Thad." The rest, of course, from triggering the bride's allergies to letting the reporter annoy the guests, was exactly the sort of thing a wedding planner was supposed to prevent.

"They can blame me for Thad if he got food poisoning from the caterer. I was the one who chose her."

"It wasn't food poisoning," Mabel said firmly.

"Well, that's a relief." Paige adjusted the too-wide neckline of her dress, which had slipped down her shoulder.

"Did you know Thad well?"

"Not really." She bent to fidget with the hem of her dress for a moment before straightening to ask, "If it wasn't food poisoning, then what was it?"

"I don't know."

Paige's shoulders drooped, and the dress slipped down again. "Then you can't be sure it wasn't food poisoning."

"The police will figure it out, but I'm absolutely sure Emily wouldn't do anything unsafe with her food." Movement in the rafters over Paige's head caught Mabel's attention. She didn't need Paige to get spooked and run somewhere else to hide. She glanced up, trying to be nonchalant, and saw the shadow of a barn cat moving away from the humans. Definitely not a bat, but Mabel wouldn't put it past Paige to freak at the thought of cats looking down at her from on high.

"Let's go on outside," Mabel said. "It's gloomy in here, and you'll feel better in the sunshine."

Paige gripped the doorknob behind her. "I'm not leaving here until I know what happened to Thad and that no one's blaming me."

"That could be weeks. You'll get hungry." Even as she said it, she knew it was the wrong thing to say. Emily was better with crises like these. At least she had been before her husband had dumped her and her patience had evaporated.

"Better to be hungry than poisoned," Paige said.

"Look," Mabel said. "I'm no good at softening bad news. So, here's the bottom line. If you hide now, you're just proving to everyone you can't do your job. It's not your fault Thad got sick, but it is your fault if you don't deal with the problem."

"But I don't know how to deal with it," Paige wailed. "No one ever said planning a wedding was hard. All the other ones I did were easy."

"Fine," Mabel said, exasperated. "You can hide if you want, and I won't try to stop you. But first you need to tell me if you've talked to the bride about what's going to happen next. Is the ceremony still happening tomorrow, or does she want to postpone until Thad is out of danger?"

Paige blinked. "I don't know. You should ask Donna."

Actually, Mabel thought, Paige should be the one asking the bride, and it should have happened already. "I will talk to her, but it would help to know what you're going to recommend."

"I don't know. Nothing like this has ever happened to me before."

"What about when you learned to become a wedding planner? Is there a book or something on best practices for different kinds of crises? The experts must have seen other situations where a member of the wedding party became incapacitated at the last minute. What's the standard response to it?"

"I don't know," Paige said. "I got my training on the job. All my friends were getting married, and I went to so many weddings that after a while I could see what could have been done better, so I started helping my other friends who were just starting to plan their events and everything turned out perfect for them. They never had anything like this happen."

"Is that how you got this job?" It would explain a lot. "You're a friend of Donna's?"

"Not exactly," Paige said. "And she's definitely not going to be my friend in the future, after all of this."

"Then how'd you get the job?"

"Oh, Thad got it for me," she said. "He met me at a wedding I did and decided I'd be the perfect gift for his business partner's wedding. Mr. Bellingham is so rich he doesn't need material things, so Thad decided to give him the perfect wedding experience by hiring me."

Thad had hired Paige *after* observing her in action? That seemed more like sabotage than a gift.

"That was...thoughtful of him," Mabel lied.

Paige sighed. "I guess it didn't work out the way it was supposed to. But it's really not my fault. It's like the day was jinxed or something. How was I to know the bride was allergic to lavender?"

"You could have asked her in advance."

"Well, I suppose, but how was I supposed to think of every little thing that might go wrong?"

Mabel bit her lip against the urge to say it was Paige's job to do just that, anticipate the problems so they could be avoided. Not unlike what Mabel herself did as an app developer, with clients who expected her to know all the relevant questions in advance to prevent glitches down the road. It was just common sense and good organizational skills. Both of which Paige lacked, apparently.

Still, Paige wasn't the only one to blame. What on earth had Thad been thinking to hire such an inexperienced and incompetent wedding planner? Had he perhaps had some ulterior motive, unrelated to the wedding couple's happiness? Paige was a pretty young woman with what was probably an attractive body beneath the extra yardage of her dress. Could Thad have been lusting after her, hoping she'd view him more favorably after he gave her something she desired, like a step up in her career? They might even have ended up in a relationship over the course of the wedding preparations, which would explain why she'd been more visibly upset by his illness than anyone else had been. But then why hadn't she gone to his side while the EMTs were working on him and insisted on going to the hospital with him? It certainly hadn't been her commitment to her duties as the wedding planner that had kept her from leaving with him, since she hadn't done anything useful since the ambulance arrived. They probably hadn't been in a relationship then, at least as far as she was concerned. Thad might have had other ideas, but she didn't sound particularly concerned about Thad's suffering, just about the consequences of his illness on her career.

Much as Mabel would have liked to blame Paige for Thad's illness, it seemed clear that, of all the people on the farm today, the wedding planner was the least likely to have wanted something bad to happen to Thad during an event she'd planned. Which was too bad, really. It would have been so satisfying to see the annoying woman removed from the farm in handcuffs, with Rainey snapping pictures for the story that would undoubtedly end Paige's career as a wedding planner. No other brides—or best men—would ever have to suffer like today's had.

CHAPTER SEVEN

"I'm going out to talk to the bride now, Paige. You can either hide in the barn some more, or you can come with me and show everyone how good a job you can do even in a crisis." Mabel didn't wait for an answer before heading for the barn doors. Behind her, she heard the rustling of a dress sleeve being hiked back up onto a shoulder, followed by reluctant footsteps.

Once outside, Mabel paused to take in what was happening on the patio directly across from the barn. The police tape had been moved so it only blocked the buffet table and the area behind it, where Thad had been found. Detective O'Connor had commandeered one of the smaller tables nearest the scene of the crime to use for interviewing witnesses—Emily was in the hot seat at the moment—and someone had moved the rest of the tables closer to the driveway end of the patio.

Joe Hansen was standing guard in the space between the two sets of tables, while the other officer was halfway back from the lavender field, escorting the wedding party and mayor to the patio, presumably to be seated in the unoccupied tables while waiting for their interviews. It was close to five o'clock now, about an hour after they'd originally expected to be enjoying the buffet. The guests were probably hungry, but even if there wasn't police tape preventing access to the buffet table, she doubted anyone would want to eat anything there, at least not until it was determined whether the food had anything to do with what had happened to Thad.

Paige caught up to Mabel. "I don't see the bride."

Mabel looked back at the group coming in from the field. Paige was right. The bride wasn't with them. Neither was the groom, and the couple wasn't out at the spot near the creek where Stan had made his phone calls earlier.

A young woman with a toddler in her arms broke away from the group and came running up to Mabel. "Restroom?"

Mabel turned to point to the left side of the barn's interior while asking, "Have you seen the bride?"

Without pausing, the woman said, "She wanted a little privacy, so she went for a walk. She should be on her way back by now. Or she might have been intercepted by her kids. They went out to your front porch to get away from their almost-stepbrother."

Mabel nodded her thanks and turned to Paige. "I'll check the porch to see if Donna's there with her kids, and you can check with the other wedding guests." If the bride wasn't with her children, they might at least be able to confirm where she'd gone. "Why don't you go help the guests get settled on the patio? Show them you're in control, despite everything, and that they don't have anything to worry about."

Paige shrugged, causing her dress neckline to slip off the shoulder again, and headed toward the approaching guests.

Mabel was about six feet away from the front corner of the house, not yet visible to anyone on the porch, when she heard a triumphant male voice, presumably Donna's son, Harlan, say, "Everything's working out even better than we'd planned. Next step is to convince Mom to hold off on the wedding until Thad has recovered. That gives us several days to stop things completely."

Mabel froze. The *next* step? The bride's children's goal was obviously to break up the Bellinghams, but what had been the *first* step in their plan? Cause someone in the wedding party to be ill? Would they intentionally hurt someone, or had they simply latched on to an unexpected occurrence they could work to their benefit?

A woman's voice, which Mabel recognized as belonging to the bride's daughter, Beryl, said, "We might even have more time, depending on how long it takes for the police to figure out what happened to Thad. We should tell Mom she can't take the risk someone else will get sick. She needs to wait until we know for sure what happened."

"Good idea," Harlan said. "If it's up to the giggling detective to solve the case, we might never get any solid answers."

Mabel heard Pixie yowl in the kitchen. Someone must have entered the driveway and would be coming into sight in another few seconds. She didn't want to be caught eavesdropping on her guests, so she hurried back in the direction of the patio. She stopped about halfway there and turned to look over her shoulder at the driveway just in time to see her friend, Rory

Hansen, park her small green pickup on the grass in front of the house near the Mini Cooper, Charlie's truck, and the reporter's car.

Rory was in her mid-forties and had a lot in common with her truck. They both showed their age, but were sturdy and built for work. Like her police officer husband, she was dedicated to improving the community, although she motivated people with the threat of her disapproval, rather than force.

Rory raced over from the front yard and started to pull Mabel into a hug before stepping back and letting her arms drop to her side. "Sorry. I'm just so worried. I had to come see for myself that you and Emily are okay. My husband texted to say someone became seriously ill at the wedding rehearsal and had to be taken to the hospital."

"I'm fine," Mabel said, "and Emily's holding up okay so far."

"Where is she?"

"On the patio."

Rory took a step in that direction, but Mabel pulled her back. "She's talking to Detective O'Connor, so you'll have to wait a bit."

"What about the victim? Is he going to be okay? What happened to him, anyway?"

"Let's go inside to talk." Now that the police tape had been moved back, it should be possible to get into the kitchen without being stopped. Especially since Rory's husband was in charge of who could go where, and he wasn't likely to stop his wife. "It might be better if we weren't overheard. And I'd like to check on Pixie. She's supposed to be locked in the office, but I saw her in the kitchen window not long ago."

They passed the tables occupied by wedding guests, who should have been chatting happily after the rehearsal, but now were as silent as if they were attending a funeral. It had to be sobering for them, seeing the police tape at the far end of the patio, and in the other direction, a detective and witness at a makeshift interrogation table.

As Mabel had expected, Joe Hansen didn't stop her and Rory from going inside, and O'Connor either didn't notice they were crossing the patio or didn't care.

Once in the kitchen, Rory said, "I'll get us both a drink while you check on Pixie."

The cat wasn't on the windowsill any longer, so Mabel headed to the front of the farmhouse. The office door was ajar, but Pixie was innocently napping on a chair as if she hadn't just been yowling about a visitor, and apparently not too traumatized by the number of people coming and going. On the way out again, Mabel made extra sure the door was securely fastened before returning to the kitchen.

Rory had poured two glasses of iced tea and set them on the table before going over to stand in front of the window and watch the activity on the patio. She turned at Mabel's entrance and settled at the table in front of her drink.

"It's got to be bad if O'Connor is here," Rory said. "More than a simple accident, right?"

"I wish I knew." Mabel dropped into the seat across from Rory and paused to take a long drink while she gathered her thoughts. "All I know for sure is that the best man passed out near the buffet table, and he was still unconscious when the ambulance took him away. I'd love to know how Thad's doing now and what made him sick in the first place, but you're more likely to get an update than I am. O'Connor certainly isn't going to tell me anything."

"He still hasn't forgiven you for showing him up last time, has he?"

"I don't think he ever will."

"I'm so sorry," Rory said. "I know you and Emily were both counting on this weekend to launch your wedding and catering sidelines."

"Skinner Farm will be fine, even if there aren't any more events in the lavender field," Mabel said, although she wasn't entirely sure it was true. The new rhubarb bed wasn't likely to be all that profitable, even once it matured enough to harvest in a couple of years, and the added expense of a farm manager's salary was going to eat up all of the usual profit from the other crops. A bad season could leave the budget in the red. Still, she had other financial resources, so she could weather a bad year or two. "I'm more worried about Emily than myself. I don't want to believe it, but it's possible something the best man ate is what made him sick. He'd been raiding the buffet table while Emily was setting up, before it was ready for diners. And the wedding planner didn't think to ask anyone if they had allergies so those foods could be kept off the menu. It's not Emily's fault if Thad was allergic to something she made, but some potential customers might still be put off by the situation."

"Poor Emily. It's really hard making a living in the food industry, even when things go well." Rory looked down at her glass of iced tea for a long moment before lifting her head and straightening her slumped shoulders. "I'm afraid I may have some more bad news for both of you. As farmers, not wedding producers. I was going to wait until after the wedding to mention it, when I thought you'd be feeling more optimistic, but today can't get much worse, so now's as good a time as any to tell you. Unless you want to wait?"

Mabel wondered if she'd been a little too hasty in rejecting Richard Wetzel's application to be the farm manager. She wasn't sure she could handle any more bad news for the farm on her own. The muscles in her neck were already tense, worse than after pulling an all-nighter hunched over a laptop to meet a work deadline. Delaying the bad news wouldn't help, though. She might as well get it over with.

"No," she said. "Go ahead."

"I just got confirmation that three of the nearby towns are adding farmers' markets this year."

"That sounds like good news, not bad. More places to sell our products."

"It's more complicated than that," Rory said. "More places to sell can be good or bad depending on whether there will be an increase in the total number of buyers. We already draw people to our site from all the towns starting new venues, and studies have shown that the demand for farmers' market products is pretty stable, so adding locations just means each place gets fewer people shopping. If you have to work at four markets instead of one to make the same number of sales, your labor costs quadruple, while the income remains the same. Or if you decide not to do the extra market sites, so you can save on labor costs, then you'll only get about a quarter of the previous year's sales."

"This is exactly why I need to hire a market manager instead of doing it myself. I never would have thought of that complication. At least not until I'd already overextended myself at all the markets."

"That reminds me," Rory said. "You were going to interview a candidate for that job today. How'd it go?"

"About as well as everything else today," Mabel said. "He thought everything Aunt Peggy and I did on the farm was wrong. I'm pretty sure he even thought the creek didn't know how to do a proper creeking. I couldn't see working with someone that negative, so I told him he wasn't getting hired. He didn't take the rejection well, so even if I wanted to change my mind, I doubt he'd consider the job. Especially after he found Thad unconscious on the ground. It freaked Wetzel out pretty badly. I have a bad feeling he's already actively spreading the word among anyone else who might be considering applying for the job that Skinner Farm is a terrible, dangerous place to work."

"You're lucky to be rid of him, then," Rory said. "And look, they say bad things come in threes. You've met your quota now, between the disrupted wedding, the increased competition with other markets, and the hiring fiasco. Things should start getting better any minute now."

The kitchen door burst open. Emily rushed inside and slammed it shut behind her. "Thad just died. And O'Connor thinks I killed him."

* * * *

Mabel paced the kitchen, staying out of the way while Rory—much better equipped to handle emotional crises—soothed the distraught Emily. Even so, it took Rory several minutes to get Emily settled at the kitchen table with a box of tissues and a glass of iced tea. Most of that time was spent with Emily sobbing on Rory's shoulder and mumbling incoherently.

Eventually, Emily took a deep breath and straightened away from her friend. "I'm sorry for freaking out like this. I was just a little overwhelmed. I know the giggling is just O'Connor's nervous habit, but it was like he was laughing at me the whole time he was clearly building a case against me for killing someone with my cooking. Even if I don't go to jail, I could lose everything once the rumors about my role in Thad's death start. I could lose my *goats*!"

"Wait." Mabel came to a stop next to the window. "Have the police even confirmed the cause of death was food-related?"

Emily thoughtfully rubbed a tissue against her dripping nose. "I don't think so. I tried to find out exactly what happened, since I was being blamed for it, but O'Connor just laughed even more than he usually does. That tells me he doesn't really know much and is trying to fake it. But the police are definitely assuming there was something wrong with the food. They took samples from everything on the buffet table."

"I'm sure they won't find anything wrong with your food," Rory said, patting Emily's back. "If the death had anything to do with what he ate, it was probably because he had an allergy. In which case, it's not your fault."

Mabel glanced out the window. "Or someone could have poisoned the food after you set it out. If it was intentional, as opposed to an unknown allergy, there are plenty of other people who are more likely suspects than you are, Emily. O'Connor should be looking into who might have had a reason to kill Thad."

"That's what I was thinking too," Emily said. "That if it wasn't just some freak accident, it couldn't have anything to do with me. I barely knew him, so I couldn't have any possible reason to kill him. I mean, I told O'Connor that the man had annoyed me by messing up the buffet and smoking too close to the food, but dealing with that sort of difficult guest is a normal part of working in food service. I worked for catering companies all through high school and college, right up until I got married, and there was always at least one guest who made things difficult for the staff. In fact, it's a good event when there's only one annoying person. I learned how to handle them a long time ago without killing anyone."

"I'm sure O'Connor will consider the other possibilities eventually," Mabel said. "People who actually knew Thad must have stronger motives than anything that could be conjured up for you."

"I don't think O'Connor's even considering anyone else," Emily said. "He seems to think none of the guests had access to the buffet table, since the whole wedding party was out in the lavender field when the body was found. It looks like he's going to go through the motions of collecting information on where everyone was when he talks to the wedding party, but I doubt he'll be looking for discrepancies in their stories the way he was in mine. I wish I could have named someone else who left the rehearsal area, other than Thad, but I was too busy to pay attention to who was where this afternoon."

Just wait until O'Connor heard I was on or near the patio when Thad made his last trip to the buffet and paid for it with his life.

Mabel sighed. "We can keep each other company in the lockup. As the only other person near the crime scene, I'm going to be right next to you on O'Connor's suspect list."

"I'm sorry," Emily said. "Renting out the farm for weddings was my idea, and now one or both of us is going to end up in jail for poisoning someone. On purpose or through unsafe food handling."

Rory spoke up indignantly. "There was nothing the least bit unsafe about your food."

Even O'Connor would know how fastidious Emily was in her food handling if he'd ever seen the commercial kitchen that had been installed in her farmhouse when she'd first started making the goat cheese she sold at the farmers' market. The place was always immaculate, and the work surfaces were kept free of anything but the equipment and ingredients she needed for her recipe, with nothing nearby that might introduce unwanted bacteria or otherwise lead to cross-contamination.

"Assuming Thad's death wasn't due to an allergy or some other natural cause, then I think it's far more likely that he was intentionally poisoned than killed with bad food," Mabel said. "And then the strength of any alibi might depend on how long the poison would take to act. If it was just a minute or two, then O'Connor might be right about no one from the wedding party being near the buffet right before Thad died. But if it could have taken longer than that for him to get sick after he ingested it, the alibis are no good. Not everyone was needed for every minute of the rehearsal and pictures, so any one of them could have claimed they needed to use the facilities in the barn, and instead popped over to the patio to put the poison in whatever Thad was eating."

"No matter what, they'll think I was part of it," Emily said sadly. "A coconspirator maybe, claiming I helped by labeling Thad's plate so they'd know which one to poison."

"We don't even know for sure that he was the intended victim," Mabel said. "The killer could have poisoned all of the food, but Thad got to it first. Plus, he ate a lot. More than most people would. Perhaps it was sprinkled around all the food and was just meant to make everyone sick, not to kill any one person, but his gluttony gave him too high a dose."

"It doesn't matter," Emily said in a resigned tone. "Even if it was natural causes, everyone's going to hear that someone died after eating my food during the very first event I catered, and potential customers aren't going to want to hear the details about how it wasn't my fault. They'll just move on to another caterer. My business is probably as dead as Thad, and I'm going to lose my goats."

"That's not going to happen," Rory soothed. "Worst-case scenario, if you lose your farm, I'm sure I can find someone to board the goats for you."

Mabel was becoming less worried about the goats and more worried about Emily ending up in prison. Not because she'd done anything wrong, but because O'Connor was incompetent and would never find the real culprit while he was set on convicting Emily. To make it even less likely that he'd succeed, he was running out of time to figure out who was really to blame. The suspects were all part of the wedding party, but not necessarily local residents. As long as they were staying here in West Slocum, they could easily be reached for questioning. Once they left after the wedding on Saturday afternoon, Mabel definitely wouldn't be able to question them, and they might even be out of O'Connor's reach if they lived far enough away.

The best chance Mabel would have to question the witnesses was if the wedding went forward as scheduled. And that was looking iffy, given the bride's children's intent to get it cancelled completely. If they succeeded, Mabel wouldn't be able to interview everyone on Saturday, and without her help, however unwanted by O'Connor, the killer was likely never to be caught, while Emily took the blame.

For everyone's sake, including Thad, who deserved justice, Mabel needed to find the bride and get her to commit to getting married the next day, before her children could talk her into a postponement that would result in a killer getting away with murder.

CHAPTER EIGHT

Mabel left Emily and Rory in the privacy of the kitchen and went outside, intent on doing everything possible to make sure no one was thinking about postponing the wedding. She couldn't ask the bride, because she was being interviewed by Detective O'Connor, while everyone else sat and waited silently. They were starting to get restless and were probably hungry too. It was a shame to let all of Emily's food go to waste, but even if the police were willing to let someone move it away from the blocked-off section of the patio so that it could be eaten, Mabel doubted anyone would take the risk, no matter how hungry they were, until the testing confirmed it hadn't been the contents of the buffet that had killed Thad. And that confirmation wouldn't be available for hours, if not days.

Mabel paused just outside the kitchen door to call Maison Becker and Jeanne's Country Diner to order enough food to be delivered for the twenty or so people on the patio. The two restaurants were longtime customers of the farm, and also the source of most of Mabel's own meals whenever she wanted something more than what her limited cooking repertoire covered. She trusted them to come up with something that would satisfy the wedding party's hunger and possibly even distract them from the less-pleasant aspects of the day, at least for a few minutes.

Confident that food would be on its way as soon as humanly possible, Mabel looked around the patio for someone other than the bride who might know whether the wedding might be called off. Paige had stayed out of the barn, but she still wasn't doing her job. Instead, she was hunkered down at a table all alone, her slumped body language shouting that she didn't want to be approached. It seemed unlikely that she'd have learned anything definitive about the wedding plans while Mabel had been in the kitchen.

The groom should have some answers, but he wasn't on the patio. Not out by the lavender field either or the area near the creek where he'd been using the phone earlier. Mabel finally caught sight of him over by the barn, half-hidden between the new-looking Mercedes-Benz SUV he was leaning against and a smaller BMW. He was on the phone again, this time talking to someone rather than reading and texting.

Mabel crossed the driveway and waved to catch his attention. She stayed several yards away to give him a minute to finish his call, and she kept an eye on O'Connor in case it looked like he'd be done with the bride's interview before she could claim the groom's attention.

Stan didn't keep her waiting long, though. He glanced at his phone regretfully before asking with only a hint of impatience, "What can I do for you?"

"I wanted to tell you how sorry I am for your loss," Mabel said as she approached.

"What loss?"

"Your best man."

Stan waved his phone dismissively. "He can be replaced."

Mabel was shocked into silence. Perhaps he hadn't heard that Thad was dead, not just sick. Or perhaps he just meant that someone else could fill in as best man. "So, the wedding is going forward tomorrow despite everything?"

"The wedding? Why wouldn't it?" Stan glanced down at the phone. Mabel could hear it vibrating against the ring he wore. "Look, I need to take these calls. Thad's death has left a huge hole in my business."

So he did know his partner was dead. And he obviously didn't care. Mabel might have understood not visibly mourning a business associate, but according to Grant, Thad had practically been a member of the family.

Mabel said, "I thought maybe the wedding would be postponed while you and your bride deal with the tragedy. If so, I need to cancel some deliveries and staff."

"The wedding planner would know what to do," Stan said. "Go talk to her and let me make my calls."

"I tried to ask her, but she didn't have an answer and didn't seem to think it was her responsibility to find out," Mabel said.

"Then as far as I'm concerned, the wedding is going forward as planned. It's taken me months to convince Donna to do this, and I don't want to have to start over from scratch." The phone had stopped vibrating, and he made a grunt of irritation. "Now, leave me alone so I can take care of the things that will actually be affected by Thad's death."

"Is there anything I can do to help?" Mabel asked. "Would you like to come inside the farmhouse and use my office?"

"Thanks," Stan said begrudgingly, "but that won't be necessary. And it would be a little too easy for my loving bride to corner me in there, where I'd have no escape route. She's not going to be happy that, unlike the wedding, our honeymoon *is* going to be postponed, so I can pick up the reins of the business again for a while."

"Isn't it up to Thad's heirs to deal with all of that?" Mabel thought of the stacks of paperwork she'd had to deal with for inheriting the farm from her aunt. That had to have been simple compared to the transfer of a multimillion-dollar business. "I thought he bought you out so you could retire."

"The deal wasn't set to go into effect until the marriage certificate was signed," Stan said. "So now it looks like I'm buying him out instead of the other way around. Ironic, isn't it? But that was in our partnership agreement, that the survivor would buy out the share of the person who died first, paying the money to the heirs."

"The police will want to know who those heirs are," Mabel said. "If you have a list of them, it would save them some time in contacting his loved ones."

"I don't recall whom he listed as his heirs," Stan said. "I didn't pay much attention to it. I never really thought I'd be in this position, since he was the junior partner. All I know is that he doesn't have any immediate family members who might inherit his assets. Unless that silly woman who claimed he'd fathered her child was telling the truth. Thad denied it, though, so I'm not sure whom he wanted his money to go to."

A spurned woman sounded like a perfect murder suspect, Mabel thought. Especially one with a child to provide for, and a deadbeat father whose wealth should have supported his child, but instead had apparently served as a shield against the legal system that should have forced him to pay up. An angry ex-girlfriend would definitely have a solid motive, but she wouldn't have been invited to the wedding, let alone the rehearsal that only the closest family and friends were part of.

"If you do find out who Thad's heirs are, would you let the police know?" Mabel asked. "Or you can give me the information if it's easier, and I'll pass the information along to them."

"I'd hoped to put off dealing with the heirs for another week or two, but I suppose it's better not to wait," Stan said. "I'll have my lawyers look into who my new silent partners are. The sooner I know, the sooner I can buy them out. Now, if you'll excuse me..."

Mabel nodded and left him to his cubicle-like space between the vehicles to continue his calls. The groom might not see any reason for the wedding to be postponed, but he also didn't seem to view his partner's death as anything more upsetting than a business setback that could be straightened out with some phone calls and a pack of lawyers. The bride might well react differently, so Mabel wanted confirmation from Donna.

As she left, she tried to imagine what the bride saw in the seemingly heartless and distant groom. But then again, relationships weren't Mabel's strong suit. Her friends had made it clear they thought she should be encouraging Charlie's attentions more than she was. She hadn't even noticed his interest in her at first, and since realizing he wanted to be more than just casual friends, she'd resisted becoming more serious about him. He was everything the groom wasn't—attentive, kind, and funny—but she still kept him at arm's length, and not entirely because she was planning to leave town soon. She just wasn't any good at relationships.

Mabel was halfway across the driveway when Stan called out from behind her, "Wait."

She turned to see what he wanted, and he came out from between the vehicles.

"There is one thing that would make me want to postpone the wedding, or at least move it elsewhere," he said. "So, maybe you can do something to prevent it."

"What is it?"

"That guy." Stan pointed toward the front of the farmhouse, where Mabel had last seen the bride's children. The reporter, Andrew Rainey, was at the side of the porch, peering through the railing. "He interrupted my work earlier to introduce himself and then proceeded as if I'd agreed to an interview. I don't do interviews. That's what I have...had...Thad for."

Mabel didn't bother explaining that she'd checked with the wedding planner, who'd okayed the presence of the reporter as part of a farm-focused story. The reporter's annoying behavior was as much Mabel's fault as Paige's. They'd both underestimated how much trouble Rainey would be, since he'd lied about his real reason for being on the farm. "I'll go talk to him and make sure he leaves you and your guests alone."

"You'd better do more than that," Stan said. "Make sure he stays away completely. If I see him tomorrow, I'll move the whole wedding back to my house. If he follows us there, I can and will have him arrested for trespassing. We should have held the ceremony there anyway. No need for all this fuss and expense. But it was the only way Donna would agree to marry me, so I went along with it. Big mistake."

Mabel would have reminded him that traditionally the wedding day fuss was mostly for the benefit of the bride, not the groom, but it didn't seem like Donna was enjoying the experience all that much either, between the allergies and the police presence.

"I'll make sure there's no unnecessary fuss tomorrow," Mabel promised and hurried over to evict Rainey.

* * * *

By the time Mabel caught up with Rainey, he'd moved from the side of the porch and was at the top of the steps, completely blocking Beryl and her brother from leaving unless they got physical with him. Given his precarious position, he was lucky they apparently shared their mother's unwillingness to be confrontational, and they weren't the type of people who would shove someone down the stairs. They had backed away from Rainey and had apparently been politely declining his requests for an interview before Mabel arrived.

Rainey had his notepad out, although the huge lens on his camera would have made it awkward to write with it in the way. "Just answer one question for me. Why was your mother crying? Before the best man died, I mean. What else made her so upset? Is she regretting the marriage?"

"That's none of your business," Beryl said, showing she wasn't quite as passive as her mother was.

"Beryl's right," Mabel said from behind Rainey, startling him into dropping his pen. "Your question has nothing to do with farm sustainability, which is the only story you have permission to pursue here."

Rainey bent to retrieve his pen, and the camera swung from the neck strap, thwapping him on the inner side of his elbow. As he stood, he said, "There's a much bigger story now. Someone died during a wedding rehearsal. It's my journalistic duty to get the story." He pointed to the press tag in his hat's band.

"Then talk to someone who has factual information on the death instead of gossip," Mabel said, shooing him to the side to make a path for Beryl and her brother if they wanted to leave. "Detective O'Connor is in charge of the investigation. He can tell you what you need to know."

"He won't talk to me," Rainey said. "Not until he's ready to make a public statement. Which is really foolish, because I saw the crime scene, and I'm a keen observer. I'm sure I noticed things that no one else did."

"He might not have realized you were here when Thad was found, rather than responding later after hearing what had happened on the police scanner. Once O'Connor realizes you're a witness, I'm sure he'll want to know what you saw."

"It might be too late by then," he said. "I can't wait much longer before I write my story or someone will beat me to it. Did O'Connor tell you anything? Can I quote you on what he said?"

"I'm not talking to you about anything as long as you're bothering the guests." Mabel didn't really know much about what had happened to Thad, but maybe she could use what little she did know to lure Rainey away from easy access to the guests.

There had to be somewhere she could stash him for a while, given that she had a whole farm, spread out over ten acres, with plenty of secluded spots. Too many of them weren't good options, though. She couldn't drag him over to the barn, since it would take him past where Stan was making his phone calls, and the last thing she needed was to be seen accompanying Rainey anywhere near the groom. The patio wasn't good either, since the bulk of the wedding party was there, and they didn't want to be interviewed. If she let Rainey inside the farmhouse, he'd be out of sight and unable to bother anyone except Pixie, but Mabel hated the idea of a stranger—especially a nosy one who couldn't be trusted not to rummage through her personal belongings—left all alone and unsupervised in her home. The only other option for stashing Rainey was out in the fields. Where he was supposed to be talking to Terry about the farm, after all.

"I'm going out to talk to my field hand," Mabel said. "You should come with me."

"And you'll answer my questions?"

"It depends on what they are," Mabel said.

"Forget it. I'm not leaving the porch."

Mabel shrugged. "Then I'll have to ask the police to remove you. Conveniently, they're right here on-site, and they aren't going to want you bothering the guests any more than the guests want to be bothered. They've been through enough today already." She started down the steps, hoping he wouldn't call her bluff. Joe Hansen might have helped her out if the detective wasn't around, but O'Connor would undoubtedly balk at having one of his officers spending even a single minute helping Mabel.

After the barest hesitation, Rainey called out, "No, wait," and hurried down the steps after her.

She looked back to see he'd tucked his notepad into a pocket and was holding the camera safely against his chest so as not to be hit by it again.

Behind him, Beryl and her brother gave her grateful smiles and went back to sitting on the wicker porch chairs.

Mabel led Rainey across the front yard toward the new rhubarb field, which was conveniently far enough from the patio that the reporter couldn't even see the guests. Or be seen by them, if he'd irritated them before and they would be happier if he wasn't around.

"What can you tell me about the body? Did you notice any signs of foul play? Something out of the ordinary?" Rainey stumbled over an uneven spot in the grass. He righted himself, clutching his camera, and continued, "Don't even try to tell me you didn't see anything. I did the background work. I know you found the body."

Technically, the farm manager applicant had been the one to find the body, but the less said about Richard Wetzel, the better. His getting hounded by the reporter would only give him one more reason to bad-mouth Mabel and Skinner Farm. Besides, she had to be careful not to say anything that might annoy O'Connor if her comment was made public. There was enough friction between them already, and talking to the reporter before the detective interviewed her definitely wouldn't mend their relationship.

Mabel hedged, "Perhaps you could tell me what you know first, so I won't be repeating the obvious."

"The victim is Thad Dalton," Rainey said promptly. "The best man and the groom's business partner."

"That's my understanding too."

"So, what else do you know?" he asked impatiently.

"Nothing more than you do," Mabel said. "You saw Thad on the ground. Probably even took pictures."

"It's not about what I know, which is plenty, but about other perspectives," he said. "You must know something more. What about the cause of death? Did O'Connor confirm it was poison?"

Mabel could speculate that, whatever had killed Thad, it hadn't been something natural, since the detective was building a case against Emily. But it was still possible Thad had died of an allergy, not intentional poisoning. Until there was a definitive answer on the cause of death, Mabel wasn't going to be the one who started rumors that could hurt Emily. "You'd have to ask the police. I'm not qualified to offer a medical opinion, and the people who are qualified aren't going to tell me or anyone else involved with the wedding, not before it's announced publicly. They're much more likely to talk to you as a member of the press."

"I'll get the official answers from O'Connor eventually, but I need more than that for a really good story. Help me out here. You must have seen something suspicious when you found the body."

She'd seen crumbs from the cheesecake bars on Thad's shirt, and near him were his empty plate and the little flag marked with his name. Rainey must have seen them, too, but she wasn't about to bring his attention to something that so clearly pointed to Emily as a prime suspect.

"I'm afraid that's all I can tell you," Mabel said as they approached where Terry was working in the rhubarb bed.

"I guess I'll have to look for a better witness, then. I know more about the crime scene than you do." Rainey stuffed his notepad into a pocket. "Do you know where Charlie Durbin is? He was with you when you found the body, wasn't he?"

Mabel hesitated. The reporter clearly wasn't going to quit looking for someone to answer his questions. If he couldn't talk to Charlie, then he'd find someone else to bother. Emily was safely inside the farmhouse, out of Rainey's reach, but there were plenty of other people he might target, like the bride—once O'Connor was done with her—or the rest of the wedding party. Given that Paige wasn't likely to run interference for any of them, Mabel had to protect them. Charlie, on the other hand, could take care of himself, and he was less likely to be fazed by the reporter than any of the guests were. He'd certainly dealt with enough press—both good and bad—in the course of his career as one of the most prolific developers in the county.

Still, no one deserved having her sic a reporter on him, least of all Charlie, who'd been a big help with designing the stage for the wedding and having his crew build it. If only she was on better terms with the detective, she could have asked him to keep the reporter from talking to any witnesses for fear of contaminating their recollections. If the death turned out to be foul play, as O'Connor clearly believed it was, then everyone on the property had to be considered suspects. And that included Rainey.

"I really don't think it's a good idea for you to interview anyone about Thad's unfortunate death right now. Maybe work on the story you came here for originally, about the farm, while you wait for the detective to talk to you. O'Connor won't like it if he finds out you're talking to his witnesses before he does. Especially since you're potentially a suspect yourself if it turns out the death wasn't from natural causes."

"Me?" Rainey squeaked. "But I was with the wedding party out in the lavender field when Thad collapsed. I only found out something happened when everyone else did, by the sound of the ambulance's siren."

"You were supposed to be talking to my field hand then, not the wedding party," Mabel reminded him.

"Yeah, yeah." He adjusted the strap of the heavy camera where it dragged against his neck. "The thing is, no one wants to read about boring old farmers. Not when they can read stories about celebrities. Millionaires and murder make for front-page stories. My being here for the death just shows what good instincts I have. I must have known there'd be something bigger when I agreed to do the silly little puff piece."

Mabel was skeptical of his supposed nose for news. He worked for a small, regional newspaper that was mostly about town politics and kids playing sports. It was a good source for basic local news, but the stories didn't require any investigation beyond searching public records for the times and locations of meetings.

Besides, Rainey's personality was clearly not well-suited for getting people to talk to him. He'd irritated Stan enough that he'd threatened to move the wedding to avoid the reporter. And Rainey didn't seem to be the least bit conscious of the fact that he'd just called Mabel old and her beloved farm boring. Not the sort of thing that would make her more inclined to cooperate with him.

"I'm afraid you're stuck talking to boring old farmers as long as you're on my property." As she spoke, she heard Pixie's yowl, faint through the walls of the farmhouse, announcing a new arrival. It had to be the food she'd just ordered. It was a welcome diversion, but she was glad Emily was inside the farmhouse, where she couldn't see the delivery and wouldn't have to see someone else's food replacing her own.

Rainey glanced at Terry in the nearby rhubarb field and wrinkled his nose. Before he could come up with some new excuse, Mabel said, "You can either interview Terry while you wait to talk to O'Connor, or you can go enjoy the take-out that will be delivered to the patio by the time you can get there. But I won't have you questioning my guests. One word to any of them, and I'll have you removed from the property."

Rainey looked at the still-empty driveway. "There's no food coming."

"You really push skepticism to its limits, don't you? I thought reporters were supposed to trust before they verify. So trust me, there *will* be a delivery vehicle coming up the driveway any second now. You can follow it back to the patio if you want." Mabel counted on delivery for a lot of her meals, as well as food for her farm workers, and she couldn't risk the drivers blackballing her because of Rainey. "Just don't say a single word to the driver. He can't possibly know anything about Thad's death."

CHAPTER NINE

A small white SUV came around the corner just as Mabel had predicted, and Rainey tried, but failed to hide his surprise.

"The food is from Jeanne's Country Diner and Maison Becker," she told him. "I'd recommend getting there quickly, because it's not going to last long."

Apparently Rainey had a stronger nose for free food than for news, so he left without any more encouragement, holding his camera to his chest as he hurried off in the wake of the delivery vehicle. Mabel didn't trust him to leave the guests alone for long, but she thought he'd be distracted for a few minutes while claiming his food, and she needed that time to talk to Terry.

If, as she'd told Rainey, everyone on the property was a potential suspect, then that included her field hand, who'd had the misfortune to be working today. Terry hadn't been anywhere near the patio after the guests arrived, and he couldn't possibly have had a motive to kill the best man, but she wanted to prepare him for possible questioning, especially if O'Connor thought it would upset her. She also needed to know if Terry had seen anything useful to the investigation, in case the detective didn't ask him the right questions. Terry was smart and observant, and Mabel wouldn't underestimate him the way O'Connor would. If Terry had any relevant information, she would make sure the detective knew about it.

Terry had his back to her and was using a spading fork to spread the mulch he'd dumped out of a wheelbarrow along about ten feet of the first row of rhubarb plants. They were tiny now, since it was their first spring in the ground after being started in a greenhouse. When they matured in a couple of years, they'd be two to three feet tall and wide, filling in what looked like too much empty space between them. The stalks were far too small to be harvested this summer, and only a few could be pulled the next year, but after that, the quarter-acre field would produce regularly for the next decade or longer, adding a new source of revenue for Skinner Farm. She was pleased with what she'd accomplished by planting it, but rhubarb didn't promise the immediate gratification that Wetzel had seemed to want and that Rainey thought his readers wanted to hear about. She'd have to find something else to distract the reporter when she got back to the patio.

She called out Terry's name to get his attention and made her way along the path nearest where he was working. "How's it going?"

Terry straightened and stretched his long spine. "Good. I should have about half the field properly mulched before it gets too dark to see the smallest plants. I wouldn't want to step on any of them after all the work we did to plant them."

When Mabel had first decided to create the rhubarb field, she'd envisioned a simple project. Just plow it in the spring—or, more accurately, hire Terry to dig up the field with the tractor, since she was still wary of big farm vehicles—and then mark the rows, quickly tucking the tiny seedlings into easily hand-dug holes. Even after she'd seen exactly how big a quarter-acre field was and how tiny the seedlings were, she'd expected it to take no more than a couple of days, just a minute or two per plant after the initial plowing. It had actually taken the equivalent of two people putting in a forty-hour week, spread out over more than six months, due to the extra prep work necessary for a perennial crop like rhubarb. After all those hours spent on a field that wouldn't even produce any income for another two years, she definitely didn't want to risk damaging even a single one of the plants.

"It's probably best that I don't try to help you, then," Mabel said. "Even in good light, I'd probably do it wrong." After all, Richard Wetzel had years more agricultural education and experience than she did, and he'd thought everything she'd done on the farm was terrible.

"It just takes practice," Terry said. "Unless you bury the plants under six inches or more of mulch, they'll be fine."

"I'll come back later to help if I can get a break from the guests before dark, but for now, we should both probably head back to the farmhouse. I came out to let you know the police might want to talk to you." She gestured at the delivery vehicle that was parked behind the cruisers with the back doors open. "And there's dinner, if you're hungry."

Terry was in his mid-twenties, old enough to have outgrown the usual adolescent hunger, but he was still so skinny she doubted his metabolism would ever slow down. He looked like he never ate, although she knew he did, because she tried to provide food whenever he worked for her, as a thank-you for his tendency to do more than his job required without ever making her feel stupid or incompetent.

"I never say no to free food." Terry leaned the spading fork against the wheelbarrow and brushed his dirty hands against his jeans. "I should wash up first."

The groom was probably still out in front of the barn, making calls and not wanting to be disturbed. "You can use the kitchen sink instead of the one in the barn, if you want." She glanced toward the porch as she walked with Terry toward the driveway. Beryl and Harlan weren't there any longer, so there was no risk of them overhearing her conversation. "Before you go wash up, though, I was wondering if you'd seen anything unusual before the ambulance arrived."

"People wearing dresses on a farm is pretty unusual."

"Besides that." They'd reached the end of the porch, and in a moment, they'd be out from the front of the house, where people could see them and possibly hear what they were saying. Mabel held out her hand to stop Terry. "I expect the police will want to know if you saw anyone wandering away from the group instead of participating in the rehearsal and pictures."

"Just the guy who got taken away by the ambulance. He was missing from the rehearsal more often than not. I could hear the photographer's frustration every time he had to rearrange everyone to make up for the guy's absence."

"That was the best man." Mabel realized Terry wouldn't have heard the latest news about Thad, and needed to be aware of how serious the situation was. "I'm afraid he died."

"Really?" Terry's pale eyebrows raised in surprise. "He didn't look old. If anyone was going to fall over dead, I'd have expected it to be the groom, not someone who was young enough to be his son."

"Detective O'Connor is treating it as a possible murder. That's why it's important to know who might have had the opportunity to kill Thad."

Terry nodded. "No one from the wedding party came over near where I was working. Probably thought they'd get dirty. Or have to do some work. The manager candidate came out to chat with me. Or lecture me mostly, I suppose. He didn't seem to be a fan of companion planting."

"He mentioned that to me too."

"He's right that it's more labor-intensive than single crops that can be harvested mechanically," Terry said earnestly, "but for a small farm, it's still more cost-effective, and it protects against a total crop failure. Weather that's bad for one is often fine for the other."

"You don't have to convince me," Mabel said. "Where did Wetzel go after he talked to you?"

"Was that his name?" Terry said. "He didn't introduce himself, and I didn't really pay that much attention after he was done with me. He was heading over toward the creek initially, but I didn't see where he went after that."

"What about the people who were here specifically for the wedding? Did anyone other than the best man step away, even for a few minutes?"

"The bride and the photographer took a break at some point," he said. "Not too long before the ambulance siren."

"I know about them. They came to the farmhouse to fix the bride's makeup."

"Other than that..." Terry paused to think before saying, "The groom spent most of his time over by the creek so he could mess around with his phone. He only joined the rest of the party when he had to be part of a picture or do his part in the rehearsal, but he was never out of sight. The only other person who didn't stay in the lavender field was the reporter covering the wedding. He seemed to be annoying everyone, and they'd tell him to leave. He'd back off a bit, but then five or ten minutes later, he'd be back in the thick of things."

"He wasn't supposed to be covering the wedding. He was supposed to be interviewing you."

"That's what I thought, so when I saw he had the press tag in his hat, I waved at him, but he ignored me to head straight on over to the lavender field. He certainly never came over to talk to me. I figured maybe, with that big camera he had, he was a newspaper photographer instead of the reporter."

"Unfortunately not." But it was interesting that the reporter hadn't been with the wedding party the whole time. "Did Rainey leave completely when he was asked to, or did he just linger in the tractor path when he backed off?"

Terry thought for a moment before saying, "A little of both. Mostly, he just lurked around the edge of where the photography was happening. But one time a guest escorted him all the way back to the parking lot."

"So, they all have alibis, except the reporter. Everyone else was out by the lavender field or near the creek the whole time."

"I wouldn't go that far," Terry said. "I can't completely vouch for everyone the whole time they were supposed to be out there. I took a few breaks myself, to use the bathroom and refill my water bottle or empty the weeds onto a compost pile. Someone might even have gone past me while I was busy and I just didn't notice. I can zone out when I'm working."

"Then no one has a really solid alibi," Mabel said, discouraged. She didn't have much time to get to the bottom of the situation before the wedding was over and all her suspects left. Especially if the wedding was postponed or moved to a different venue.

"Sorry I couldn't be more help."

"It's not your fault. Close surveillance of guests isn't part of your job description."

"Shouldn't the wedding planner know where everyone was?" Terry asked.

"She should, but... Did you meet her?"

He laughed. "Yeah. She wanted me to make the lavender plants taller. She seemed to think they should grow at shoulder height and above, like she'd confused them with lilacs."

"When was that?"

"Right around when the bride and photographer went to the farmhouse," Terry said. "Actually, after she left me, she went to the barn instead of back to the lavender field. I'd forgotten about that. I didn't see her come back."

So, the planner was unaccounted for around the time of Thad's death. That was interesting.

Terry interrupted her thoughts. "Is there anything else you need to know, or can I ask you something?"

"Sure, but I don't know how Thad died. Or how or why."

He waved a dismissive hand. "Not about that. About the farm manager. What are you going to do now that you've rejected your one and only qualified candidate?"

"I don't know exactly."

"You're not planning to put the farm back up for sale, are you?"

"That's no longer an option," Mabel said, although she wished it were. She'd only considered hiring a manager after it had become clear she wouldn't be able to find a buyer who would continue to farm the land instead of turning it into condos. Now it looked like hiring a manager could take years instead of weeks, and she hadn't planned to stay in West Slocum that long. She'd already had to deal on her own with last fall's garlic planting, then the six-month-long project of starting the new rhubarb field, and finally the spring seeding of butternut squash. At this rate, there wouldn't be anything left for the manager to manage, not even the final project of the year in October, harvesting the squash. "I'll have to place some more ads and be patient. The right person has to be out there. I just need to figure out a way to reach him."

"You could change your required qualifications, making them a little less strict."

"I got them from a book on hiring a farm manager," Mabel said. "And confirmed them with several other sources."

"I know, but..." Terry hesitated. "It's not my place, and you can tell me I'm overstepping if you want. It's just, well, you know how I love the theory of agriculture, and some great texts have been written about it, but sometimes they're written by people without much hands-on experience with the real world. That's what I've learned while working for various farms while in school. The theory I learn in classes always needs a little adjusting sometimes for individual circumstances, like the way growing zone maps are great in theory, but they might not be quite right for a given field, because of microclimates within a zone and even within a single parcel of land. Farming is very much not a one-size-fits-all endeavor. You need to tailor the academic stuff to fit your individual needs. I think that's probably true of the hiring process, too, not just the crops."

"I'm stuck in a catch-22 then," Mabel said. "If I had the expertise necessary to tailor the qualifications for my perfect farm manager, I probably wouldn't need to hire a farm manager at all."

Terry looked like he was going to say something else, but the delivery driver called out, "Hey, are you Mabel? I need a signature before I leave."

"I've got to deal with this," Mabel told Terry. "We'll talk more later about what I need in a farm manager."

"I'm sure you'll figure it out," Terry said before loping off in the direction of the food.

He had more confidence in Mabel than she did in herself when it came to the farm. Especially after Wetzel had listed all the things he thought she'd done wrong. Still, today's interview had given her one more thing to look for in the ideal candidate: an attitude that stayed as positive as Terry's even against the backdrop of a suspicious death.

* * * *

Mabel signed the delivery driver's paperwork and let him know she'd added a tip for him when she'd placed the orders. He thanked her and left, and she continued over to the patio to see if O'Connor had finished interviewing the bride.

Beryl Markos had taken her mother's place at the table with the detective, and her brother, Harlan, was waiting anxiously for his turn, seated at the table closest to them, with his chair turned sideways so he could watch his sister. He had a paper napkin from Jeanne's Country Diner in his hand, which he was twisting into a rope. Everyone looked slightly on edge at the prospect of being interviewed by a police detective, but Harlan seemed more nervous than the other guests. He was close enough to the interview that if he strained, he might be able to pick up parts of it, but not so close that O'Connor, never good at noticing small details, was likely to pick up on the eavesdropping. Every once in a while, his hand twitched as if he'd started to raise it to get his sister's attention, perhaps in response to something she was saying, and then had caught himself and let his hand fall back into his lap.

The bride was nowhere in sight, which was a problem for Mabel's finding out if the wedding was still on, but at least she was safe from the reporter. Rainey was on the patio, talking to a pretty young woman whose toddler was playing at her feet. He started to take the child's picture, but the woman said something that Mabel couldn't hear and held out her hand for the camera. She was probably worried about her child's privacy and intended to erase the digital picture, Mabel thought, except instead of scrolling through the images, the woman raised the camera to her face, fidgeted briefly with some settings and then took a rapid series of pictures of her child before handing the camera back to the reporter. The expression on her face clearly said, "*That's* how it's done." Then she scooped the toddler up in her arms and carried him over to where the line for food had begun to peter out.

The patio was quiet, considering there were twenty or so people getting or eating their food in small groups. Mabel was relieved to see that Emily hadn't come out of the farmhouse, so she wasn't forced to see her food being replaced. The other bit of good news was that the reporter had apparently taken Mabel's threats to heart, so when the young woman left to get her food, Rainey didn't try to follow her or look for other guests to interview. He remained seated with his lunch at an otherwise empty table to watch everyone without trying to talk to anyone.

Joe Hansen and the other uniformed officer kept an eye on everyone from unobtrusive spots on the edge of the patio. Mabel made a mental note to save them something to eat in case they got a chance to take a break.

The wedding photographer flitted around, taking pictures and doing his best to improve his subjects' glum expressions. Charlie Durbin shared a table with Terry and four members of the wedding party who hadn't been introduced to Mabel, but looked to be bridesmaids and their partners. The only member of the wedding party who was missing, other than the bride, was the groom. Stan was still over by the barn, using his phone. Someone had brought him a meal, though, and the remnants of it littered the trunk of the BMW that was serving as his desk.

Stan's son, Grant, sat alone, one table farther away from where O'Connor was interviewing the guests than the bride's son was. Grant picked at the food he'd unpacked from the two boxed meals in front of him, one from Jeanne's Country Diner and one from Maison Becker. Unlike the bride's son, Grant was sprawled in his seat as if he didn't have a care in the world, oblivious to the detective's interview, but he must have been paying attention, because as soon as Beryl pushed her chair back to stand, marking the end of her interview, he jumped to his feet and headed in her direction.

As he passed Harlan, who had also stood and started toward the interview table, Grant said, "Where do you think you're going? I'm tired of waiting, and I can't leave until I give my statement. I'm going next so I can get this over with."

"The detective said he wanted to talk to me after Beryl," Harlan said mildly. "But if you want to go first, go ahead."

"Why are you being so nice?" Grant frowned for a moment, then his face cleared. "Oh, I get it. I know what your plan is. You want to ask your sister what she said and make sure your stories match before you talk to the cops. Well, I'm not going to help you get away with whatever you two have done to ruin today. Go on, go tell your lies. I can wait a few minutes longer, I suppose. It'll be worth it, watching you squirm, trying to figure out what Beryl might have already said so you won't contradict her."

Harlan silently shook his head in exasperation as he resumed his walk over to the detective's makeshift interview table. Grant wandered off in the other direction to where about a dozen boxed meals, twice that many water bottles, and a smattering of soda cans were still laid out.

The little confrontation reminded Mabel of the missing wedding planner. Paige should have been keeping the two sides of the family apart, but of course, she was nowhere in sight. Perhaps she'd gone with the bride, wherever she was. But that left Mabel to keep Grant from bickering with Beryl the way he'd done with her brother. That meant engaging him in small talk, not something she was suited for. Next time she hosted a wedding, she was making it a condition that she didn't even have to be on the property while it happened. She could spend the day at the library. At least there she'd only risk hugs from everyone's favorite librarian, Josefina.

Fortunately Mabel didn't have to make up a reason for following Grant over to the food table. She hadn't eaten since breakfast, and it was almost six now. She was starved, as well as curious to see what the respective restaurants had made.

Mabel pasted on a smile and asked Grant, "How's the food?"

"Adequate." Grant opened a box from Maison Becker, removed the brownie, and closed the box up again. As he repeated the action with the next meal, he added, "Surprising, really. I wasn't expecting much in the way of decent meals in this podunk town. It's not up to my standards, of course, but it's edible enough. Probably better than what the original buffet would have been."

She bristled at the insult to Emily's food, but now wasn't the time to argue with a guest. Or bring his attention to the person responsible for the food who might eventually be implicated in Thad's death. Mabel forced herself to say, "I guess we'll never know how good it was."

Grant laughed snidely. "We know one thing. It was deadly. Thad died for his gluttony."

"I hadn't heard that the cause of death has been determined," Mabel said, hoping to head off the spread of rumors that would tarnish Emily's reputation even after they were proved false. "Are you sure it had anything to do with the food?"

Grant shrugged. "Had to be something he ate. It certainly wasn't natural causes. Thad was healthy as a horse, even if he ate like a pig."

Maybe she could introduce some doubt that would keep him from spreading his rumor. "So, Thad wasn't a workaholic like your father? The kind that can lead to heart disease and sudden death?"

"Thad wasn't like that at all," Grant said. "Father isn't either actually. Not in any negative way. They both found their passions, and could earn a good income from something they wanted to do all the time, so they did. Thad was happiest when he was working. Just like my father is. Not that the girlfriend cares what makes him happy."

"I heard your father was planning to turn the business over to Thad tomorrow," Mabel said. "What's your father going to do now?"

"We haven't discussed it yet," Grant said. "But I bet he's secretly thrilled he doesn't have to quit now. And the girlfriend can't stop him, in the circumstances. Not unless she wants to live in poverty."

Mabel doubted very much that poverty was a possibility, given the couple's obvious wealth even before selling the business. "He could look for someone else to buy him out."

"Maybe," Grant said, "but I think it's more likely Father will use the situation as an excuse to keep working, despite what the girlfriend wants. She's always been jealous of his time spent with anyone but her. All he has to do is find a new junior partner, who can be the face of the business, while Father is the brains of it, and things will be back to the way they were."

"What about you?" Mabel asked. "Have you ever considered joining his business as a junior partner?"

"Not an option," he said without hesitation. "I'm already following in my father's footsteps as an entrepreneur. He understands I'm not interested in his particular field, so I'm blazing my own path."

"Where's it leading you?"

"Here and there," he said. "I've started a few companies already, but none of them was quite right, so they didn't go anywhere. I've got something new underway, and it feels right, but you never know until it all comes together."

Grant was pushing forty, which seemed a little late for finding his passion when he'd had all the opportunities a wealthy father could provide. Mabel had known she wanted to work in the tech field as far back as she could remember. Not everyone found their true calling as early as she had, but they usually had at least some strong interests and were invested in the outcome of their pursuit of them. The blasé way Grant talked about his dead-end start-ups and his lack of full commitment even to his latest endeavor made her wonder if he was more of a dilettante than an entrepreneur.

Grant's father appeared next to him and abruptly announced he needed to talk to his son in private.

"You can use the front porch if you'd like," Mabel said. "I don't think anyone's out there now."

Stan grunted his agreement, then gestured for his son to follow. Grant jumped to obey, abandoning the bravado he'd shown Mabel and apparently forgetting that he was in a rush to get his police interview over with.

Relieved that she no longer had to keep Grant out of trouble, Mabel resumed her delayed search for the bride. Not just to discuss the status of the wedding, but also to make sure that O'Connor hadn't unduly traumatized her with his inept questioning.

CHAPTER TEN

Mabel headed across the driveway to see if the bride and the wedding planner were inside the barn again. On the way, she saw the young woman who had put the reporter in his place a few minutes earlier. She was seated next to her son in the back of a small pickup truck a little to the left of the barn, near the path to Emily's Capricornucopia. The vehicle had been one of the first to arrive, memorable both because of its bright yellow color and because of the signs on the doors and tailgate, which advertised the Linden Photography Studio.

The woman looked to be in her early twenties, of average height and extremely pretty, with a softly rounded face and generous figure. She dressed with more functionality than fashion, in a light blue cotton sweater and navy pants. She almost matched her toddler's outfit of a long-sleeved blue T-shirt and jeans. The two of them were entranced by a tortoiseshell cat on the ground about six feet away, peering back at them warily. Billie Jean was a relatively new member of the colony. She'd given birth to five kittens the previous fall while Mabel had been fostering her. After her babies were weaned and adopted out, the momcat was spayed and released to the barn. She remained too feral to live indoors, but over the past few months, she'd come to tolerate being around human beings as long as they didn't get too close.

The toddler was reaching his arms out over the raised tailgate, making a grabbing motion with his hands, and saying something that was probably his word for "soft, cuddly, creature." The woman kept the child restrained with a hand on the back of his waistband, and Billie Jean didn't seem particularly frightened, although that would undoubtedly change if the toddler were down on the ground with her. Still, it was unusual that she hadn't already run away and instead was preening for the child.

Animals were generally considered to be good judges of character, sensing when they should run away from someone who wished them ill. For all anyone knew, they could identify people who'd committed violent crimes like murder, but if so, they had no way to communicate that information to humans. And just because Billie Jean seemed to like the woman and her son, it didn't necessarily mean they were both good people. They certainly looked innocent enough, but history had shown that serial killers could be both angelic-looking and charismatic, so their neighbors never suspected the bodies in the basement.

Billie Jean turned to look at Mabel, then apparently decided there was one human too many in her vicinity, so she trotted away and into the woods.

Mabel detoured toward the truck. "I'm sorry," she told the young woman. "The barn cats aren't friendly. There's one inside the farmhouse who likes people if your son would like to meet her later on."

"He'd *love* to meet her, but he's never been around pets before, and I'm not sure he understands that animals can't be tossed around like toy trucks." She released the toddler now that the temptation to dive over the edge was gone, so he could crawl around the bed of the truck. "I'm Lara, by the way. Photographer's assistant."

"Mabel. I own the farm."

"It's beautiful," Lara said. "Would you mind if I take some pictures for my portfolio tomorrow? Not as part of the wedding, I mean. I've got my own camera in the truck's cab. I took some pictures of my son earlier, but I didn't want to do landscapes without your permission."

"I'd be honored." Mabel wished the reporter and the manager candidate were as appreciative of the farm's natural beauty as the photographer's assistant was. "I'm looking for the bride. Have you seen her recently?"

"She's hiding out in the barn," Lara said. "I'm supposed to tell anyone who's looking for her that she needs some privacy."

"That's understandable. I promise not to bother her for long, but I really need to know if she's still planning to go forward with the wedding tomorrow despite losing the best man. The groom says it's still on, but I just want to be sure she agrees."

Lara wrinkled her nose. "Of course Stan wants it to go ahead. It's just a business deal for him."

"Still, he lost his business partner, so I'd think he'd be rattled at least a little. He seems awfully unconcerned about Thad's death."

"That's just how Stan is," Lara said. "He never shows his feelings, for good or bad. He's known for it. He could be furious or euphoric while he's talking to you, and you'd never be able to tell. Even Donna can't always figure him out."

Mabel wondered how Lara knew so much about the groom and whether her information was reliable. "He must have expressed his feelings to Donna at some point. She is marrying him, after all."

"Oh, that's just business too," Lara said. "Something to do with estate planning. I don't know all the details, but apparently there are financial benefits to a spouse, rather than a girlfriend, inheriting assets. He'll do anything to avoid paying taxes. Even get married."

"It sounds like you know the family well." Much better than a wedding photographer's assistant would be expected to know the client.

"The bride's my godmother," Lara said while stopping her son from climbing over the tailgate to pursue something on the far side of the truck over in the woods. "She really stepped up when my mother died. I was about my son's age at the time, and she treated me like another daughter. I've known her and Stan for as long as they've been together."

"You must know Beryl and Harlan, too, then," Mabel said. "They don't seem terribly happy about this wedding. I heard them talking about some plan to postpone it, if not cancel it outright."

"That sounds like them. They're well-intentioned, but they're wrong about Stan. They think he's abusive toward their mother." Lara pulled her son onto her lap in the nick of time before he went over the tailgate headfirst. "Stan can be a bit arrogant and self-centered, but no more than most men, I suppose."

She sounded bitter for someone so young. Although she'd probably been not much older than eighteen when she'd had her son. If the father was a deadbeat—emotionally, financially, or both—it could easily have soured her on men.

Lara continued, "And if Donna wants to marry Stan, then it's really none of the kids' business. Beryl and Harlan should stay out of it, and so should Grant. It's not like any of them live with Donna and Stan or even spend much time with them. I probably see them more often than their biological children do."

"You must have known the best man too."

"Of course." Lara let her son go free again and turned to watch for a moment as he toddled toward the far end of the truck bed. She faced forward again to say, "Stan always mixed his work with his personal life, so I ran into Thad at their house all the time. It will feel strange not to see him there in the future."

"I'm sorry for your loss."

"We weren't close or anything," she said, "but it's still a shock. I mean, he was so young."

Just another example of how Lara seemed older than her actual age, Mabel thought. Thad had been a good fifteen years older than Lara, and here she was, lamenting how young he'd been.

A thump from the other end of the truck's bed caused Lara to turn around again. The toddler had slipped and fallen onto his bottom while trying to climb over the side. He'd already gotten back up on his feet and was tackling the obstacle again, apparently intent on chasing after Billie Jean, who'd returned from the woods and was walking toward the truck on the way back to the barn.

Lara jumped to her feet, and as she raced over to grab her son, she said, "Sorry. Gotta go. Sometimes Harry takes after his father a little too much, always chasing after something he shouldn't touch."

* * * *

Mabel stopped just inside the barn doors to let her eyes adjust to the dimmer light. She should have been able to spot the bride's pale lavender outfit even half-blinded, but Donna wasn't anywhere in sight. She'd probably stepped into the bathroom.

The wedding planner was there, though, her intense perfume drawing attention to her while her dark purple dress camouflaged her in the shadows. Unlike earlier, she wasn't actively hiding. Instead, she leaned with feigned nonchalance against one of the huge back tires of the tractor that had been parked inside to leave all the space in front of the barn open for parking.

It seemed like an odd place for her to be loitering, until Paige said, "Oh, it's you," then turned toward the deeper shadows behind the tractor. "It's okay. It's just Mabel."

The bride peered out cautiously. "The reporter didn't follow you, did he?"

Mabel automatically looked behind her and through the open barn doors, as if Rainey might have snuck in behind her. He wasn't there, and when she looked past the doors, over to the patio, she saw first his distinctive hat and then the rest of him seated alone in the same isolated corner spot on the patio where she'd last seen him.

"No," she said. "He's on the patio. Alone, not bothering anyone."

Donna heaved a long sigh. "I know I said he could be here today, but I didn't think he'd pester me and Stan nonstop. First about our relationship and then about poor Thad."

"I'm sorry." Mabel joined the other women near the tractor. "I've told him to leave the wedding party alone. I'd have kicked him off the property as soon as I heard he'd been bothering people, but by then the police had ordered everyone to stick around until the interviews are all finished. I'll make sure Rainey doesn't come back tomorrow, though. Assuming the wedding is going forward on schedule."

"I don't know." Donna's mascara had run again, and she reached up to dab at it ineffectively with what looked like a crumpled paper napkin from Jeanne's Country Diner. "It seems so disrespectful to Thad to go ahead like nothing happened, but some of the guests live pretty far away and are already traveling to West Slocum for the wedding, and it wouldn't be fair to them to change things at the last minute."

"Stan told me it was definitely going forward tomorrow, but I wanted to check with you too."

"I suppose he's right, as usual. But there's so much to consider. We definitely have to postpone the honeymoon." Donna let her hand drop from her face and smiled. It was the first time Mabel had seen her look even a little happy, and it made her radiant, despite the mascara streaks. "Actually, it's terrible of me, I know, but I've been thinking I might go on the honeymoon by myself. I've always wanted to see Alaska, but Stan could never take time away from his work to take a trip where he might be out of touch for a day or two at a time. I waited for years so he could see everything with me, but now he's going to have to go back to work until he can find someone to take over his business. And that could take years. Especially since once we're married, I won't have any leverage left to convince him to retire. His accountant told him we needed to be married for tax reasons, and I said I'd only agree if he retired. We had a deal, and it's all changed now, because he *can't* retire. It would be unreasonable of me to ask. The business he built would die, and I can't do that to him." Donna's smile had faded as she spoke, and she dabbed at her eyes again. "Sorry to unload on you. Too much information, I'm sure. But I just don't know what to do now."

"It's okay," Paige said airily. "You don't have to decide right now. We'll do whatever you want, whenever you make up your mind. It's no big deal."

Mabel felt the urge to slap Paige. It might not be a big deal for her, but it was for everyone else. There were contractors and guests to notify. And

Emily needed to know whether her catering services would be needed so she could make the food.

"I'm sorry," Mabel said, "but you really do need to decide now. Not this exact minute, but in the next hour at the latest. Before the detective says everyone can leave. Your wedding party needs to know whether to prepare for tomorrow, and I need to know whether to cancel everything. For starters, the caterer needs to know, and so do the florist and the quartet."

"Oh, right," Paige said. "I forgot about them."

Just like she'd forgotten to ask about allergies and forgotten to make sure the guests were comfortable and given food and drinks while waiting for the police to interview them. Mabel had done more planning for the wedding than Paige had.

"That's all right," Donna told Paige, taking the young woman's hand and patting it. An outsider might have thought Donna was the planner and Paige was the anxious bride. "You had no way of knowing what would happen today. Why don't you take a break, and I'll go talk to Stan right now and get it all figured out."

"Good idea," Paige said, heading for the bathroom. "I'm going to freshen up first."

Donna made a scooting motion with her hands, then turned to Mabel. "Do you happen to know where Stan is so I can hash this out with him?"

"He was heading for the front porch with his son," Mabel said. "Stan wanted a quiet place for them to talk."

"Oh, dear." Donna looked around for a place to put her soggy napkin before giving up and sticking it into a hidden pocket at her hip, causing a small lump in the otherwise smooth line of her perfectly fitted dress. "I was hoping Stan and I could have some privacy. Somewhere our kids couldn't intervene."

"You can use the farmhouse kitchen if you want," Mabel offered. "The door's unlocked. Just don't let the cat outside if you see her."

"Thanks." Donna hesitated. "It's not that I don't value our children's opinions, you know. It's just better that Stan and I work everything out on our own. My kids romanticize their memories of my first husband, so they don't think Stan is good enough for me. And Grant isn't very good at sharing. He wants his father all to himself."

And his father's money, Mabel suspected. For his various start-ups that turned out not to be his passion, after all. The marriage would give Donna and possibly her children a legal claim against Stan's estate, a permanent one that wasn't likely to be terminated even if the couple broke up or Grant contested his father's will. Mabel could ask her lawyer back in Maine about claims against an estate, she thought, only to stop short at the realization that he couldn't ever advise her again. It had been long enough that she sometimes forgot he was gone, and then the renewed memory was like losing him all over again.

Donna and Stan were going to go through that sort of belated heartache, remembering their friend's death every time they thought of their wedding. Mabel didn't envy them that pain. She couldn't bring Thad back to life, but she might be able to make the memories a little less terrible by making sure Detective O'Connor did his job thoroughly and offered a little justice by arresting Thad's killer.

CHAPTER ELEVEN

As soon as Donna headed for the front porch, Mabel looked toward the patio to see what Detective O'Connor was doing. He was still in the same spot as before, but now one of the bridesmaids was seated across from him for questioning.

It would be some time before O'Connor ran out of other options and condescended to question Mabel, so she decided to stay in the barn to do some interviewing of her own as soon as Paige came out of the bathroom. Terry had said the wedding planner was unaccounted for around the time Thad died, and Mabel didn't trust O'Connor to delve deeply into everyone's alibis, so she intended to find out where Paige had disappeared to.

Mabel also planned to insist that Paige do what she'd been paid to do, even if Donna was willing to let her off the hook. It was time for the wedding planner to earn her fee instead of leaving it up to others to do her job.

While Mabel waited, she made some notes on her phone about what she needed to do before the next morning, depending on whether the wedding went forward or not. There was almost more work for her to do, she thought, if the wedding was cancelled than if it happened as planned. Perhaps Donna could be persuaded to go forward as planned if she heard how much work it would be to reschedule, and how unfair it would be to the contractors.

Paige emerged from the bathroom a couple minutes later, as fresh and radiant as the bride should have been, with no sign that she had a care in the world. Even the too-large neckline of her baggy dress was neatly balanced on her shoulders.

"We need to talk," Mabel said.

"About what?" Paige slumped and the neckline slipped down one arm.

"About where you've been all day when you should have been working," Mabel said. "You weren't out by the lavender field with everyone else when the rehearsal wrapped up. Where were you?"

Paige fidgeted with the wandering neckline. "I can't remember."

"Try harder."

"I think I might have left early to use the bathroom. Trying to get in ahead of the rush."

"How long were you there before the rehearsal ended?"

"I don't know. Maybe half an hour?"

That was a long time to spend in the barn's rustic bathroom. It didn't exactly have much in the way of amenities. "What else did you do in that time?"

"Nothing."

Mabel gave her a skeptical look.

"Okay, so I climbed into the tractor and sat there for a while and cried. I'm not usually a baby like that, but it's been a difficult day. Even before Thad went and died."

"When did you leave the barn?"

"As soon as I heard the sirens." Paige frowned. "You sound like a cop. But you're not, and you're not my mother either. I don't have to tell you anything."

"All right," Mabel said. "Never mind the past. We can discuss the future. I need to know what you'll be doing to make things go smoothly tomorrow, assuming the wedding goes forward."

"My work is done," Paige said with a shrug that caused her neckline to slip farther down her arm. "All I have left to do is show up and admire how my planning turned out."

"Are you sure you've planned a wedding before?" Mabel asked incredulously. "All the way to the end?"

"Of course." Paige straightened proudly and tugged the neckline back into place. "I helped with five perfect weddings and was in charge of three of them all by myself."

Mabel's mind boggled, but she reminded herself that it didn't really matter if Paige was telling the truth. She needed to keep both herself and Paige on point. "I assume none of them was cancelled or postponed at the last minute, so perhaps you haven't had to deal with that sort of thing before."

Paige shook her head.

"Then we can make a plan together," Mabel said briskly. She didn't have any experience with wedding cancellations either, but she was good at anticipating problems for a project and creating flowcharts to make sure that all possibilities were covered while she worked on an app. "Let's think about what needs to be done if this one is postponed. For one thing, the contractors—starting with the florist, and the quartet—all need to be contacted. Will you take care of that?"

"I can't." Paige tugged at the neckline that had fallen again. "I don't have their contact information. It's all in my computer at home and in the cloud, which normally I could access with my phone, but there's no service here."

Fortunately, most of the contractors were local people Mabel had recommended, except for the photographer, who could be told in person, and the quartet that Paige had hired on her own, without getting any local recommendations. She would have to contact the musicians when she got back to her hotel and had internet access. "Never mind the local contractors. I'll take care of them. Unless there's anyone you hired without telling me."

"Not that I can think of," Paige said. "But what about the guests? Someone needs to let them know, too, if it's postponed, and I can't access their information either."

Mabel drew the line at offering the use of her own internet access. She didn't trust Paige not to crash it somehow. If it weren't so late in the day already, Mabel would send Paige to the local library to use their internet to access her files, but it would be closing soon, and getting the information couldn't wait until it opened again the next morning. By then, the guests would already be on their way to West Slocum.

"It shouldn't be much longer before the police let everyone go home," Mabel said. "Contacting the guests, and the quartet you hired, can wait until then. Your hotel should have wifi for your phone."

"I'm not staying at a hotel," Paige said. "The Bellinghams offered me a room at their house."

"They must have internet access you can use."

"Yes, but—"

Whatever new excuse Paige was going to offer was cut off by the photographer, Ken Linden, rushing into the barn. "Have you two seen Donna?" he asked. His elegant suit was slightly disheveled, and there was a look of panic on his face. "She's missing, and her kids think something terrible has happened to her, maybe even the same thing that happened to Thad. We've got to find her."

* * * *

Mabel allowed herself a moment to imagine being able to go hide inside the farmhouse until the weekend was over, or go screaming to her car, where she could leave and never return, like the manager candidate had done. But she wasn't like Wetzel or Paige, who ran away from problems. Otherwise, she'd have long since sold the farm to the first person who made an offer, not caring what happened to it, and gone back to Maine.

Besides, she didn't really think anything had happened to Donna. She was fine, but at this point, a rumor was all it would take to send the whole wedding party into a panic.

"She can't be dead." Paige clutched at her ribs, pulling the oversized dress tight against her torso. "My new career will be ruined if the bride dies."

Mabel was fairly sure the woman's future as a wedding planner was already deader than Thad, but all she said was, "Donna is either out on the front porch or else in the kitchen with Stan." Normally they wouldn't have been able to get to the kitchen door without anyone noticing, but nothing about the day was normal, and everyone was distracted by the presence of the police, so they probably hadn't been paying much attention to their surroundings. "I asked her for a definitive answer on whether the wedding will be postponed after Thad's death, and she wanted some privacy while she discussed the options with Stan."

"Oh, thank goodness." Ken thumped one hand over his heart and closed his eyes briefly as if saying a quick prayer of gratitude. When he opened them again, he told Mabel, "I should have known there was a simple explanation for her absence from the patio. I guess we're all on edge, or I'd have realized there's no reason to think there's any continuing danger. Thad's death was a fluke, after all, nothing to do with anyone here, as I'm sure the detective will come to realize pretty quickly."

Mabel wasn't that optimistic, but it wouldn't help to have Ken and others second-guessing O'Connor. She planned to do enough of that for everyone.

Ken then turned to Paige. "I need to talk to Mabel for a moment. Would you mind mingling with the guests for me and distracting them from all the delays? You're good with people."

"I am, aren't I?" Paige brightened, and practically skipped as she left the barn.

Once she was out of earshot, Ken said, "I'm sorry you've had to deal with Paige. I tried to convince Donna not to accept her help, but you probably noticed how kindhearted Donna is. She's naturally trusting of everyone, even when she should know better, so she believed Thad when he said Paige was fully qualified for the job. I could tell from the beginning that the only reason he recommended her was that she was his latest girlfriend.

He changes them so often I can't keep track. But they're always young and pretty and naïve like Paige."

The wedding planner had downplayed her connection with Thad, and it could have been a relatively innocent attempt to hide the truth in order to convince everyone she'd gotten the job based on merit, not who she was sleeping with. But now Mabel had to wonder if there had been a darker reason for hiding their relationship. It could have been because she was planning to kill Thad and wanted to claim she had no reason to want him dead. Mabel had discounted Paige as a suspect earlier, since she'd seemed to be the only person who didn't dislike Thad. The equation changed if they'd been in a relationship.

Significant others were always at the top of the list of suspects in any murder investigation. If Paige had been Thad's girlfriend, that automatically meant there were a number of possible reasons to have wanted him dead. He could have cheated on her or been abusive or, while it was hard to imagine, he could have been perfectly innocent and Paige had been the one taking advantage of him, and was now ready to cash in on his estate. In any event, Paige definitely had potential motives, and she'd also had the opportunity to kill Thad since she had no alibi for the time when he'd sneaked back to the patio the last time. That meant Paige had just become a serious suspect, as far as Mabel was concerned, and she never would have known if the photographer hadn't mentioned the couple's relationship.

Mabel might have originally preferred to hire a local photographer instead of Ken, but he was turning out to be a fortunate choice. Any other businessman would have given up as soon as things started going wrong, and the bride would have had no one to lean on.

"Paige's mistakes aren't your fault," she told him. "Were you able to get some good pictures after Donna fixed her makeup?"

"I think I've got some adequate material to work with, but I really want the pictures to be perfect. Donna deserves the best. I'll be spending a lot more time in the studio than usual, Photoshopping the images so the bride doesn't look like she's crying in most of them. On the plus side, the lavender field really is stunning, so I won't have to clean up the background much. I'm cautiously optimistic that Donna will be pleased with the final versions."

"The police might want to see the raw pictures if it does turn out that Thad's death wasn't an accident or natural causes. The time stamps might be useful for confirming alibis."

"It may take some time. Image files can be really large, and with the number I take, it's time-consuming to download," he said.

Mabel bristled at being treated like she was computer-illiterate. Then she reminded herself that he probably had to explain basic digital matters to clients all the time, like she herself did, so it wasn't personal.

"I'm sure the detective would appreciate whatever help you can give him," Mabel said. "The pictures might help to establish who was where when, which could be helpful once they've confirmed the cause and time of death."

"Of course, of course," Ken said. "I'm happy to do anything to help. I'll make sure the police get a full download of everything on my cameras as soon as I possibly can. Now that I don't have to search for Donna, I'll be able to start working on it while I wait for the detective to let us leave."

"What about the camera your assistant has? She mentioned having her own and using it to take pictures of her son. She might have caught some of the wedding party in the background."

"I'd forgotten about that," Ken said. "Although I shouldn't have. I gave it to her, after all, as a birthday present. She's my daughter, you know, and it won't be long before she becomes the main photographer in the family, and I'm demoted to assistant. She has an amazing eye for detail and composition."

That would explain why he'd been so accepting of her bringing her toddler—his grandson—to work. "If you wouldn't mind getting the images from her for O'Connor, I'd appreciate it."

"Of course," Ken said. "Although I don't think there will be any that include the wedding party. She mostly focuses on nature, rather than people, except for her son, of course. I think it's a waste of her talents, because she's so good with people. She understands how people feel, and she can use that to get the subjects to relax and forget about the camera. I just wish she wasn't quite so caring about other people outside of the photography sessions. She's a lot like Donna in the way she gives everyone the benefit of the doubt, even when they're trying to cheat her, so she gets hurt a lot, also like Donna."

"Both women are fortunate to have you in their lives, then," Mabel said. "I should get back to the patio now. The detective must be almost finished with his interviews, and I need to ask him if his forensics team will be done with the patio in time to use it for the wedding tomorrow. Assuming it happens."

"I'll come with you," Ken said. "I haven't had a chance to grab any food yet, and I'm starving. Thank you for ordering it."

"I hope there's something left for you. Last I knew, Grant was going through the boxes and pulling out his favorite bits."

Ken laughed. "That sounds like him. From the way he acts around free stuff, you'd never know he has a substantial allowance from his father, twice what the average person earns in a full-time job, and all tax-free."

"Doesn't Grant have a job?" Mabel asked. "He told me he was an entrepreneur."

"In his imagination maybe, but I think he likes the idea of being a businessman a lot more than he likes the reality of it. It's like he still has a child's image of what a job is. He throws himself into creating the pretty façade and all the basic material that goes into a business plan, like the name and a vague mission statement, but he always bails right around when it's time to do the hard work of putting a plan into operation."

Mabel wanted to ask more about Grant and whether he might have been jealous of Thad, enough to have wanted him dead, but she could hear raised voices down the driveway toward the front of the house. Beryl and Harlan were in the driveway, yelling at Officer Joe Hansen about needing help to find their mother.

Joe was good at his job, particularly at keeping the peace. If the situation had escalated to yelling, he might need some help. Preferably from a civilian, rather than police backup. Paige should have been the one handling difficult guests, but she wouldn't think to step up to deal with a problem, and even if she did, she was more likely to make the situation worse than to calm anyone down.

"I'd better go see what the problem is," Mabel said.

"And I should go find Donna to make sure she hasn't let Stan steamroll her in the decision about the wedding. I'll check the kitchen first, if that's okay with you."

Mabel nodded, and Ken jogged in the direction of the back door while Mabel headed down the driveway.

CHAPTER TWELVE

Joe Hansen was making soothing sounds at Beryl and Harlan, although the exact words were drowned out by the combined voices of the bride's children.

"What's wrong?" Mabel asked Joe.

He bent toward her, invading a bit of her personal space, but it was necessary so she could hear him over the panicked voices of Beryl and Harlan. "They want me to start a missing-person search," he said calmly. "They think something's happened to their mother. Normally, I wouldn't be concerned, since it's been less than an hour since the last time they saw her, but given what's already happened here today, I'm going to have to kick the issue up the ladder to someone who has more authority."

"Do I count?" Mabel asked. "Because I can tell you their mother is perfectly fine."

"You're sure?"

"I am."

Joe turned back to the bride's children and starting speaking to them very quietly. The specific words were inaudible until, after a full minute, first Harlan, then Beryl quieted enough to hear him. Then he raised his voice to say clearly, "Your mother is safe."

"Not as long as Grant is anywhere near her, she isn't," Harlan said.

His sister added, "He's missing too. He's probably got her somewhere and he's feeding her poison, just like he did with Thad. Grant's already spent a good chunk of his inheritance, and he's desperate not to share the rest with anyone else. He'll do anything to get his hands on his father's money and keep Mom from getting her fair share."

Harlan nodded emphatically. "His first attempt to stop the wedding didn't work, so now he's going to make sure his father can't marry our mother by killing her."

"Relax." Mabel thought they were right that Grant wanted to stop the wedding, and he seemed self-absorbed enough to be oblivious to the possibility that stopping it would hurt his father as much as it hurt Donna. He might even be able to justify to himself anything he did, even murder, as a legitimate means of self-preservation. What didn't make sense to her, though, was that he might think killing Thad was a good first step. The best man's death could get the wedding postponed and give Grant more time to try to talk his father out of the marriage, but there was no guarantee it would result in cancelling the wedding permanently. If Grant was intent on murder, the bride would have been a much more effective target.

Mabel continued, "I don't know for sure where Grant is, but I do know where your mother is, and she doesn't want to be disturbed."

"She'd want to see us," Beryl said. "I won't be able to relax until I've seen her for myself."

"How about if I go confirm that she's okay?" Mabel asked.

"Only if we can come with you."

At this rate, the entire wedding party was going to end up in her kitchen, and Pixie would escape the office again to see what was happening, and then she might even go outside as people came and went through the kitchen door. The way things were going today, it would probably turn out that one of the wedding party was deathly allergic to cats, and Pixie would hunt them down and scratch them and they'd end up in the hospital.

There was no dissuading Beryl and Harlan, though, so Mabel led the little parade toward the kitchen. She stopped at the door, signaling for everyone to stay where they were. "I'm going in first to see if she wants to talk to you."

"Of course she does," Harlan and Beryl both said simultaneously.

"This is still my home, and I'm not inviting you in until I'm sure your mother is ready for you."

Joe moved to stand between the siblings and the door. "Mabel's right. Give her a minute to go inside first and get the all clear."

They mumbled their assent, and Mabel slipped inside. The bride was, indeed, perfectly safe, although she wasn't exactly "fine." She was sitting all alone at the huge trestle table, and this time the red puffiness of her eyes wasn't solely due to an allergy to lavender. The tears rolling down her face meant she was either extremely unhappy or intensely allergic to cats as well as lavender. Pixie was on the table, butting her head against the seemingly oblivious bride's shoulder. Mabel supposed she should have expected Pixie wouldn't stay where she was supposed to during the rehearsal and wedding, closed door or not. The cat never did take no for an answer, whether it came to her yowling or her demands for attention, so why should she accept the limitation of a closed door? If the farm hosted weddings in the future, it might be necessary to put Pixie in a securely locked crate during the events. The animal control officer had reclaimed the one that Billie Jean had raised her kittens in, but Mabel would get her own crate if it was the only thing that could keep Pixie safe.

It took a moment for Donna to realize she had company, and when she did she wiped her face on another napkin from Jeanne's Country Diner. There was a whole stack of unused ones on the table, surrounded by a dozen more that were crumpled into soggy little lumps. She sniffled and said, "I'm supposed to tell you that the caterer went on home and would like you to call her when you get a chance."

"Thanks." Mabel hovered near the door, prepared to use her body to keep it shut if necessary. The bride was miserable enough, and she deserved some alone time if she wanted it. "Where's Stan?"

Donna shrugged. "He had to take a call. I'm not sure where he went."

"Is it okay if I let your kids in?" Mabel asked. "They're worried about you."

"Go ahead." She smiled through her tears. "They'll knock the door down otherwise, and we've had enough mayhem already."

Mabel opened the door, and the kids, who must have been leaning against it, trying to hear what was going on, tumbled inside.

"Mom," Beryl and Harlan called out in harmony as they rushed to envelop her in a group hug.

Harlan added, "What did Stan do now?"

"It's not like that," Donna said, pushing them away and encouraging them to sit across from her so they wouldn't smother her. "I'm just tired, and the allergies—"

"Mom," Beryl interrupted. "We know it's not allergies. Stan did something to upset you. He always does, and you cover for him. Just because he doesn't experience normal human emotions is no excuse for him being cruel to you."

Mabel scooped up Pixie, just in case she was adding to the allergic reaction, and took her into the front of the house to close her inside the office again. Not that it would do much good if Pixie decided she was bored. She did have a favorite napping place there, so maybe she'd settle down now that she'd checked out the bride and her family. There shouldn't be any new arrivals that would trigger a yowling, so Pixie might be willing to sleep for a while.

Returning to stand unobtrusively where the hallway opened into the kitchen, Mabel found Harlan and Beryl had settled across from their mother as she'd asked them to. Beryl was saying, "We just want you to be happy."

"I am happy," Donna said. "Or I will be, once this weekend is over."

Mabel stepped forward. "Does that mean the wedding is going forward as planned tomorrow?"

"Yes. Absolutely," Donna said. "And please tell the caterer—Emily, is it?—how sorry I am not to have had the chance to enjoy her buffet today. I'm planning to eat extra tomorrow to make up for it."

"But Mom, you can't go forward with the wedding now," Beryl said. "You only agreed to marry Stan if he retired, and he's already gone back to work. He's never going to take you seriously if you give up on your ultimatum now."

"No, we worked out a new agreement," Donna assured both her children. "It would be foolish to insist that he not work right now, before he has someone to take over from him. Stan promised to retire as soon as he finds a new person to buy the business."

"That could take forever," Harlan objected.

"It could, but it won't," Donna said confidently. "If he doesn't retire within a year, he's agreed to volunteer with me at the food pantry every time I go for two whole years after that, and you know how much he'd hate that."

Harlan waved his hand dismissively. "He'll just come up with more excuses when the time is up and he doesn't have a new buyer for the business."

"That's what I think too," Beryl said. "Remember when he promised to take two weeks off every year for a vacation, and then reneged, claiming he'd taken every single Sunday off, and that added up to more than two weeks."

"I remember," Donna said. "That's why I made him put a big chunk of money into an account that I have sole control over as a guarantee for his good behavior. If I'm not satisfied at any point, then I can donate the whole thing to the food pantry. He'd hate losing that much money even more than he'd hate doing the volunteer work."

Donna wasn't the quite the doormat her kids and Ken obviously thought she was.

Harlan asked, "Are you absolutely sure marrying Stan is what you want, Mom?"

"It is." Donna reached across the table to take one of his hands and then one of Beryl's into hers to make sure she had their full attention. "Listen to me for once. I love Stan, and he loves me. Truly. He just doesn't do public displays of affection. And he doesn't talk about his feelings. But he shows me how much he cares by the way he acts with me when you're not around."

"I don't know..." Harlan said.

"Stan may be okay," Beryl said doubtfully. "But what about Grant? You won't be safe in a house where he can come and go as he pleases. He killed Thad, and you could be next."

Donna let out a little gasp. "Why on earth would you think that?" She released the kids' hands and sat back. "What about you, Harlan? Do you think Grant is a murderer too?"

He nodded, crossing his arms over his chest. "Grant is evil."

"That's ridiculous," Donna said. "Grant might be a little inconsiderate of other people, but he isn't a monster. He'd never kill anyone."

"Sure, he would." Harlan leaned forward and put his hands flat on the table. "Grant never liked Thad. Considered him a rival for his father's affections. That's exactly how he views you too."

"Stop that," Donna said. "Grant is your family. He's been your stepbrother in effect for years, and it'll be official tomorrow. I expect you to behave accordingly."

Harlan made a gagging noise. Grant wasn't the only person who could be inconsiderate of others.

Mabel's phone pinged, and she hoped it would provide an excuse for her to leave and let the family work out their issues in private. She glanced at it to see a text from Joe Hansen that Detective O'Connor was looking for her, and now that he finally wanted to hear what she had to say, he was getting worked up over having to wait.

It was O'Connor's own fault, she thought. He'd been playing petty power games by making her wait to be interviewed. He could have talked to her and Charlie first, which would have made the most sense, since they'd been the ones who'd found the victim, but he'd opted to save them for last instead. No one ever liked to be last for anything, and O'Connor was using the timing as a reminder that he was the person in control, not her. It was tempting to make him wait now, but it wasn't worth the risk of his one-sided feud with her escalating. Especially since he was already threatening to blame Emily for Thad's death. Mabel wouldn't put it past O'Connor to try to charge her as an accomplice if he arrested Emily.

Mabel hurried to the kitchen door. No point in antagonizing O'Connor any more than necessary.

* * * *

Mabel felt like she was part of a hostage exchange as she and Charlie passed each other, with him leaving O'Connor's table and her taking his place. If they were in a movie, Charlie would have grabbed her and run off with her before she could be mistreated by the detective. But this wasn't a movie, and she wasn't a helpless victim who needed saving, and Charlie respected her ability to rescue herself. Which was how it should be, but there was a brief moment as she heard the detective giggle in anticipation, when she wished she wasn't quite so independent.

O'Connor had a folder on his desk, along with a stack of a dozen legal pads, only one of which had anything written in it. Enough sheets of paper had been flipped over for there to be one for each member of the wedding party. His phone lay faceup on the table near his right hand, leading her to wonder if he was recording the interviews. It wasn't active at the moment, but that could change.

"Am I the last witness?" Mabel asked as she sat, trying for some small talk.

"For now," O'Connor said with a snicker. He flipped over the latest used sheet of his pad and picked up his pen without touching his phone to turn on the recorder app. "Officer Hansen tells me you and Durbin just happened to be on the patio and saw the victim where he had collapsed, even though there was a table blocking your line of sight. Would you care to explain that?"

O'Connor had done his best to make her being on her own patio seem suspicious, but it would only be playing into his hands if she became defensive. She'd had a good reason to be where she'd been when she'd spotted Thad, but explaining about his earlier ravages of the buffet table would only remind the detective that his favorite suspect, Emily, had been annoyed with the victim for ruining her hard work.

Mabel tried to sound helpful instead of critical. "Richard Wetzel drew our attention to the situation. He was at the buffet table, sampling the food, so he likely had a better view than Charlie and I did."

O'Connor frowned down at his pad and flipped back to the top sheet. "Where is this Wetzel anyway? He's not on my list of witnesses. Did he get sick and die too?"

"Not as far as I know. He left before the police arrived."

"Why didn't you stop him?"

There was no pleasing O'Connor. If she tried to help, he complained that she was interfering in police business. If she didn't help, he thought she was obstructing the investigation.

"I was a little busy trying to get medical help for Thad."

He giggled. "That turned out well, didn't it?"

She didn't need a reminder that Thad had died, despite the EMTs quick response and best efforts to save him. Mabel swallowed her irritation and pulled out her phone. "Would you like Wetzel's contact information?"

"Is he a friend of yours?"

"No. He was here for a job interview."

"Ah." O'Connor smiled triumphantly. "So, he's working for you and will tell me whatever you want him to say?"

"More likely he'll tell you I'm stupid and incompetent, maybe even malicious and evil." Mabel scrolled through her emails to the one with Wetzel's résumé attached, so she could find his address and phone number. "The interview didn't turn out the way he'd hoped."

"I'd like to hear that directly from him." O'Connor used his pen to point at her phone. "Give me what you've got on him."

Mabel read out the information he needed, having to repeat the number twice and spell the street name three times before the detective got it right. It would have been easier to just text it to him, but for a young guy who'd grown up with technology, O'Connor was incredibly old-school.

"I'm not sure Wetzel will have much information to share," Mabel said. "He's from out of town and didn't even know there was going to be a wedding here today. As far as I know, he didn't know anyone else here."

"I still need to talk to him. He might have seen something useful." O'Connor laughed knowing. "Or *smelled* something."

"You think Thad was poisoned?"

O'Connor giggled and looked down at his pad as if he realized he might have said, or at least implied, too much. "It's a possibility."

In other words, O'Connor definitely thought poison was involved. "I guess it's a good thing I arranged for replacement food to be delivered for the wedding party."

"It wouldn't have mattered if people had eaten from the buffet," O'Connor said. "Thad was targeted, and only his food was affected."

"How do you know that?"

"You must have seen the plate on the ground next to him." O'Connor chuckled at what he thought was an instance of catching Mabel in a lie. "It had a little flag with the victim's name on it. Made it easy for the killer to target the right person."

"Unless everything was poisoned before it ended up on that plate, and the flag was just a coincidence," Mabel said. "I hope you're checking samples of the rest of the food."

"Of course," O'Connor said. "But I'd really like to know who made it so easy for the killer to identify Thad's plate."

"I'm sure you'll find out eventually." Just not from Mabel. She wouldn't lie to the detective, but she also didn't feel obligated to offer information he hadn't directly asked her about.

Mabel had a belated thought that maybe he already knew who had created the little flag, having heard it from Emily herself, and was looking to see if Mabel would volunteer the information. Except that required much more planning ahead than she thought the detective ever did.

Perhaps she could set him on a different path from the one that led to Emily. "Did anyone tell you that a local reporter, Andrew Rainey, was here before Thad was found? Not just after the police and ambulance were called. Rainey was supposed to be doing a story on the farm, but he spent most of his time harassing the wedding party. Thad escorted him away from the rehearsal in what must have been a humiliating incident. Is he on your list of witnesses?"

O'Connor laughed nervously as he ran a finger down the top sheet on his legal pad. "He's not on here either. He hasn't left like the other guy, has he?"

"I wish he had, but he's still here somewhere," Mabel said. "I'm planning to ban him from the farm as soon as you're done with him."

"I'll talk to him next." O'Connor flipped back to the sheet intended for Mabel's interview and tapped it with his pen for a long minute. "I guess I'm done with you for now. You aren't planning on leaving town any time soon, are you?"

"No." Mabel wasn't much of a traveler, and she couldn't move back to her home in Maine until she finally hired a farm manager, which wasn't likely to happen anytime soon. It was still annoying to be told she *couldn't* leave if she wanted to. "Not unless you count visiting adjoining towns. They're planning new farmers' markets, and I need to check them out before next month's harvest."

"That should be okay. Unless I decide differently." His laugh undercut the threat. "You can go now."

"One question first," Mabel said. "I was wondering when you think the forensics team will be finished with the patio. There's supposed to be a wedding reception here tomorrow."

"Seriously?" O'Connor laughed as if he'd just heard a brilliant joke. "They trust you to host the wedding after their best man got killed during the rehearsal?"

"They do," Mabel said. "I just confirmed it with the bride. The wedding is going forward as planned. She wouldn't agree to that if she thought I had anything to do with Thad's death."

"Ha! That's not what she told me."

Mabel thought he was just trying to get a rise out of her, but she had to wonder if Donna had said something implicating Emily and by extension, Mabel, who'd recommended her. If so, given the bride's accommodating personality, it had probably been the result of leading questions from O'Connor. And Mabel couldn't ask him what the bride had said, or there would be a lecture on minding her own business and not thinking she could do a professional detective's job. She already had that one memorized and didn't need to hear it again, especially given that recent history had proven that the advice was wrong.

"Regardless of what the bride thinks of me, she told me the wedding is still happening here tomorrow. I need to know if we'll be able to use the patio."

"The team will take as long as they need." O'Connor got to his feet. "I'll let you know when they're done."

"I understand." More than he might realize. She'd made a mistake in letting him know she needed to use the patio. Now he'd make sure it was tied up for days. If she complained, he'd impose even broader restrictions, and she'd be lucky to be allowed inside her own house while the forensics work was happening. She'd just have to figure out somewhere else on the farm to hold the reception. Too bad it couldn't be out in the lavender field, because of the bride's allergies, but the less time Donna spent in the middle of the pollen, the better.

"Oh, I almost forgot," O'Connor said with a nervous laugh that made it clear he thought he was being cunning. He picked up his phone and scrolled until he found what he wanted and turned the screen toward Mabel. "The photographer sent me this when I asked if he had a shot of the victim that I could use. He said this was the only one that didn't include the entire wedding party."

It was a picture of Emily handing an overflowing plate of food to Thad. He looked sublimely happy and carefree, while she looked like she was gritting her teeth with the effort of keeping from dumping it over his head.

Rather than rising to the bait, Mabel just said, "Ken Linden is an extraordinary photographer, isn't he?"

O'Connor's laugh sounded forced for once, as if he was only pretending to be amused rather than unable to quash an involuntary reaction. "Just remember, I'll be keeping a close eye on you." He glanced over toward the path that led to Emily's farm. "And on your friends."

CHAPTER THIRTEEN

As Mabel stepped away from the detective's table, she could hear him on his phone asking Joe Hansen if Rainey had left yet. O'Connor laughed at the response and said, "Then find him. I want to talk to him."

Mabel wanted to talk to him, too, but first she needed to check on Emily. Hiding at home wasn't like her. Mabel was always happy to retreat into her home, but Emily liked people and had been so excited about sharing her food with guests, and not entirely because she needed the money. She was a natural-born nurturer of both animals and humans.

Charlie intercepted her before she could send Emily a text to check on her. "How'd it go with O'Connor?"

"Not well." Mabel got out her phone. "Give me a second, and I'll explain. First, I want to make sure Emily is okay." She sent a text to that effect and kept the phone in her hand, hoping for a quick response.

"Okay, we can talk now." Mabel glanced back at where O'Connor was pacing beside his interview table, presumably waiting for the reporter. "You might want to keep your distance from me, though. O'Connor is threatening to harass my friends until he gets a confession from someone, and I don't think he cares whether the person is guilty or not."

"I'm not going anywhere," Charlie said. "O'Connor can't hurt me or my business. I do a lot of volunteer work for West Slocum and contribute to local charities, so people respect me. A good portion of the town's population has bought a home I built or renovated, and they've been happy with my work. They won't believe any negative rumors about me."

"I wish Emily was that well established here, instead of just starting her catering business," Mabel said. "She's more susceptible to O'Connor's harassment, and she doesn't need this kind of stress on top of her divorce."

"I'll do what I can to make sure people know she's a good person." Charlie patted his stomach. "And a great caterer too. She dropped by my work site last week with a batch of her cheesecake bars when she was testing the recipe. Said she wanted to get a male opinion, but she brought enough for my whole crew, both men and women. Everyone agreed they were perfect, except there weren't enough of them."

"It really is a shame all her work for today's buffet was wasted."

"What about tomorrow?" Charlie asked. "Will Emily be catering the wedding itself?"

"Unless she's arrested in the meantime. I talked to the bride right before O'Connor interviewed me, and she said she's going ahead with the wedding as planned. She specifically mentioned looking forward to Emily's cooking."

"Then everyone will see how great Emily's food is, so you don't need to worry."

"I do, though. The wedding planner should be the one anticipating problems and preventing them, but she's not capable of it, so I know things will keep going wrong." Mabel glanced over at the table where she'd last seen Paige chatting with a bridesmaid, but the planner had disappeared again. Joe Hansen wasn't anywhere in sight either, probably searching for Rainey, but his uniformed colleague was going from table to table, apparently telling the members of the wedding party they could leave now. "I can't begin to understand why Thad hired Paige to plan his partner's wedding. He had to have known how unsuited she was for her chosen career. It was almost as if he wanted things to go wrong, while retaining plausible deniability." *I thought she knew what she was doing,* he'd say. *I was just trying to help.* And no one could prove otherwise, despite the terrible outcome.

"Is Paige really that incompetent?" Charlie asked. "Everything looked good to me."

"Except for the dead body, you mean," Mabel said. "Not that what happened to Thad was her fault. But trust me, Paige has no idea what she's doing, and every time something goes wrong, she disappears. Like now."

"Still," Charlie said, "I think you're being a bit harsh, suggesting any problems were intentional. Why would someone want to sabotage a wedding after he'd agreed to be the best man? Besides, I thought I heard that Thad was going to be the sole owner of their business as soon as the wedding was official. Why would he want to risk that?"

"I don't know," Mabel said. "Maybe he was afraid of the responsibility."

"Like you're afraid of commitment?" Charlie asked.

"I'm not afraid of commitment. I'm staying here to run the farm until I can find a good manager, aren't I?"

"Not that kind of commitment. I know you're determined to protect your aunt's legacy and you'd never even think about breaching your employment contract with your boss. I meant more personal commitments. Like agreeing to be my date for the wedding tomorrow."

She glanced down at the phone as if it had pinged, even though it hadn't. "I'm going to be working."

"That's not the real reason." His tone was calm but certain.

Charlie wasn't going to let it drop, she decided, so she put the phone away. If Emily hadn't returned the text yet, she was probably busy and wouldn't get around to it for a while.

"You know the real reason," she said. They'd gone on a few dates in the last six months, but they'd just been a bit of fun for them both, not something that was building to a long-term relationship. Everything had been casual, like some business events he'd attend, a talk at the library, and a group hike in the woods. Going to a wedding with someone was different. It felt *serious.* Like they might have a future together. Which they didn't.

Charlie had agreed to a no-strings-attached relationship, but he'd also made it clear he wanted something more when and if she was ready. It wouldn't be fair to him to hold out that possibility when she knew she was planning to return to Maine where she belonged as soon as she could get the new farm manager hired and settled in. And Charlie's work wasn't the kind of thing that could be transported to another state. As he himself had just mentioned, he'd worked hard to establish a solid local reputation as a quality developer, and it had taken years to get to this point. She couldn't expect him to give that all up for her.

Mabel checked her phone again, hoping Emily might have responded and given her an excuse to end the uncomfortable conversation. No such luck.

She dropped the phone back in her pocket. "I'm sorry, but I'm just not ready to be part of a serious couple."

Charlie paused briefly before saying lightly, "I'm never serious."

"And I always am," Mabel said. "That's another reason why it wouldn't work for the long term."

"We could make it work. Or at least try. I understand that you're afraid of getting close to anyone after all the loss you've had in your life. Everyone in your original family, both by birth and by choice, is gone now. It's time for you to create a new family."

She hadn't consciously thought much about the fact that everyone she'd grown up with was completely gone now. She'd been too busy to think about anything over the last few months, between the series of big rush jobs she'd done for her boss and searching fruitlessly for a farm manager. But Charlie was right. She'd lost her parents when she was a child, her grandparents when she was in grad school, and her aunt a year ago. Then last fall she'd lost her long-term lawyer, who'd been like another grandfather to her. If she continued to dwell on it, she'd start crying, and there'd been enough of that today already.

"Now isn't the time to discuss anything but the wedding. We can talk after it's over and Emily's safe from O'Connor's misguided suspicions." Mabel got out her phone again to confirm she hadn't missed a ping. "I'm worried about Emily. You saw me send her a text, and she hasn't answered yet. That's not like her. You haven't seen her recently, have you?"

Charlie paused, and Mabel thought he might insist on an answer about their relationship, but after a moment, he said, "I haven't seen Emily since she went inside the farmhouse after she was interviewed by O'Connor. She isn't still in there?"

"No," Mabel said. "The bride told me she'd gone home."

"She's probably out with her goats, then."

He was probably right. Emily sometimes turned off her phone when she was out with the herd, so she could give them her full attention. Or she could be meditating. She turned her phone off for that too.

"What about the reporter, Andrew Rainey? Have you seen him recently?" Mabel asked. "He was on the patio long enough to get some dinner, but he seems to have disappeared since then, and O'Connor's looking to interview him. I want to make sure he's not bothering any of the guests again. He was making a pest of himself earlier, and I'm afraid he'll be even worse now that he's got a murder to cover."

"I'll go see if I can find Rainey if you want to go next door and check on Emily." Charlie added, "It's going to be all right. O'Connor is crazy to suspect her of murder. Emily wouldn't hurt anyone unless they were threatening her goats."

Unfortunately, Mabel thought, that didn't clear Emily as thoroughly as Charlie thought. Thad had undermined the success of her catering by ravaging the buffet, which in turn threatened her financial stability, which she needed in order to keep her goats.

It was probably a good thing O'Connor had never heard Emily's frequent claim that she would do absolutely anything to keep her goats.

* * * *

Separating Skinner Farm and Capricornucopia was a wooded area deep enough to offer complete privacy to the two properties. The path between them was used frequently most of the year, and recently it had seen even more traffic than usual as Emily transported supplies and equipment from her house to Mabel's in preparation for the wedding rehearsal dinner. As a result, the ground was free of fallen branches and other tripping hazards, which was fortunate, because the sun was setting and there were shadows everywhere.

Mabel emerged from the tree line and paused at the closed gate to view the next-door farm. Emily was in the nearest field, seated on a mat in a classic, cross-legged meditation pose. She was surrounded by grazing goats that seemed oblivious to her presence.

Now that she knew Emily was safe, Mabel was reluctant to interrupt. She started to turn away, but Emily called out, "It's okay. I'm done. And I want to hear the latest on what's happening at your place. I would have stayed to help with the guests, but it felt like everyone thought I was going to kill them next, so I thought they'd be more comfortable if I wasn't there."

"No one blames you." Mabel unlatched the gate and went over to the back porch.

"O'Connor does." Emily stepped up onto the porch, draping her yoga mat over the railing. "And I bet he's been doing more talking than listening with the witnesses, so everyone must know by now that I'm a suspect."

Mabel couldn't say Emily was wrong, and she couldn't think of anything else that would be both reassuring and true. How did other people find the right words in fraught situations?

"You look more upset than I feel." Emily dropped into one of the half-dozen wicker chairs on the porch. "Once this is over, I need to teach you to meditate. You look incredibly tense. I'm guessing that means you don't have any good news for me."

Mabel dropped into an adjoining chair. "I'm afraid not. O'Connor is in charge, after all."

"He only thinks he is," Emily said. "He can't stop you from investigating on your own property. You'll figure it out."

"I'll do my best." Mabel had her doubts, but she kept them to herself. No need to undo all the calm Emily had achieved with her meditation. "Mostly I just came over to see if you were okay. And to see where you think we should set up for the reception tomorrow. I think O'Connor's going to keep the end of the patio blocked off with police tape just to spite me. I was thinking we could put the buffet and tables in front of the barn, and move the parking onto the grass in the front yard."

"Will they even want me to cater it?" Emily asked. "I thought they might have decided to hold the reception somewhere else."

"I talked to Donna about it, and she's looking forward to your catering tomorrow."

"I'd feel better about that if we knew who killed Thad," Emily said. "For all we know, Donna did it, and she's planning to knock someone else off tomorrow and frame me for both murders."

"Donna's just about the only person who couldn't have killed Thad," Mabel said. "She's the center of everyone's attention. She couldn't have slipped away unnoticed. Even when she came to the farmhouse to fix her makeup, she was accompanied by the photographer, who can give her an alibi for the time she was away from the lavender field."

"Well, that's one suspect down, twenty-plus to go," Emily said. "Who do you think is the most likely?"

"I don't know yet," Mabel said. "What about you?"

Emily shrugged. "It could be anyone, I suppose. If you'd asked me this morning, I'd have said Thad was more likely to kill than be killed."

"Did you see anyone leave the rehearsal in the half hour or so before Thad was found?" Mabel asked. "You were out near there at that point, weren't you?"

"You want to know if I have an alibi?" Emily's eyes widened, and she lost some of her recently acquired calm. "You don't really think I might have done it, do you?"

"No, no, of course not." Emily had had means, motive, and opportunity, but murder just wasn't something she would do. Or at least it hadn't been something the pre-divorce Emily would have done. Now... "No, I was just thinking that you had a better opportunity to see who was where at the relevant time than I did, since I was inside the farmhouse with the bride and the photographer."

"I didn't have much better of a view than you did. I was in the gazebo most of the time, huddled there with the impossible Paige, barely aware of what was going on at the rehearsal and photographs."

"Try to think back to then anyway, just in case you did notice something."

Emily looked out toward her goats for long moments before saying slowly, "I remember seeing the bride leave with the photographer, and then they came back with Thad." Her words came more quickly as she explained, "I wouldn't have noticed, except Paige pointed out both events. She wanted to go with the bride, and then when they came back, she wanted to be in the pictures. Anything to avoid having to go over the details I needed to know. I swear, if that woman has ever organized an event for more than six people, I'll eat my goats' hats."

Mabel brought Emily back to the topic of what she'd seen during the rehearsal and photography. "So, you missed the scuffle between Grant and Rainey?"

"Oh, wait. I did see that. It was the one time Paige was glad to be in the gazebo with me instead of out doing her job, since otherwise she'd have had to be the one to break up the argument. We heard some yelling and turned around to see what was going on. I thought it was just silly posturing by Grant and Rainey, nothing serious, or I'd have sent Paige out to deal with it whether she wanted to or not. In any event, Thad got involved right after Rainey fell down, before Paige or I could do anything. Thad helped Rainey to his feet and stayed between him and Grant." Emily's eyebrows lowered. "That's odd, come to think of it. I don't think Thad did one other considerate thing all day. Ironic if his involvement in that confrontation got him killed. He was surprisingly kind to Rainey. Although I suppose it could have just been so he could use escorting the reporter back to the patio as an excuse to raid the buffet again or have another cigarette. Or both."

Mabel realized she didn't know when the two men had come back to the patio together, since Thad had nipped back to the food more than once. "When was the scuffle? Before or after the bride came to the farmhouse to fix her makeup?"

Emily thought for a moment. "After," she said. "Definitely after. The only reason Thad was there at the time was because Donna and Ken had dragged him back with them a few minutes earlier."

"And then Thad and Rainey came back to the patio together?"

"I didn't see where they went," Emily said. "But they must have, right? Where else would they go? Thad ended up on the patio for sure, and Rainey probably went with him, at least most of the way, to see if he could get an interview after striking out with Grant and his father."

"That does seem likely," Mabel said, "but speculation isn't evidence I can bring to O'Connor."

"Where else would Rainey have gone?"

Mabel shrugged. "The barn. The front porch. He could even have decided to take a walk in the woods to clear his head."

"He'd better not come over to my house," Emily said darkly. "I'll sic the goats on him if he tries to interview me. The last thing I need right now is a newspaper article picturing me as a murder suspect. My husband would have a field day with it, showing it to the judge and demanding an immediate sale of Capricornucopia before I got sued for wrongful death."

It could be worse, Mabel thought. The newspaper article might just be a precursor to Emily's arrest if O'Connor had his way.

CHAPTER FOURTEEN

Mabel made sure to latch the gate behind her on the way home so the goats couldn't follow her. She'd only gone a few feet along the wooded path when Rainey stepped out from behind a bush with a palm-sized pair of bird-watching binoculars in his hand.

Mabel glanced over her shoulder to confirm that he would, indeed, have had a clear line of sight to Emily's back porch from where he'd been watching. She doubted he could have overheard them, unless he had an equally tiny parabolic microphone, which seemed unlikely. Not impossible, though, given that Rainey had clearly come prepared to spy on the wedding party. Had he heard Emily's threat against him?

Rainey stuffed the binoculars into the pocket of his tweed jacket, adding to its rumpled appearance. "Well? What did Emily say about her role in Thad's death?"

So, he didn't have a microphone, Mabel thought.

"Emily had no role in Thad's death whatsoever," she said.

"Is she willing to say that on the record? I'm available to interview her right now if she wants to give her side of the story."

"Is that what you're doing out here? Getting ready to harass her?"

"It's not harassment," Rainey said. "It's journalism. Besides, that's not why I was here. I'm meeting a witness to see if I can confirm my suspicions about how Thad Dalton died."

"You're meeting in the woods?"

He shrugged. "It's where the story called me."

"What story?"

"I can't say. I never betray a source."

Mabel wasn't convinced he actually had a source or a meeting, but she was willing to humor him that far. "Tell your source to stay out of my woods. And stay out of them yourself."

"I just follow the news," he said loftily.

"Right now, you need to follow the path back to the patio," Mabel said. "Detective O'Connor has been looking for you, and he's not happy about your slipping away from there."

"I'm always happy to assist the police. As long as they don't ask me to reveal my sources."

"I think he just wants to know where you were when Thad was killed, and what you saw while the EMTs were working on Thad." She'd almost said *while you were bothering the EMTs*, but she'd stopped herself before saying something that would just annoy him. Perhaps if she praised his journalistic skills, pride in his work would cause him to brag about what he planned to tell the detective. "As an experienced reporter, you might have noticed something that no one else did."

"I just might have," he said smugly. "But I'm not telling you."

Oh well, it had been worth a try.

"I understand," Mabel said evenly. "And I hope you'll understand that after you talk to O'Connor, you're banned from my property. You aren't welcome here ever again."

"We'll see about that." Rainey stalked off, and Mabel followed closely to make sure he didn't wander off the path again or otherwise avoid being interviewed.

Unfortunately, that meant that they both emerged from the woods together, and O'Connor saw them walking next to each other. He hurried over to meet them in the middle of the driveway.

"Where have you been hiding him?" O'Connor shouted at Mabel. "You knew I was looking for him."

"He was in the woods." Mabel didn't want to mention why she herself had been in the woods, since the less time O'Connor spent thinking about Emily, the better. "He told me he'd been meeting with a confidential source."

O'Connor laughed and turned his ire on Rainey. "Confidential, huh? I don't think so. This is a murder investigation, and you're a witness, so you'd better not be keeping anything secret from me."

Rainey squared his shoulders as if planning to martyr himself, but followed meekly as O'Connor led the way to the interview table on the patio.

Mabel headed in the same direction, keeping a discreet distance. All of the members of the wedding party had left, and the remains of their boxed dinners were scattered across the tables. It was almost fully dark, so she went into the kitchen to turn on the outdoor lights. She couldn't call Emily to come over to get the place ready for the next day until O'Connor left, so Mabel went outside again to begin collecting the trash.

O'Connor and Rainey didn't seem to notice her or try to keep their voices low. She heard O'Connor ask Rainey where he'd been when Thad was killed, and Rainey claimed he'd been talking to Terry in the garlic field. O'Connor had laughed but apparently accepted the answer.

Mabel knew it was a lie, though. Rainey had claimed that alibi with her, too, but Terry had denied ever talking to the reporter. And she knew which one she trusted to tell the truth.

She sighed. It would be so much simpler if O'Connor would accept her help and treat her as an ally instead of an enemy. Then she could tell him that Rainey was lying. On the other hand, maybe it was just as well she couldn't tell the detective that Rainey's alibi was false. It would only put Terry in the hot seat and make it obvious that he didn't have an alibi either for the time of the murder. So far, O'Connor seemed to be overlooking Terry as a possible suspect, and she'd just as soon keep it that way.

Rainey didn't say anything else of interest as Mabel cleared the last table and tied up the trash bags for Emily to take away later. By then, the two men had moved on to a discussion of the members of the wedding party, which seemed to be nothing more than an excuse to share gossip, rather than useful information. She decided there was no point in eavesdropping any longer and headed for the back door.

Inside, she found Pixie had let herself out of the office again. She was sitting in her favorite windowsill in the kitchen, where she could keep an eye on any activity at the barn. Mabel looked out over the cat's shoulder, but didn't see anything interesting out there. All of the vehicles were gone from the parking area, while the driveway held Joe's cruiser and O'Connor's SUV.

She made a mental note to arrange for a dead bolt to be added to the kitchen door. Pixie had always contented herself with just raising an alarm about visitors, but now that she'd learned to open the office door, she might try the exterior one too. Outdoors wasn't safe for a housecat. Pixie might think she was tough, but she didn't have the survival skills the ferals did.

While Mabel was double-checking the back door was secured, she decided she should also fix the wonky doorknob that could be opened without a key by anyone who knew how to bump just the right spot. As evidenced by Thad's death, the farm wasn't necessarily safe for human beings either. She'd feel more comfortable for herself, not just for Pixie, if there was a dead bolt between her and creatures whose opposable thumbs made them particularly good at opening doors and committing murder.

* * * *

Despite what O'Connor undoubtedly had hoped, the forensic team hadn't needed to work on the patio for the entire night and into the next day. Mabel had heard them leave around midnight, and then everything had been quiet until around eight in the morning, when Pixie began yowling about vehicles arriving every ten minutes or so. After about an hour of trying to ignore the increasingly frequent alarm-cat sounds, Mabel gave up and rolled out of bed.

By the time she made it down to the kitchen, the patio was free of any sign of the previous day's tragedy. Someone had removed the police tape, and there were no returning forensics technicians or uniformed officers who might dampen the mood. The trash bags had also been cleared away—presumably by Emily, not the forensics team—and fresh linens had been laid out for the late-afternoon reception. Additional round tables had been set up to accommodate the hundred or so guests invited to the wedding. The weather was even cooperating, with bright sunshine and picturesquely fluffy clouds.

Mabel hadn't planned to be up so early. The ceremony wasn't until two, so she hadn't seen any reason not to stay up until four working on a time-sensitive project for her boss, expecting to be able to sleep in while the highly competent contractors set up for the wedding.

She poured herself the last serving of iced tea from the pitcher in the fridge, hoping it had enough caffeine to wake her up. It was going to be a long day.

While she gulped down her drink, she stood near the window and watched the activity on the patio. The wedding planner, who should have been overseeing the setup, was—unsurprisingly—nowhere in sight. Fortunately, the contractors had considerably more experience than Paige did, so they didn't need much supervision.

A cooler filled with champagne was tucked up against the house in the shade at the far end of the patio, while at the opposite end near the driveway, Rory Hansen, who could always be counted on to support her friends, was wearing a matching server's uniform of black pants and t-shirt with a white apron. Both she and Emily were laying out glasses, napkins, and utensils on the round tables. There weren't any chairs yet, since they were all out in the tractor path next to the lavender field for guests to use during the ceremony. The rental company's crew was there, too, lining them up in front of the stage that backed onto the lavender field. The florist was out there decorating everything that wasn't already a flower, and the quartet Paige had hired was setting up in the path to the left of the field.

Mabel finished her tea, grabbed Pixie from her favorite kitchen windowsill, and shut the cat into the office. Not that the closed door would keep Pixie there for long if she wanted to escape, but it was the best that could be done for now. The farmhouse was old, and the rooms upstairs had even less secure doors than the ground-floor office. When she finally had time to hire someone to fix the lock on the kitchen door, she'd have the other doors made more secure too.

The caffeine was starting to kick in, so Mabel headed outside to see if she could help with the reception setup.

Rory caught sight of her almost immediately. "Oh, good, you're up." She continued making her way around the table, laying out utensils as she went. "I need you to tell Emily that everything is going to be fine. She won't believe me."

Emily was in the white-aproned catering uniform that was as flattering on her as a designer outfit, but her usually sunny expression was cloudy and her eyes were red, as if she'd been awake all night. She paused to look at Mabel hopefully.

"It's going to be fine," Mabel said, trying to sound like she meant it before quickly changing the subject. "Where's Paige? Shouldn't she be here helping?"

Rory snorted. "It's probably better she's not here, from what I've heard. The florist knows what he's doing, and so does the rental chair crew. The musicians seem to know what they're doing, even if they look a bit rough around the edges for a quartet, and, of course, Emily has the food under control. Plus, I brought Joe with me this morning to help. Not in uniform—it's his day off—so there won't be any unpleasant reminders of what happened yesterday. I sent him out to the lavender field in case an extra hand is needed there."

"I should have stayed in bed, then," Mabel said. "No one needs me."

Emily smiled, although it wasn't as effortless as usual. "We always need you. We're counting on you to protect our friend's—your aunt's—farm."

"Exactly," Rory said. "Oh, and Terry's here, and he brought some friends like he promised, to help with parking."

Mabel looked around her. "Where is Terry?"

"He drove the tractor down to the beginning of the driveway," Rory said. "Paige insisted it needed to be out there, festooned with some balloons that the florist brought, so people would know they'd found the right place. She said something about a tractor adding to the setting's quaint factor."

"Has she actually seen the tractor?" Mabel asked. It was fairly new and sleek, as far as farm equipment went. Nothing like the rusty, old clunker Paige probably had in mind from nostalgic images of long-ago agriculture. "Because I'm not going to trade it in for a quaint one just for today."

"Don't worry," Rory said. "I'll keep an eye on Paige so she doesn't do too much damage. I'd have stopped her from demanding that the tractor be used as décor if it had been a real problem, but Terry said he didn't mind. You and Emily don't need to deal with her."

"Thanks."

Emily had moved on to the next table and was humming to herself as she laid out linen napkins. Rory called over to her, "We'll be right back," as she took Mabel's arm and nudged her toward the farmhouse kitchen door. "We're just going to get something to drink."

"I'm not thirsty," Mabel said. "And I finished the last of the iced tea. There's bottled water out here on the patio, though, if you need a drink."

"I'll help you make some more tea." Rory tugged hard in the direction of the kitchen and lowered her voice. "I need to talk to you. Privately."

Mabel glanced back at Emily, who was facing the other direction. Despite the humming, Emily seemed tense. Rory had to have noticed it, too, and she probably had a plan for helping.

"I understand now," Mabel said. "You don't have to drag me along anymore."

"Good." Rory briskly closed the distance to the kitchen and let them both inside. Once the door was closed behind them, she said, "Emily is convinced all the guests will have heard what happened yesterday and blame her, so they'll be afraid to eat her food now. She was still asleep when I arrived this morning, and that's not like her at all. You know what an early bird she is. It's a good thing she hired me to help today, or she'd probably still be in bed with the covers over her head, trying to come up with a way to get someone else to do the catering at the last minute."

"She might be right about people being afraid of her food." Mabel went over to the sink to fill the electric kettle. Even though making more iced tea was only a cover story, now was a good time to restock her fridge. "I'm sort of surprised Detective O'Connor wasn't camped out on Emily's porch when you got there this morning. He obviously considers her the prime suspect and doesn't seem interested in looking at anyone else. And he doesn't believe in keeping his cards close to his chest, so he's probably telling everyone what his theory of the case is."

Rory took a seat at the kitchen table on the side that let her look out the window to make sure Emily wasn't heading in their direction. "He's definitely blabbing to everyone at the police station. Joe told me O'Connor's been strutting around, acting like he's got a huge serial murder case on his hands, and he's going to be responsible not just for the one yesterday, but dozens more that Emily committed and were overlooked until now. Joe thinks O'Connor's already practicing his speech for when he's awarded a special commendation for making the arrest."

Mabel sighed. "Meanwhile, he's nowhere close to finding the killer."

"He did make one breakthrough," Rory said. "They found your farm manager applicant late last night at a bar, so O'Connor went to talk to him. Apparently, Wetzel was too drunk to be questioned, though. They arranged for him to stay in a local hotel overnight to sober up. He may have already been interviewed this morning."

"I wish I could think of a reason why Wetzel might have wanted Thad dead, because then he'd be a suspect instead of just a witness." Mabel retrieved the canister of her favorite tea blend and added the loose tea leaves to a large glass pitcher. "But I suppose it's possible Wetzel had a motive. Plus, he had the opportunity, since he was on the patio alone for a while before the body was found, and he'd been wandering the farm unsupervised before that."

"Do you think O'Connor is capable of figuring that out?" Rory said. "Emily might feel better if she knew someone else was being looked at for the murder, especially since it's not someone she knows, so she doesn't have to feel bad for him."

"I wouldn't mention it to her just yet," Mabel warned. "I'd love to blame Wetzel, too, but I think it's much more likely the killer is someone who was in the wedding party. Some of them, maybe all of them, had known Thad for quite a while through their connection to the bride and groom. Given how much of a jerk he was, anyone who'd ever had to interact with him might well have disliked him intensely. And the more often they had to be around him, the more likely he'd have angered them. That means the people who were part of the wedding are much more likely to have had a motive than someone like Wetzel, who'd only met Thad once, shortly before his death, assuming they met at all."

"If it's about motives, shouldn't that rule out Emily too? She couldn't possibly have had any reason to kill Thad."

"I wish that were true," Mabel said. "Unfortunately, she'd had a rough morning, dealing with Paige's incompetence, and then Thad started messing up the buffet she'd worked so hard to make look pretty. O'Connor would say that was a last straw, she snapped, and she killed him."

"Being a garden-variety jerk is no reason to kill someone. Least of all with poison. I'd understand if she'd hit him, but poison takes planning. Besides, Emily would never get violent unless it was in self-defense or to protect her goats," Rory said. "She's a firm believer in turning the other cheek."

Not always, Mabel thought as she turned to pour the boiling water into the glass pitcher. She'd heard Emily threaten to kill Paige. It had just been a joke, of course, but that wasn't what O'Connor would think if he heard about it. He'd consider it proof that Emily was psychotic and willing to kill anyone who annoyed her. But if that were true, Mabel herself would probably be dead. She wasn't always the easiest person to befriend, and Emily had frequently been irritated by Mabel's determination, first, to sell the farm, and more recently, to hire a manager so she could be an absentee owner.

"It may be silly to consider Emily the prime suspect," Mabel said as she set a timer for when the tea would be ready for filtering out the leaves, "but I think she'd better talk to an attorney as soon as possible. My attorney doesn't handle criminal cases, but I can ask him for a referral."

"I can take care of that," Rory said. "Joe will know who the best local defense lawyers are."

"I hope she won't need anything more than a quick consultation," Mabel said, "but it could get complicated if the real killer isn't arrested before today's wedding reception is over. The most likely suspects—the members of the wedding party—will all be scattered by the time it ends tonight at six. I don't even know how to contact most of them. I should be able to find out from the wedding planner, but, well, it's Paige, after all, so I'm not optimistic."

"So, who are the possible suspects other than Emily?" Rory asked. "Joe wouldn't tell me any details."

"Pretty much everyone who was at the rehearsal. Probably not the mayor, who's officiating at the ceremony and hadn't met Thad before yesterday, but other than that, I can think of obvious motives for the groom, the bride, and their children. Thad was the groom's business partner for years, and it sounds like he socialized with him, too, so everyone in the family has known him and interacted with him during all that time. Stan's son was jealous of Thad, I think, and Donna's kids are desperate to stop the wedding, although killing someone is a bit extreme. More generally, anyone who knew him, which I think probably includes the bridesmaids and ushers, could have had a bad past experience with him, and then something happened yesterday to bring the old wounds to the surface. Even Paige knew him, since he was the one who hired her to plan the wedding."

"So, the entire wedding party is on the suspect list," Rory said. "Anyone else?"

"The photographer was here, along with his daughter, who's his assistant, and her toddler," Mabel said. "I think we can rule out the kid, at least, but any adult who knew Thad has to be considered a suspect. Ken and Lara must have met him through their connections to Donna. Ken has been her friend for a long time, and Lara was Donna's godchild."

"So, there's really no one you can rule out?"

"Terry Earley and Charlie Durbin were here yesterday, but there's just no way either of them killed Thad," Mabel said. "Other than that, I'm keeping an open mind. At this point, everyone in the wedding party seems equally likely suspects. Except maybe for the bride."

"There must be someone you think is more likely than the others."

"Not really," Mabel said. "It's hardly surprising, though. It feels like a long time since Thad died, but it's been less than a day. I never really suspected the killers of either my aunt or Graham Winthrop until much later that that, after the evidence piled up. You didn't either."

"True." Rory stared out the window toward where Emily was working. "I hate it when a friend's in trouble and there's nothing I can do about it. I start envisioning all sorts of impossible scenarios for fixing the situation."

"Me too." The timer for the tea rang, and Mabel turned to pour the finished tea through a filter and into a second pitcher. "Yesterday I found myself wishing the barn cats could tell me who killed Thad. They always seem to be aware of everything that happens on the farm, especially when it involves human beings, so they can keep their distance from anyone who might hurt them. It would be so much easier to solve crimes if humans could do that, too, so we could identify guilty people with an additional sense that worked as clearly as sight or hearing."

"Emily would say we do have such a sense," Rory said. "I know that sometimes I'll meet a person who makes my skin crawl, and I make sure to stay far away from them and later I'll find out they did something terrible. Unfortunately, not everyone gets the creeps from the same person, so I suppose it's not all that helpful to prove who's guilty and who isn't."

"What worries me is that Detective O'Connor seems to rely on his gut instinct, rather than actual evidence, when he develops a theory of the case, and then he won't look at anything that doesn't fit his theory. He'd love to pin the murder on me, but even he can't really come up with a motive for me, so he's going after one of my friends. I think arresting Emily would be almost as satisfying for him as putting me in jail."

"We won't let anything happen to Emily."

There wasn't much that Rory or even her police-officer husband could do if O'Connor charged Emily with murder. Joe couldn't risk his job by openly criticizing a superior officer, and Rory wouldn't do anything to undermine her husband's career. That left Mabel to make sure Emily wouldn't suffer for being a friend of someone who'd made an enemy of O'Connor. If he wouldn't do his job and find the real killer, then Mabel had to.

She already knew that the issue of motive wasn't going to solve the case. Opportunity might be more useful. She needed to figure out where everyone was around the time Thad ingested whatever had killed him. Perhaps she could convince Ken or his daughter to give her a set of the time-stamped pictures they'd already given to O'Connor, so she could build a clearer timeline.

As she was trying to come up with a reason to give them for why she wanted the digital images, one that didn't require her to say that O'Connor was incompetent, the kitchen door flew open and Terry Earley raced inside. Gasping for breath, he managed to say, "The wedding planner is losing it."

CHAPTER FIFTEEN

Terry had traded in his worn jeans for pristine khaki pants and paired them with one of the t-shirts Mabel had had printed with the Skinner Farm logo for the valet drivers.

"What's Paige done now?"

Terry leaned against the kitchen door and took a moment to catch his breath. Then he said, "First, she told me I needed to park the tractor out in the middle of the road or no one would see it in time to turn into the driveway."

"I hope you told her that wasn't an option."

"I did," Terry said. "I knew you'd back me up. But then Paige stomped off toward the farmhouse, and when I returned from parking the tractor where it was visible but not a traffic hazard, she was picking on Emily, telling her she's doing everything wrong. I thought you'd want to know."

"Definitely."

Rory jumped up from the kitchen table. "I promised to deal with Paige. I'll go run interference."

"Good." Terry helped himself to half a glass of the still-cooling tea and rummaged in the freezer for ice cubes. "Someone needs to intervene before Emily kills the wedding planner. No one wants a second body turning up this weekend."

"Let me know if you need backup," she said as Rory passed, although the other woman was far better at getting people to do things than Mabel was, as evidenced by the fact that she was still living in West Slocum looking for a farm manager and not back home in Maine.

That won't be necessary." Rory closed the door behind her.

Terry carried his glass over to the table and sat down with his back to the window. "I've been thinking."

In her experience, he thought about food almost all the time, either what he was going to eat or what he was going to grow, and Mabel realized the fruit basket on the table was empty. Emily usually offered a reminder when it needed refilling, but she'd been distracted lately.

"What's on your mind?" Mabel went over to the fridge to see if there was anything in it that wasn't intended for the wedding reception and could be offered to Terry as a mid-morning snack.

"This summer's farmers' market," he said. "Has Rory told you about the new markets opening up nearby?"

Mabel nodded and pulled out the three leftover boxed meals from the previous day's dinner delivery. "I was planning to go check out the other markets and talk to their managers after this weekend is over. Rory said there was a risk of fewer buyers coming to the West Slocum market, now that there's more competition." She dropped the boxes on the table in front of Terry.

"I thought she might have said something like that." Terry claimed one of the boxes and upended it to consider the contents. "Some of the other local farmers may see a drop in sales, but you don't have to worry about it."

Mabel's stomach growled, reminding her she hadn't had anything but tea for breakfast. She reclaimed one of the boxes. "Why shouldn't I worry?"

"Because your aunt Peggy did a brilliant job of branding her product as the best garlic on the East Coast," Terry said triumphantly. "People will make a separate trip for the best of something."

"I'm still worried for everyone else. Even if we don't lose buyers, others could. And then it becomes a big problem for everyone, including us, if the market doesn't attract enough buyers." Mabel unwrapped the sandwich from her box, which turned out to be ham and cheese. Not her usual breakfast, but it would do in the circumstances. The brownie was missing, presumably thanks to Grant's picking through the offerings the day before. "I'm not sure the town could justify having a paid market manager if business falls off."

"That's what's so brilliant about Peggy's branding. It benefits everyone, not just you. As long as people are making a separate trip for your unique product, they'll realize they might as well skip the other markets and buy everything else they need here too. At least if you advertise that it's the only location that has your aunt's garlic, so they aren't looking for it at the other places."

"I hope you're right."

"I am. I can even send you some case studies if you want." Terry's box hadn't been robbed of its brownie, and he apparently didn't have any qualms about early morning sweets, since he wolfed down half of it before adding, "Even if I'm wrong and people do split their business among several different markets, the odds are that the new ones won't last more than the first season. It's hard to start one up, and most fail pretty quickly, like any new business. Once the organizers realize they can't compete with existing sites, they'll shut down. Any good vendor at the new markets will join West Slocum's, making it even stronger in the long run."

"So all I need to do is keep the farm afloat for a year or two until things settle down." It should have been reassuring, but it just reminded Mabel of how much of a long-term commitment she'd made to her aunt's legacy. The app world was all about the short-term, getting things up and running quickly, before a competitor could establish itself as the front-runner.

Terry seemed to pick up on her anxiety. "Don't worry about the added competition yet. Whoever you hire to manage the farm will know how to survive a single season's challenges. If it's not the weather reducing the harvest, it's price fluctuations. Anyone with experience will have been through a few bad seasons and lived to tell about it."

"That's assuming I can find a qualified farm manager."

"You will." Terry looked at the packet of chips that Mabel had set aside from her breakfast. "Are you going to eat that?"

"You can have it," Mabel said. "There's probably another in the last box."

Terry got to his feet and collected her chips before rummaging through the contents of the last box. "I'll share them with the other valets. I should go make sure they've set up the markers for the parking area."

Mabel made a shooing motion and got up herself. She heard the door open and close as she headed in the opposite direction to check on Pixie in the front of the house. The cat was napping in her favorite spot in the office, so Mabel backed out of the room and secured the door as best she could before returning to the kitchen. As she cleared the table, she thought about what Terry had said about the upcoming market season. He always went above and beyond his job description, like he had just now, thinking of ways to reassure his boss before she could panic about the farm's future.

Too bad Terry hadn't applied for the manager position. He'd be perfect, although he was probably planning to go back to his native England as soon as he got his graduate degree in the next year, so he wouldn't be interested in a permanent job in Massachusetts. She could certainly understand someone wanting to get home again, and she couldn't expect him to stay just to help her out.

Raised voices out on the patio reminded her that now was not the time to dwell on her plans for hiring a manager. She had more pressing concerns. If anything else bad happened during the wedding, she could forget about ever holding another event on the farm, and, worse, Emily's new catering career would be over.

* * * *

Mabel had never before seen anyone who could resist Rory's gentle but inexorable guidance, but the wedding planner was apparently immune. Emily was off to one side of the patio, looking on in obvious horror while Rory tried to reason with the planner. Paige ignored them both while rearranging everything that Emily had spent the morning setting up on the patio. The first two tables nearest the driveway had been shoved aside to make a wider central aisle, even though it meant that half of the seats were inaccessible because they were too close to the chairs for other tables. Neatly folded linen napkins were being tossed into the center of each table, where eventually the florist would have to move them to install the centerpieces. The utensils from both sides of each place setting were gathered together and laid out diagonally across the space where the dinner plate would eventually go.

Paige stepped back to survey her handiwork and announced, "That's how it should be." She had traded in yesterday's oversized purple vintage dress for an equally baggy white linen caftan, the lower half of which seemed inspired by jodhpurs, with the sides puffing out from hip to knee before narrowing again at the ankles. There must have been hidden pockets in the extra side fabric, because Paige wasn't carrying a purse or phone. "I specified avant-garde, not all traditional and boring."

Poor Emily looked like she wanted to run back home and hide under her blankets again. She might even be reconsidering whether keeping her goats was worth having to deal with Paige and others like her. No matter how much Emily loved her goats, it had to be a close call.

Rory kept her patience somehow and said, "We'll take care of redoing the table setup now that we know what you want. Why don't you go out to the lavender field and make sure it's ready for guests?"

"I've done all I can out there," Paige said. "I chose the musicians myself, so I'm sure they'll be fine. I wish I could say the same for the florist, but I only hired him because Donna insisted, and he's been impossible to work with. I tried to explain what he was doing wrong, and he just ignored me. Can you imagine? Me? The wedding planner?"

Mabel wished she could ignore Paige, too, but she couldn't. The farm and Emily both needed to be paid for the weekend's events, and even more, they needed not to be blamed if things continued to go wrong. And Paige was intent on making a mess of everything. Now that Rory had failed to control her, Mabel had to try, although she wasn't sure what more she could do. Rory always appealed to a person's better nature, and that obviously hadn't worked, so maybe it was time for a different tack.

Mabel went over to tell Rory, "I'll take care of this if you'd like to go back to Emily's farm with her to get the next batch of supplies."

Rory glanced at Emily, who had a pleading look on her face, then nodded. She strode over to the driveway, snagging Emily on the way to the path through the woods between the two farms.

Paige destroyed another place setting, thumping the utensils haphazardly on the table. "Everything's going wrong, and no one will do what I say. I'm the wedding planner. I'm in charge."

"Not anymore." Being conciliatory hadn't worked, and Mabel was better at bluntness anyway. "We don't have time for your childish tantrums. There are only a little more than two hours until the ceremony, and I can hear Pixie yowling inside, so the photographer has probably just arrived to set up, and the bridesmaids and ushers will be next. It's too late for you to change anything now. So either accept the way Emily is arranging everything on the patio or you can go home. I won't have you on my property any longer if you're going to harass the contractors."

Paige spun to face Mabel. After a moment of silent shock, she sputtered, "You can't do that."

"I've already made arrangements to remove the reporter who was here yesterday if he shows up again," she lied. "Having another person removed won't be any trouble for me at all."

"If you make me leave, no one will ever have a wedding here again."

"Good," Mabel said, although she doubted Paige had that kind of power. "This one was just an experiment, and it's been far more trouble than it's worth. Largely because of you and your unreasonable demands. We're not going to put an expensive tractor out in the middle of the road, and we're not going to change the menu at the last minute, and we're not going to move the tables so people can't sit at them."

"You could at least let me fix things the way I want them, even if the caterer won't do it for me."

"No." Mabel had dealt with plenty of app-development clients when they'd wanted last-minute changes, and Paige's demands were no different. There was always a whole list of impossible changes that would waste too much of her time before they finally offered to settle for just one of their requests, which would be a hassle to do, but not impossible like the rest of their items. She'd often suspected they'd done it intentionally, starting with what they knew was impossible, so that the lesser request would seem reasonable only by comparison to the original one. That suspicion had led to her firm policy of refusing to make any changes without a significant additional payment, which had cut down on the unreasonable requests.

What Paige was asking for now was completely unreasonable, and Mabel was done with coddling her. "If we let you redo the tables, you'll just want more terrible, last-minute changes. That's not an option. You have two choices for what happens next. You can agree to relax, step back, and enjoy the event quietly, only alerting the contractors if someone's in danger, or you can leave right now."

"I can't leave," Paige said. "I need the guests to know I was the one who planned the wedding so they'll hire me for their own events."

"Are you sure you want to claim credit for this weekend?" Mabel asked. "You set the wedding in the middle of a site the bride is highly allergic to, and then the best man died, and a reporter harassed everyone."

"None of that was my fault." Paige picked up another set of utensils, but absently held them to her chest instead of placing them back on the table. "I'm sure it would have been a lot worse without me. The whole wedding was a farce from the start. The groom only cares about his work, the bride is a doormat, and all of their kids are greedy little monsters. Thad told me the marriage was doomed before it was even official."

"If Thad thought it was such a bad idea, why did he agree to be the best man?" And why had he hired someone with as little empathy and interpersonal skills as Paige to plan the wedding? Having her around was guaranteed to take a possibly fraught situation and make it worse. "Wasn't he a friend of the family? Didn't he want them to be happy?"

Paige shrugged. "He and Stan weren't really friends. Just business acquaintances. Thad had to be nice to Stan and his bride until the marriage certificate was signed, and then the buy-out agreement would take effect and it would be too late for Stan to change his mind about selling."

"What would have happened to the agreement if the wedding had been canceled?" Was it possible that Thad had *wanted* the agreement to fall apart? Had he come down with buyer's remorse, maybe thinking he was paying too much for the business? What if he'd thought that delaying the wedding would allow him to renegotiate for a lower price? So he'd hired Paige, not as an honest gift, but because he'd known how terrible she was at her job, and he was hoping to sabotage the wedding by setting her loose on it? "Could Thad have wanted to ruin the wedding so he could get out of the deal with Stan?"

"Of course not," Paige said. "Otherwise he wouldn't have hired me to plan the wedding."

"Unless he hired you, not to make things go smoothly, but to sabotage them instead."

Paige thumped down the gathered utensils she'd been hugging without looking at where they landed. "That's ridiculous. I've planned five of my friends' weddings, and all of them were perfect. One of them even had twenty guests and they all told me how good of a job I'd done."

Paige was sufficiently earnest in her defense that it seemed likely she was doing her best, and was simply incompetent, rather than that she was intentionally sabotaging the wedding. That didn't let Thad off the hook, though. He must have had an ulterior motive in hiring someone with such little experience. Planning five weddings, none exceeding twenty guests, was not a long enough résumé to qualify Paige for the Bellinghams' modest but still significantly more complicated event. Thad must have known that. He never would have hired someone with that little experience for his business. So, why had he done it for his partner's wedding?

"How well did you know Thad before you got this job?"

"Pretty well," Paige said, relaxing a little and picking up the abandoned utensils again. She went around the table, changing the place settings to her "avant-garde" style as she spoke. "We lived together for a few months. But it's not what you think. He respected my skills. I'd already left him before he hired me for this wedding."

So, Mabel thought, there were two obvious explanations for why he'd hired someone he had to know didn't have the necessary expertise to do the job. He'd either been trying to win her back to his bed, or he'd been trying to sabotage the wedding. But which one had it been?

Another thought struck Mabel. What if their separation had been Thad's idea, not Paige's, as she claimed, and she wanted revenge for being dumped? She could have hounded him into hiring her, telling him she needed the job to advance her career, while she'd really been planning to use it as an opportunity to kill her ex-lover.

"Your breakup must have been amicable if he was willing to hire you for an event that was important to him."

"I don't think he even noticed I'd left him." Paige stepped back to view her handiwork. "He's like Stan in that the only thing he really cares about is his work."

"You must have resented that while the two of you were together."

"I did," Paige said. "But I'm no doormat like Donna. I know my own worth, and I'm not settling for someone who doesn't appreciate me. Besides, I found someone much better just a few weeks later, and I never would have met him if I'd been stuck with Thad."

Unless Paige was a brilliant liar, which didn't seem likely, it sounded like she had definitely been over Thad before this weekend, with no residual anger toward him and therefore no reason to want him dead. Unless there'd been some sort of new falling-out yesterday. "You didn't mind working with an ex for this wedding?"

"I wasn't really working *with* him," Paige said. "He just wrote me a check and then told me to hash out all the details with Donna. So, that's what I did."

"What about yesterday?" Mabel asked. "What did Thad think of the work you'd done for the wedding?"

Paige narrowed her eyes. "Are you trying to suggest I might have killed Thad because he insulted my work? That's ridiculous. He told me everything was perfect, from the setting, to my outfit, and even my perfume. But for the most part, I was much too busy to have anything to do with him. The only thing he might have considered inadequate was the buffet, and I never even got to check out the food display until after he was dead, and then it was too late to do anything to fix it. Which is too bad, really, because from what I saw from behind the police line, the presentation was completely inadequate. I'm going to pay closer attention to the buffet today. I'll be watching over every move the caterer makes."

"No, you won't." Mabel was distracted briefly by the distant sound of renewed yowling from Pixie. Someone else was arriving, although it was too early for guests. Probably someone in the wedding party, either a bridesmaid or an usher, who'd been advised to arrive at least an hour before the event. "You're not getting near the caterer today. Remember what I told you? You don't bother the contractors unless it's something serious, or else I'll have you escorted off the property."

"The food presentation *is* a serious problem if it's not done right."

"Perhaps at another wedding that might be a possibility, but not with the current caterer. She knows what she's doing and has a great deal more experience than you do." I glanced down the driveway to where Joe Hansen was huddled with three young men in their valet t-shirts. I nodded in his direction. "Remember him from yesterday, when he was in uniform?"

Paige nodded.

"He's married to Rory, the woman you were arguing with a few minutes ago. I'm sure he'd be happy to make you leave if I ask him to."

"I guess I'll let the buffet's presentation slide this once," Paige said loftily. "It's a shame, but if anyone asks why it was so inadequate, I'll tell them it was the fault of the site owner, who wouldn't let me fix it."

"You do that. I'm happy to accept the blame." Especially, Mabel thought, since she doubted anyone would find any fault with the buffet. At least as long as Paige didn't touch it.

In any event, Mabel had a bigger problem than the wedding planner right now. The car that had provoked Pixie's latest yowl had just come to a stop beside Joe Hansen and the sign for valet parking. The driver wasn't a guest or a member of the wedding party or anyone else who belonged on the farm. It was the reporter, Andrew Rainey.

CHAPTER SIXTEEN

By the time Mabel made it over to the car, Joe Hansen had taken Rainey's keys and was seated behind the wheel in his role as a valet.

"Wait," she called out. "Rainey isn't staying."

"I have a right to be here." Rainey held up the camera hanging heavily against his chest and gestured with his free hand toward his fedora with the press ticket in the band. "I'm following up on a story."

Joe stayed in the car, but didn't put it in gear.

"There's nothing to follow up on here," Mabel told Rainey. "If you really want a story, go talk to Detective O'Connor at the police station."

Rainey smirked. "I already did. That's why I'm here. They're closing in on a suspect, and she's here." He turned to stare at the patio where Emily and Rory had returned with a handcart loaded with bins that presumably contained elements of the buffet dinner. "I'm here to document the arrest."

"No one's going to be arrested here today," Mabel said. "As far as I know, the police haven't even confirmed the cause of death. It could still have been natural causes."

"Oh, they know the cause of death all right," Rainey said. "They might not know the exact chemical composition, but it was definitely poison. O'Connor confirmed it. Not that I was surprised. I've got a real nose for news, like I told you yesterday. I knew it was poison just from what I observed at the crime scene while the EMTs were working on the victim, but it's necessary to get a quote from a source before publishing a story."

"Are you sure you should be covering this investigation?" Mabel asked. "Isn't it a conflict of interest if you might be a suspect? You were here at the time of the murder, after all, and you were even seen with Thad shortly before his death. He was escorting you away from the rehearsal, I believe, after you had an argument with the groom's son."

"That was nothing," Rainey insisted. "The kid just wanted me to put a plug for his start-up in any story I wrote, and I wouldn't do it, so he called me a few names and then I tripped over something. It certainly wasn't worth killing over. I've experienced much worse while pursuing stories. Angry people are part of the job."

"Still," Mabel said, "you must be a suspect, at least in theory. You were nearby when Thad died and for quite a while before that. How do we know you didn't sneak onto the patio and poison his plate?"

"Because I wasn't there," Rainey said. "After Grant yelled at me, Thad saw it as an excuse to go back to the patio to start raiding the food. I wasn't going to waste any more time with him, so I went and talked to your field hand."

Mabel knew that was a lie, but she didn't want him to know that she knew quite yet. She had to wonder why he was lying, unless maybe he really had killed Thad and needed an alibi, but it might be better to wait to question him further until she knew more about the exact timeline and who else did or didn't have an alibi.

Rainey continued, "I never went anywhere near the patio until after I heard the sirens. I don't care if you want to suspect me, though. I know more about what really happened than anyone else does, and it had nothing to do with me. I'm just here to get confirmation of what I already know so I can finish the story."

"You'll have to get that from the police, then, not from talking to any of the wedding party or guests," Mabel said, "They're off-limits to you. This wedding is a private event, not a public one, so you don't have any right to be here. If you're right, and there's an arrest, you can cover that, but you can't hang around like a vulture or mingle with the guests. I think you're wasting your time, but I can have a chair set up on the front porch for you, so you'll be able to see if O'Connor shows up like you think he will, and then you can interview him. But you have to promise to stay on the porch, not wander around the rest of the property. That's my final offer. Otherwise you need to leave right now."

Rainey peered at her suspiciously. "What are you afraid I'll find out if I'm not kept away from the guests?"

Mabel released a huff of frustration. He really did take professional skepticism to extremes. "I'm not afraid of anything, except that you'll upset the guests the same way you did with the wedding party yesterday."

"I was just doing my job."

"And today you can do it from the porch," Mabel said firmly. "The only other option is for Joe to give you back your keys so you can leave."

"No, no," Rainey grumbled. "I'll stay on the porch. Just until the cops show up to make their arrest. You can't expect me to keep my distance then. The public deserves to know what the police they pay for are doing."

"Just remember, if you leave your assigned seating to bother the guests, I'll have you removed, and then I'll report you for interfering with witnesses in an ongoing police investigation." Mabel knew she was on shaky ground, since she herself could be accused of the same thing, probably with more truth to the claim. But she couldn't think of anything else to threaten Rainey with. "You can only leave the porch if O'Connor shows up."

"What if he sends someone else to make the arrest?"

Of course Rainey would split hairs when it came to restrictions on his actions. Why couldn't he be that exacting when it came to claiming he knew who the killer was and how the murder had happened?

But Rainey was right about one thing. The local residents deserved to know the truth when it was determined, and it wouldn't look good for her or Emily if she sent Rainey away and then the police did show up to arrest Emily as the reporter had predicted. Rainey was sure to then claim that Mabel had been trying to cover up the truth. "You can observe the arrest, regardless of who makes it."

Unfortunately, if Emily was arrested, Rainey's story would be misleading. It would be accurate to the extent it reported that an arrest had been made for Thad's murder, but the rest of the truth—whether or not the arrested person had actually committed the murder—might never be known. Rainey would move on to another story, and O'Connor would close his investigation, while Emily, falsely accused of murder, would have to live with the half-truth for the rest of her life. Even if she was released eventually after someone else was shown to be the real culprit, or she was found not guilty at trial, Emily would still pay a heavy price, both emotionally and financially, for having been accused of murder.

There was no point in telling Rainey that he might be contributing to a miscarriage of justice. He'd apparently made up his mind about Emily's guilt even faster than O'Connor had. Mabel had more important things to do than argue with Rainey. If he was right about O'Connor's plans for an imminent arrest, she was running out of time to find the real culprit.

* * * *

Mabel didn't trust Rainey's reluctant promise to stay away from the guests until the police arrived, so she needed to take some extra precautions. Mabel told Joe he could park the reporter's car, but that it should be somewhere easily accessible in case Rainey didn't follow the rules she'd laid out and he had to leave. Then she escorted the reporter over to the porch to make sure he at least started out where he belonged.

Next, she enlisted Terry and his friends, who were waiting for more cars to park, to keep an eye on the reporter. She gave them her cell phone number and asked them to text her if Rainey set even one foot off the porch. One of them didn't have a cell phone, but said he'd be glad to tackle the reporter if he tried to leave.

"Not a good idea." Part of her would have liked to see it happen, but Rainey's expensive camera would probably break and she'd have to pay for the repairs. "Just let someone else know if he leaves the porch, and they can text me."

Mabel stayed and chatted with the valets for a few more minutes, sending meaningful glances toward Rainey occasionally, until she was convinced he would stay put for a while.

Terry ran off to park an arriving car, and Mabel excused herself from the rest of the group, saying she had a million things to do before guests started arriving in the next hour or so. She'd left her excuse vague enough that they'd assume she was preparing for the wedding, but what she really needed to do was figure out who had killed Thad or at least make sure O'Connor had all the necessary evidence.

She wished she could get a copy of the time-stamped pictures from the photographer so she could see who might have had the opportunity to have poisoned Ken. She couldn't imagine him releasing them to her, not just because they were his work product, but also because of privacy issues. He wouldn't last long as a professional photographer if he gave his work away for free and shared personal pictures with anyone who asked for them. The best she could do was to make sure Ken had sent them to the detective and hope that O'Connor would actually look at them.

Ken and his daughter and grandson should be out setting up their equipment near the lavender field, so Mabel left the front yard to head in that direction. As she passed the patio, she considered stopping there first to warn Emily that the police had confirmed Thad had been poisoned. Emily wasn't there, though, just Rory, leaning against the front of the buffet table and drinking from a bottle of water. About a quarter of the serving dishes had been laid out already, mostly filled with salads and breads. At one end, the buffet's floral centerpiece and smaller arrangements for the individual tables were clumped together, awaiting more artful distribution later.

"Where's Emily?" Mabel asked.

"She went back home to put the finishing touches on the rest of the food," Rory said. "She should be back in about an hour. She said she didn't need my help because she's going to pack everything onto the tractor's cart. She wanted me to stay here and guard everything from Paige and any guests who might show up early and be tempted to raid what's already laid out for the buffet."

"Good idea. As long as you're on the lookout for trouble, would you add Andrew Rainey to your list of possible problems? He's in time-out on the front porch, but I'm pretty sure he'll sneak away the first chance he gets. If you do see him, would you ask your husband to escort him off the property? Or text me if you can't find Joe."

"Sure."

"Meanwhile, if anyone's looking for me, I'm going next door to talk to Emily."

"Before you leave, I think he's looking for you." Rory pointed past Mabel at where a young man wearing a shirt that identified him as being an employee of the florist stood at the edge of the patio, looking uncertain.

Mabel went over to see what he wanted. Apparently she was needed out at the wedding stage to check the decorations and sign to accept them. The florist had spent the last half hour looking for the wedding planner, who seemed to have disappeared again. He couldn't wait any longer for someone to sign off on the work, since he needed to get to another site for an evening wedding. Mabel had no idea where Paige was, and it would undoubtedly be faster and less traumatic if the florist never had to deal with the wedding planner again, so she postponed her talk with Emily to go out to check on the decorations and if Ken was still there, to ask him about forwarding the pictures to O'Connor.

As soon as she got out to the field, before she could talk to Ken, the anxious florist pounced on her and led her over to the wedding stage. While reviewing the décor there, Mabel happened to look back toward the farmhouse in time to see the reporter sneaking across the driveway toward the barn. Her phone hadn't pinged with a message from Terry or the other valets, so Rainey had somehow escaped their notice. She glanced over at the patio, and Rory was kneeling behind the buffet table, breaking down a cardboard box, where she didn't have a clear line of sight to the reporter.

Mabel understood why Rainey would slip away, but why was he heading toward the barn instead of the lavender field to question the ushers who were milling about? Perhaps the perpetually absent wedding planner was in the barn, and Rainey had seen her go in there, so he'd decided to test Mabel's threats by trying to interview Paige. Mabel didn't have time to go stop him right now, but once she was done with the florist, she'd track Rainey down and have him escorted off the property by Joe Hansen. Talking with Ken about the photographs would have to wait. O'Connor wasn't likely to look at them in the next hour or two, if he looked at them at all.

Half an hour later, Mabel had seen all the decorations, and signed the document acknowledging she was satisfied with the work. Paige would probably complain later that the flowers had all been done wrong, but if she was going to disappear at a critical moment, then it was her own fault things weren't done to her specifications.

Just as she finished with the florist, Mabel's phone pinged. A text from Terry said that he was really sorry, but Rainey had disappeared while they were busy with several ushers and bridesmaids arriving all at once. She sent a text back to let him know it wasn't his fault, and she was on her way to take care of it now.

Mabel jogged back to the barn to take a look inside in case Rainey was still in there, so she could turn him over to Joe Hansen for removal. She'd have settled for just finding the wedding planner without the reporter, so Paige could be encouraged to do her job. She had definitely been there recently, judging by the lavender perfume in the air, but it was starting to fade. It only took a minute more to confirm that Paige wasn't there any longer, and neither was Rainey.

They could be anywhere on the farm's ten acres, together or separately, and she didn't have that much time to spare right now. Once Rainey emerged and was bothering a member of the wedding party, she'd hear about it and have him removed then.

Meanwhile, she still needed to talk to Emily about the police determination that Thad had been poisoned, and the conversation needed to happen before there were too many guests around. It would be better if they could talk at Emily's house, where they wouldn't risk being overheard, and fortunately, the tractor she'd planned to use to transport the rest of the food wasn't anywhere in sight, so she must still be at home.

Mabel was about thirty yards down the path between their two properties—half the width of the woods—when she noticed a hat lying on the edge of the path. It was gray with a wide band, like the fedora Rainey had been wearing, she thought. It couldn't be his, though, could it? She'd warned him to stay out of the woods, and he wouldn't have had any reason to risk her anger, not when the people he most likely wanted to ambush for an interview would be out near the lavender field. Unless perhaps he'd decided to finish what he'd started the day before and try to get a reaction out of Emily by accusing her of poisoning Thad.

Mabel bent to grab the hat, planning to take it with her on the mission to rescue Emily from the reporter, but her gaze fell on a shadow about thirty feet off the path. It was much too wide to be a fallen branch and too short to be an entire fallen tree.

She took a step off the path and squinted to get a better view. She still couldn't see any details in the fairly thick shade, but it struck her that the deeper shadow vaguely looked a torso, with two sprawled legs and an arm reaching above a head.

Mabel froze. There was a reason why the shadow looked like a body. That was exactly what it was. Someone was lying facedown on the forest floor. Once she knew what she was looking at, she could make out the gray tweed jacket that she recognized as belonging to the same person who had lost the fedora. The reporter, Andrew Rainey.

She dialed 911 first to ask for both police and ambulance, and then called Joe Hansen's personal number as she carefully made her way through what she could now see was the disturbed underbrush between the path and Rainey to see if he was still alive. There was enough blood on the side of his head that she suspected checking for a pulse would be futile. Still, she bent to touch his neck and confirmed her suspicion that he was already dead.

Joe answered his phone just then, so she said, "There's another body. Halfway down the path between Skinner Farm and Capricornucopia."

CHAPTER SEVENTEEN

There was nothing Mabel could do to help Rainey, so she returned to the path, trying not to contaminate the crime scene any more than she already had. It felt like hours passed while she was waiting, but it was probably only sixty seconds later when Joe Hansen ran up to her and then carefully made his way through the underbrush to squat down next to Rainey and check for the pulse that Mabel knew wouldn't be found. After a few seconds, he shook his head and stood before returning to the path to wait with Mabel for a more official response.

"I'm sorry," he said.

"Me too." She was sorry the reporter was dead, sorry that it had happened on her property, and even more sorry that O'Connor was going to see it as somehow her fault. Or Emily's.

Joe looked like he wanted to say more, but he was in an awkward position as an off-duty police officer. He couldn't take charge of the scene, and at the same time, he couldn't simply be a friend to the person who'd found the body and was therefore a potential suspect.

"It's okay," she told him. "I'm just glad you're here now while we wait for the official responders."

They waited in comfortable silence for the next five minutes until the EMTs—a different pair than the day before—and a uniformed officer arrived at a jog, and then another ten minutes until Detective O'Connor finally ambled up the path.

He chuckled as he caught sight of her. "What is it about you and dead bodies? Having people die on your farm isn't exactly good advertising for it."

"You never know." Mabel was done with coddling him and trying to soothe his ego. She wasn't any good at it, and it didn't work, not as long as he was nursing his grudge against her. She might as well just be herself. "Perhaps I should offer a murder-mystery weekend package. People love them."

"Not when real bodies are involved," O'Connor snapped, clearly annoyed that Mabel hadn't accepted his judgment that the farm was doomed. "So, what's the scoop?" He waved one hand toward the activity around Rainey's body.

"I'm afraid there won't be any scoops today. At least not by the reporter, Andrew Rainey. That's him in the brush." She remembered she'd held on to Rainey's fedora since first picking it up and handed it to O'Connor. "I found this next to the path, and then I saw the body. You'll also find a lens cap a couple of feet away from it. I saw it on my way back from checking his pulse. I think it belonged to Rainey. The camera itself should be around here somewhere too."

"The forensics team will find it. Assuming the crime scene isn't completely compromised by civilians." O'Connor glared first at her and then at the EMTs. "They always make a mess."

By then, the EMTs had already stepped back from the body and were packing up their equipment while the uniformed officer looked on. Mabel's first inclination was to defend the EMTs. She certainly hoped that if she were ever assaulted, the first responders would do whatever was necessary to keep her alive, rather than letting her die just so O'Connor would be able to gather evidence against her killer more easily. But if she sided with the EMTs, it would only make O'Connor more convinced that they were doing something wrong. Given how he was always looking for ways to get petty revenge on her, she could imagine him trying to get the EMTs in trouble with their boss.

She settled for saying, "I'd better go let everyone know they need to stay away from this path."

"Just don't give them any details about what happened here," O'Connor said. "I don't want people concocting stories about their innocence before I get a chance to interview them."

Did that mean he thought someone else had killed Rainey, not her? She decided to give him the benefit of the doubt and agree to his request to be discreet about what had happened. "I'll just tell them there was an unfortunate accident."

"I suppose that's okay," O'Connor said. "And tell them no one can leave until I've interviewed them. Do you have a list of who's here?"

"I'd have to get it from the wedding planner," Mabel said, trying not to let her reluctance show in her voice. O'Connor would think she was trying to sabotage his investigation, when she was just anticipating how difficult it was likely to be to get the information from Paige. "I can tell you who was here in terms of contractors, but I don't know which guests or wedding party members have arrived or what their names are."

"Just get me a full list as soon as you can."

"The wedding planner will have that information. I'll go look for her now. Once I have it, I'll text it to Joe Hansen, who can forward it to you," Mabel said. "Paige should be out by the lavender field where the ceremony will be held, but I haven't seen her recently, so it will take a few minutes to find her."

"If the ceremony's way out there, then what was the victim doing here?" O'Connor indicated the body.

"I have no idea." That wasn't quite true. There were two highly likely possibilities for what Rainey had been doing in the woods, either because he was stalking Emily or because he was meeting Paige to dig up dirt on the wedding. She wouldn't mind telling O'Connor about the possible rendezvous with Paige, but there was no way Mabel would mention a possible connection between Emily and the dead man. "Last I knew, Rainey was heading for the barn, but he must have continued past it and headed into these woods instead."

"So you weren't following him?"

Mabel shook her head.

"Then what were *you* doing out here instead of with your guests?"

Mabel didn't want to have to admit she'd been on her way to talk to Emily about her possibly impending arrest, since the detective would undoubtedly consider that tampering with his investigation. There was no point in completely evading the question, though. O'Connor was sure to connect Emily with the crime scene before long, even without Mabel's help. "I was on my way to the farm next door to see if Emily needed any help with packing up the food for today's reception."

"And did she?"

"I never made it that far. I saw Rainey's hat on the ground, and when I picked it up, I saw him in the brush."

"So, where is Emily now?"

"I assume she's still at home," Mabel said, uncomfortably aware that it meant Emily didn't have an alibi for the time of Rainey's death.

The sudden grin on O'Connor's face suggested he was thinking the same thing.

Poor Rainey, she thought. It looked like he'd been right that Emily would be arrested today, but he wouldn't be the one writing the story.

* * * *

Mabel would have liked to continue down the path to Emily's house to let her know about both the poisoning confirmation and the latest disaster, but not with O'Connor watching. He would assume she was helping Emily escape or perhaps concocting a false alibi for her, when all Mabel wanted was to make sure her friend was okay. With a killer on the loose, it was possible Rainey wasn't the only victim today.

Reluctantly, Mabel turned in the other direction, heading for the patio to let Rory and the valet team know what was going on, so they could steer people away from the crime scene. Once she was out of sight of O'Connor, she texted Emily: *Are you ok? Call me.*

Mabel emerged from the tree line to see that the photographer and his assistant and the toddler had finished setting up their video equipment in the lavender field and had come back to loiter in front of the barn with their cameras to capture the arrival of the guests and wedding party.

Lara was kneeling next to her toddler, who was lying on his stomach in front of the barn, happily making a mess of his light blue shirt. It was easy to forget how young Lara was, since she had such mature confidence and seemingly boundless patience for parenting. She was a stark contrast to the immature incompetence of the wedding planner, who was about the same age.

Ken stood on the other side of the child from his daughter, and a few feet in front of them all was a black-and-white tuxedo cat, Jonesy, named after the fictional character, Tom Jones, in recognition of the cat's lecherous ways before being neutered. He'd been the first cat Mabel had met on Skinner Farm, when he'd come out of the shadows to rush past her on the night she'd first arrived, startling her into almost falling off the front porch. He was one of the older cats in the colony, probably close to ten years old, and had lived on the farm all his life. He'd been feral initially, but by the time Mabel had inherited the farm he'd domesticated himself, and he was one of only two of the barn cats that liked to be petted. He still didn't like living indoors, so he continued to live with his colony in the barn.

Jonesy rubbed against the toddler's head, encouraging more attention, eliciting a gurgle of glee from the child and an impatient sound from the photographer.

Ken had one camera around his neck and another in his hand, which he waved at his daughter. "It's time to get back to work. I can take care of the arrival shots here, if you'll go back to the lavender field and cover the guests once they get there."

Lara got to her feet. "Just one more minute, please. We don't get to be around animals very often."

"You've got to go now," Ken said irritably, raising his foot as if he were going to kick Jonesy to remove the distraction.

Mabel shouted "No!" and raced to stop him.

Lara did the same thing and got to her father first, placing herself between him and the cat so if anyone was kicked, it would be her.

Ken froze, Jonesy sprinted to the safety of the barn, and the toddler began to cry at his new friend's disappearance. Lara bent to scoop up the crying child and began murmuring soothing words. "It's okay, baby. We'll get you your very own cat as soon as we get home."

"We're not getting a cat," Ken said, but he sounded like he knew he'd already lost that battle.

"The shelter in town always has some lovely, friendly cats who need a home," Mabel said. "The animal control officer owes me a favor, so I might be able to arrange for you to visit after hours today or tomorrow if you'd like."

"Thank you, but it's probably best if we wait until we get home. I'm sure we can find the perfect pet at our local shelter." She glared at her father. "Or better yet, a pair of them, since I've heard that animal advocates say cats do best with a feline companion."

She turned her back on Ken, propped her son on her hip, and stomped up the tractor path toward the lavender field.

Ken stayed behind, looking down at the extra camera in his hand for a moment. When he looked up again, he said, "I'm sorry. It's been a difficult couple of days. I wouldn't have hurt the cat. I promise."

"Just to be safe, you'd better stay away from the barn cats for the rest of the day." Mabel wasn't willing to take any chances with their safety, and she wasn't entirely convinced that Ken would have refrained from kicking Jonesy if she and his daughter hadn't been there to stop him.

Her initial dislike of Ken reasserted itself with a vengeance, despite all the good work he'd done, taking on responsibility for smoothing over the wedding planner's mistakes and trying to cheer up the bride. Mabel had originally chalked her instinctive negative reaction to resentment that he'd been chosen over a local photographer, but maybe her gut had been trying to tell her something else, something serious. Maybe Ken had just been pretending to be so kind and instead was really a horrible person, someone who would take out his anger on a defenseless animal. Not that Jonesy was entirely defenseless. Ken might well have lost that battle. Still, Mabel was glad they didn't have to find out how tough the cat was. The EMTs didn't need any more victims to patch up, and the farm didn't need a reputation for guests getting mauled in addition to poisoned and bludgeoned.

"I was just angry, and I wasn't thinking," Ken said. "I'm so frustrated by everything that's gone badly this weekend, and just as one thing gets under control, something else happens. And now we've needed a second ambulance in less than twenty-four hours."

"It has been a difficult weekend," Mabel agreed, although she wasn't prepared to forgive Ken yet. He could have vented his frustration in a less harmful way, kicking the ground or the barn doors. A living creature shouldn't have been an option, no matter how upset he was.

"This was supposed to be Donna's special weekend," he said, "and now all she's going to remember is murder and ambulances and police interrogations."

"It will get better," she said with more optimism than she felt. What was it that Emily always told her when Mabel was overwhelmed with the challenges of the farm? That positive thinking could fix most problems? She wasn't sure about that, but it was worth a try. "Once the wedding and reception are over, the happiness will outweigh everything else. The pain will be forgotten. Like with childbirth."

"Assuming there's nothing worse waiting in the wings." Ken absently adjusted the large lens on his camera although it was pointed at the ground. "There's still plenty of time left before the day is over for someone else to get hurt."

"It sounds like you want to postpone the wedding," Mabel said. "I know that's what her kids want. Grant too. But I thought you supported the marriage."

"I do. I've worked with her fiancé a bit over the years, doing pictures for the website and the like, so I know he's an okay guy. I wouldn't have offered to photograph the wedding if I didn't think he'd be good to her."

"So, you don't think Stan might have killed Thad, perhaps in a falling-out over the sale of the business?"

Ken looked toward the road as if hoping a new arrival would give him an excuse not to answer. Pixie hadn't yowled, so he wouldn't see anyone coming up the driveway anytime soon.

Finally, he said, "Look, I hate to say anything bad about the dead, but Thad wasn't an easy person to be around. Worse when he was particularly stressed out, like he's been over the change in the company's ownership. He could get under people's skin, testing to see how far he could push them before they snapped. And Stan's been known to snap when angry. Never with Donna or her kids. He'd never hurt them. But someone else? Someone in the business world, someone like a partner if Stan felt like he'd been betrayed somehow? I guess it's possible."

Mabel could picture the groom killing Thad, coldly and methodically, which fit with poisoning. But if the murder had been planned, then why do it this weekend, when it might cause the wedding to be postponed? The only way it made sense for Stan to be the culprit was if he'd done it in a fit of rage, but that just didn't fit what she'd seen of him. "Stan seems very much in control of his emotions and actions, not the sort who'd lash out in anger."

"Oh, he is cool as a cucumber most of the time," Ken said. "But that's just on the outside. He hides a lot of what he's feeling, and I've known him long enough to have seen him lash out angrily a few times. And it's been a fraught weekend, after all, what with the wedding and Paige's incompetence. He really lost his temper for a bit yesterday with that reporter who was begging him for an interview. I had to hold him back while Thad dragged the reporter away."

"I heard it was Grant who got into the fight with the reporter," Mabel said.

"It was, but Stan started it. Grant was just trying to protect his father."

And then Thad had helped the reporter to his feet, which might have looked like he was taking Rainey's side in the argument. That perceived disloyalty might not be enough, on its own, to lead to murder, but it could have been a final straw dropped onto existing problems between the best man and the groom. Or his son.

"Do you think it's possible Grant killed Thad on his father's behalf?"

"No, no, of course not," Ken said, although he didn't sound entirely convinced. "Grant and Thad were like brothers."

That wasn't much of a defense, Mabel thought. Throughout history, beginning with Cain and Abel, siblings had been known to resent each other and even resort to murder.

"Your pictures might be able to show that neither Grant nor his father had the opportunity to kill Thad, and also show who did have that opportunity," Mabel said. "Were you able to send them to the detective yet?"

"I've been a bit distracted," Ken said. "I need to concentrate on taking new pictures right now, but I'll take care of it as soon as the wedding is over, while people are getting set up for the reception."

"Thanks," Mabel said. "In the meantime, perhaps you could keep the guests calm while you're taking pictures. Unfortunately, Thad wasn't the only person to have an unfortunate accident this weekend. Today's ambulance was for the reporter, Andrew Rainey."

Ken froze for a moment and then shook his head as if dispelling whatever image he'd been seeing. "No, no. You can't suspect Stan of attacking the reporter. It's not possible. He isn't even here yet. He's been at home with his son all day, I believe. They were out searching for a tux so Grant could be the best man. That gives them both an alibi, right?"

"Maybe. But if they weren't together, it might raise some questions. After all, they did both have a fight with the reporter yesterday."

"Stan only yelled at the guy. It was Grant who knocked him onto the ground."

"I was wondering about that," Mabel said. "Why did Grant even get involved? I would think his father was more than capable of dealing with a pesky reporter."

"It started out reasonable enough. Grant stepped between his father and the reporter, and suggested that Rainey should leave or they'd call the police. The reporter said he'd go if Grant would agree to an interview in his father's place. Grant apparently planned to talk about his new start-up to distract the reporter from his original story, but as they started to leave, it became obvious that Rainey only wanted to talk about Stan. Grant's always been sensitive about living in his father's shadow." Ken nodded thoughtfully. "Now that I think of it, Grant is definitely a solid suspect in yesterday's murder if not what happened today. Much more so than Stan. Grant certainly had the opportunity, and I'm sure the police will notice his absence from most of the group pictures. He kept disappearing whenever he could get away with it, which was most of the time, since his father was too busy texting to notice what his son was doing."

"I'm sure the police will figure it out, once they have your pictures," she lied. "But in the meantime, I need to keep everyone away from the crime scene in the woods without getting them upset. And someone needs to let the bride and groom know why the ambulance is here and make sure they don't spread any panic. Normally, I'd ask the wedding planner to talk to them and ask them to keep it quiet until the police are ready to interview witnesses, but Paige has disappeared, so it's up to me."

"Do you really have to tell them?" he asked. "I mean, right now? Can't you let Donna enjoy the day, and you can tell her later?"

"I suppose it wouldn't hurt to wait," Mabel said. "But I'm going to have to tell Paige, so she can help to make sure everyone stays away from the crime scene. I don't want to have to ask the detective to put up police tape across the path if I don't have to."

He groaned. "Definitely not. It would be a constant reminder. And it's bound to end up in the background of some of the pictures. I could edit it out, but it would be annoying to do."

Too bad there wasn't a way to digitally edit real life to remove the killer from the farm, along with the police tape.

CHAPTER EIGHTEEN

Mabel watched as Ken headed for where two sedans and an SUV were lined up in the driveway, waiting for the valets. In the other direction, the musicians Paige had hired were starting to perform for the guests who'd begun to seat themselves out near the lavender field. There were four members of the band, so she supposed they technically qualified as a quartet, but they certainly weren't playing the classical or traditional background music she'd been expecting. They looked and sounded much more like a thrash metal band with their aggressive, loud performance.

At least it would drown out the sounds of any police activity heading to and from the latest crime scene.

Finding the body had caused Mabel to lose track of time. A glance at her watch told her there was just under half an hour left until the ceremony. Guests would be arriving at an ever-increasing pace, and she had to make sure they didn't get curious about the ambulance and wander over to the crime scene in the woods. Since Paige still wasn't anywhere in sight, perhaps Terry could help make sure everyone stayed away from the ambulance that blocked the path to the crime scene.

She was on her way to have a chat with him when she noticed that Emily was on the patio, redistributing the small floral arrangements clustered at the end of the buffet so that each of the individual tables had a centerpiece. When had Emily returned? The answer might either establish an alibi for her at the time of Rainey's murder or give O'Connor even more reason to suspect Emily of murder.

Mabel detoured over to the patio. "I thought you were still at home."

"Nope." Emily seemed almost back to her usual sunny self. "I've been back for ages."

"Before the ambulance arrived?"

"Definitely." Emily stepped back to peer at the most recently placed centerpiece, and then moved it a couple of inches to her right.

Mabel wanted to question her more about the exact timing and who might have been able to corroborate it, but then O'Connor would start accusing Mabel of coaching a witness. She could wait for the details. "Then where's your tractor? I thought you'd planned to use its cart to bring over the last of the food."

Emily laughed. "I meant to, but then I remembered how determined Paige was to have a quaint tractor parked out in the middle of the road. Mine's much older than yours and closer to her image of what a tractor should look like, so I decided to leave it at home. Otherwise, Paige would waste my time trying to get me to switch it for yours out at the end of the driveway. Keeping it out of sight seems to have worked too. Paige hasn't bothered me, and I've been able to hear the guests walking past the patio talking about how lovely everything looks."

Emily seemed so happy, and all Mabel could think was that she had to burst her friend's bubble by telling her about the latest corpse and the risk that she'd be blamed, especially after poison had been confirmed as Thad's cause of death.

Maybe Mabel didn't have to tell her quite yet. As Ken had suggested, what was the harm in letting everyone enjoy the event, and then they could hear about the bad news later when it wouldn't taint their appreciation of the day?

"Speaking of Paige," Mabel said. "Have you seen her? I need her to take care of something."

"She's been missing for a while, and I was kind of hoping she was the reason for the ambulance," Emily said. "Nothing too bad, but perhaps a panic attack or something. Is that horrible of me?"

"It's perfectly understandable," Mabel said.

"So, if it wasn't Paige who needed medical help, then who was it?"

"It doesn't matter right now," Mabel said. "I'll explain later, but you've got work to do, and I've got to go find Paige."

"I can at least tell you she's not in the farmhouse, unless she sneaked up to the second floor to hide, which seems too rude, even for her," Emily said. "I went inside to check on the bride, as well as the food I'd piled up on the kitchen table. Donna was alone in there, except Pixie had gotten out of the office and was sitting in her favorite windowsill, so I scooped her up and put her back where she belonged."

"Wait. The bride is here already? In the house?" Mabel turned automatically to look down the driveway where two cars were idling while waiting for a valet to park them. "Then where's the limo?"

"There is no limo," Emily said. "Apparently Donna decided to call the company this morning to ask if it could arrive a few minutes early, and they said it wasn't coming at all and it was too late to book a car for today. Apparently Paige had only gotten a quote and hadn't made the actual reservation."

Disappointing, but not surprising. "Maybe that's why Paige has disappeared again. She's hiding because she's afraid of how Donna is going to react to that big of a mistake."

"Donna seems more resigned than angry. At least with Paige. Stan's definitely in the doghouse. He drove them both over here himself after the limo fiasco, but something must have happened between the couple on the way. I saw the end of their argument, because the valets let the car pass the normal drop-off spot, so Stan could park outside the barn where the limo was supposed to go. As soon as he braked, Donna hopped out and then shouted something about how, if she'd known, she'd have canceled the wedding. Stan said surely she just meant postpone, and she said no, she really meant she'd cancel. Permanently. And she was still considering calling it off. Then she stomped into the farmhouse. Stan apparently decided to let her cool off, and headed into the barn with his phone after he tossed one of the valets his keys."

Interesting, Mabel thought, wishing she knew exactly what Stan had done that was so bad. Had he killed Thad and Donna had found out somehow? Finding out she was about to marry a murderer would certainly be grounds for calling off a wedding. Mabel wouldn't even blame her. At this point, a last-minute cancellation wouldn't be as bad for the reputation of both Skinner Farm and Emily's new catering business as everything else that had happened this weekend. Especially if O'Connor had his way, and Emily was arrested and Mabel was considered an accessory to the crime.

"You seem awfully unconcerned about the possible late cancellation," Mabel said.

Emily adjusted the vase on another table. "I am. I lost sight of what matters for a while, but Rory reminded me that whatever goes wrong today can't be any worse than Thad's death."

Mabel suppressed a guilty wince. A second murder felt more than twice as bad as just one, and it didn't help that the police were going to consider Emily a likely culprit in both cases. "I hope Rory's right, but I won't feel

LAID OUT IN LAVENDER

better until the wedding and the reception are both over and everyone's made it home safely." Everyone except Rainey, at least.

Emily laughed. "You're such a pessimist. Today is going to be lovely, whether the couple gets married or not. I'd hoped to get some referrals out of this job, but the way things have turned out, it might be best if everyone just forgot this weekend ever happened, and we'll both start fresh with the next booking."

Mabel had a feeling the Bellingham wedding—or the last-minute jilting—was going to be remembered for a long time, especially with Rainey as the second victim. The murder of someone from out of town would have been a one day's wonder on the local grapevine, but when someone local was killed, that made it personal and scary. His death would undoubtedly be on everyone's mind until the killer was caught and convicted.

Still, she didn't want to ruin Emily's good mood, and fortunately Rory had just come out of the farmhouse with a warming tray and was carrying it over to the buffet table at the far end of the patio. Mabel could use that as an excuse to leave before Emily figured out she hadn't been told the whole truth about why the ambulance had been called. "I should go see if Rory knows where Paige is."

"Would you let Rory know I'll be in your kitchen for a while? Everything out here is all set, and I have a few things left to do inside so we'll be ready for the reception."

"Of course." Now there was no chance Emily might overhear the conversation about what had happened to the reporter.

Rory had already finished setting the warming tray in its assigned spot and was about to return to the kitchen when Mabel intercepted her. "Emily's gone inside, and we need to talk privately. Did Joe tell you why there's an ambulance over by the woods?"

"I'm afraid so." Rory flicked a glance toward the farmhouse. "He said not to tell anyone. And that includes Emily. I guess it's better for her if she doesn't know until later."

"I just hope her ignorance won't turn into a problem for her," Mabel said. "If O'Connor doesn't already know it's Emily's house at the other end of the path, it won't take long for him to figure it out. And then he'll hear that she was in the woods herself shortly before I found Rainey dead. You wouldn't happen to know exactly when she returned, would you?"

"I didn't check the time, but she got back here maybe ten or fifteen minutes before I saw you heading toward her house."

Mabel had seen Rainey heading for the barn fifteen or twenty minutes before that, so he'd been killed sometime in that half hour before she'd found him. And Emily had been at home, without an alibi, for most of that time.

"I wish I'd known she'd already returned." Then she wouldn't have gone looking for Emily, and she wouldn't have found Rainey's body, and the bride could have had her wedding without any further tragedy. Rainey would still have been dead, so she felt a little guilty at the thought that everyone's enjoyment of the day would have been predicated on the poor man's body lying out there for hours before it was found. "I didn't see Emily on the patio, so I thought she was at home and went looking for her."

"She must have been inside the farmhouse. She went in there almost immediately after returning, so she could put most of the food inside. And then she stayed in the kitchen to calm Donna down."

"The photographer seems to be the only person who can soothe Donna," Mabel said.

"I can go get him if you'll keep an eye on the buffet."

"That's not necessary."

"But you said—"

"I know, I know," Mabel interrupted. "But he's busy."

"Not for long if the bride cancels the wedding," Rory said.

"We'll call him in if it comes to that," Mabel said, "but only as a last resort. He gets on my nerves."

"He seems okay to me."

"You didn't see him threaten to kick the barn cat, Jonesy."

Rory's eyebrows rose. "And Ken's still alive?"

"He didn't follow through with the threat," Mabel said. "His daughter stopped him. Which is fortunate for everyone. I wouldn't have wanted to explain to the detective why Jonesy mauled a contractor or why I cheered him on. I may have to tell Emily we can't do weddings here if there's a risk to my cats."

"Emily would understand," Rory said. "I'm not sure she wants to do any more catering after this weekend. She was doing pretty well this morning before the bride arrived, but Donna's anger at Stan has to have reminded Emily of her feelings toward her own husband. She's pretending it didn't bother her, but I don't know how long she can last like that. And catered events are always fraught, for one reason or another. I'm not sure she's strong enough to handle it right now."

The end of Emily's catering career wasn't even the worst possible future for her. Not when there was still a chance that she'd be arrested and then convicted of a murder or two, and end up spending the rest of her life in prison instead of meditating with her goats.

An outraged screech emerged from the kitchen, a distinctly human sound, not Pixie's yowling.

Mabel said, "It sounds like Emily couldn't calm the bride down."

"It was quiet for a while, but then Stan barged inside a few minutes before you showed up, so things started to heat up again," Rory said. "Maybe Donna's kids could help. I saw them heading for the lavender field a few minutes ago."

"More likely, they'd just make it worse," Mabel said. "I'm going to try one more time to find the planner and then she can talk to Donna. Otherwise, I'll get her kids to talk to her."

"Are you sure you want to find Paige? Things have been running so smoothly without her around." Another outraged screech filtered out of the farmhouse. "Well, everything except for the bride threatening to cancel the wedding. And Rainey's death." Rory wrinkled her nose. "Okay, I guess you'd better find Paige, after all."

* * * *

After confirming that Paige wasn't hiding in the barn, Mabel went out to the front of the farmhouse to ask Terry if he had seen the wedding planner at any time after Rainey had sneaked off the porch. She also needed to get Terry up to speed about the body on the path to Emily's house, so he could keep guests from wandering where they didn't belong.

One of Terry's friends had just taken the only waiting car to the parking area, and the other two were waiting next to the STOP HERE sign, while Terry loitered a few feet away, checking his phone.

Mabel hurried over. "Have you seen Paige recently?"

"Not since she finished chatting with Rainey on the porch." He grinned as he pocketed his phone. "We've all been hoping she'd stay out of sight."

"Wait. She was talking to Rainey?" Mabel demanded. "Why didn't you text me?"

His grin faded. "You didn't say he couldn't have visitors."

Mabel took a deep breath. "I know. I'm sorry. I'm just a little on edge. When were they together on the porch?"

Terry shrugged. "I don't know exactly. It was right after you left. If you'd turned around, you'd have seen her coming up the driveway fifty meters or so behind you. They didn't talk for long. Just a minute or two."

Given Rainey's subsequent escape to the woods, and the brevity of their conversation, it sounded like they'd been arranging to meet up somewhere private. If Paige was spilling confidential information about her employer to a reporter, she wouldn't want to be seen. And if they had had a secret rendezvous, it confirmed Mabel's earlier suspicion that Paige might well have had the opportunity to kill the reporter.

"Did you see Paige at all after she left the porch?"

Terry shook his head. "We got busy right around then, and I didn't notice much besides where we were parking cars until the arrivals slowed down again."

It was still possible someone else could give Paige an alibi, but for now it looked like she had both opportunity and means to kill Rainey. Given the blood on the reporter's head, he'd probably been hit with a fallen branch, which anyone could have found in the woods. Or possibly, she thought, Rainey had been killed with his own camera. It hadn't been hanging around his neck when she'd found the body, and the lens had looked heavy enough to inflict some serious damage on a human skull.

There was just one more piece of evidence Mabel needed to make it a slam dunk that even O'Connor couldn't ignore. What was Paige's motive? Perhaps Rainey had threatened to report on something that would put the final nail in the coffin of Paige's career as a wedding planner. She might have thought she could recover from this disaster of a wedding if the relatively small number of guests and participants were the only ones who knew about her failures. Having a story about her incompetence published online, even by a small newspaper, where it could be found easily by potential clients, would be impossible to overcome. Even Paige would have to see that.

Terry interrupted her thoughts anxiously. "You know I'm really sorry we missed Rainey's escape, right? It's just that there were all those people arriving and getting impatient, and the next time I had a minute to think, I turned around, he was gone. I texted you as soon as I knew."

"It's not your fault," Mabel reassured him. There was nothing more Terry could tell her about the wedding planner, so she changed the subject. "There's something else we need to discuss."

Terry's face brightened. "Yeah?"

"It's about the ambulance."

His happy expression faded. "Oh. I thought you... Never mind. What about the ambulance?"

Mabel heard a yowl from Pixie, indicating another vehicle had just entered the driveway. She didn't have much time before another guest would arrive, and this wasn't something she wanted overheard. "Over on the porch. This has to be just between us."

The porch didn't offer much privacy, but it was enough as long as they kept their voices low. Once there, she said, "There's been another death." She held up a hand to stop him from asking who it was. "O'Connor doesn't want me to talk about it, so I'll just say it's not someone you're close to."

Terry glanced at where one of his friends was taking the keys from the latest guest to arrive. "You want me to keep everyone in the dark, right? No point in upsetting the wedding guests."

"Exactly," Mabel said, grateful she didn't have to explain every little thing to him and she could trust his discretion. "I'd appreciate it if you'd steer everyone away from the ambulance. Not lie to them exactly, but if you could give them the impression that it's nothing major, that would be great."

"I'll tell them it's here as a safety precaution, and have the other guys say the same thing," Terry said. "It's sort of true, even if it's the investigation's safety at issue, not the guests'."

"That's perfect." Mabel never would have thought of that angle. "I don't know what I'd do without you."

He shrugged sadly. "You won't need me once you hire a farm manager. At least not for anything more than manual labor."

Mabel would miss having Terry around when he finished school and went back home. He was reliable, knowledgeable, and usually upbeat. She really should have considered him for the farm manager job before she started advertising, but she'd been stuck on the recommendations in the books she'd read, which had convinced her she needed someone with managerial experience. This weekend had shown her that all she really needed was someone with the agricultural expertise she lacked, plus basic reliability and good judgment. Terry had all of those qualifications, and unlike Wetzel, he didn't make Mabel feel inadequate.

"Actually, the farm manager job is also something we need to talk about," she said. "Just not right now. But if you have some time tomorrow, we should sit down and discuss whether you're dead-set on returning to England as soon as you've got your degree, or if you'd consider sticking around and managing Skinner Farm."

"Are you sure?" Terry's expression was guarded, as if he was trying not to get his hopes up about something he desperately wanted. "I don't have all the experience you wanted, and I'll need to get your approval a lot in the beginning until I get more experience, so it might be a while before I can handle it on my own, and I know you're in a hurry to get back to Maine."

He was right that having an inexperienced manager would complicate matters. She'd only been planning to stick around for a few months after hiring the manager, just until he settled in, but that had been based on the assumption that all he needed to learn was what was unique to this particular farm. Terry had a bigger challenge, in that he'd need to learn how hands-on management differed from theory, and that would take longer than a few months. Long-distance employment like she herself had for app development wasn't right for all projects. With the inexperienced Terry as the manager, she'd have to supervise in person for longer than she'd planned. Still, she thought it was worth the sacrifice to protect her aunt's legacy, keeping the farm something Peggy would have been proud of. Terry would do that, while someone like Richard Wetzel would not.

"I'm sure, and we can figure out the details later. On Monday, I'll talk to—" She cut herself off before automatically naming her longtime lawyer in Maine. "I'll talk to Quon Liang about the legal technicalities of getting you a green card or whatever else you need."

"Brilliant!" Terry's face unfroze, revealing his obvious joy. He bent to pull Mabel into a hug before stopping himself. He hesitated, uncertain of how to express his gratitude and enthusiasm without invading her personal space, but after a rapid-fire trio of yowls from Pixie, he stepped back and said, "I guess I'd better get back to work. Sounds like more guests are on the way."

CHAPTER NINETEEN

Mabel intended to resume her search for Paige by checking in with the bride, but then she looked down the driveway and saw the groom's son tumble out of the driver's seat of a new-looking SUV, and he was obviously drunk. One of Terry's friends was politely trying to get the keys from Grant, but he was playing keep-away and finding it hysterical.

Mabel went over to rescue the annoyed valet. "I'll take care of this if you want to go get the next car."

The valet didn't hesitate before jogging over to the Jaguar idling behind the SUV. That driver seemed a little reluctant to hand over the keys to his expensive car, but the young man promised he'd put the car in a "special" spot where it couldn't get damaged. Mabel wasn't aware of any such separate location, but the reassurance worked, and the driver handed over the keys before going around the front to join up with the female passenger.

"Just follow the sound of the band," the valet told the guests. "And stay away from the ambulance. It's guarded by police dogs."

That was news to Mabel, but, like the promise of a "special" parking spot, it seemed to be effective, since the couple hugged the side of the driveway away from the ambulance as they made their way to the lavender field.

Mabel turned back to Grant. He'd leaned his back against the driver's side door of the SUV and closed his eyes as if he planned to sleep standing up. She hoped he'd grown bored with his keep-away game now that no one was playing with him. "Are you ready to hand over your keys now?"

Grant opened his eyes and frowned. "Why would I do that? No point in sticking around, now that the wedding's off. I just wanted to see the look on the Markos brats' faces when I tell them about the cancellation. That'll only take a minute, and then I'm going back to my celebrating."

"The wedding is still on," Mabel said, hoping it was true. "The bride and groom are both here, along with the bridesmaids and ushers and about half the guests. You need to sober up if you're going to be the best man."

"I'm always the best man." Grant giggled at his pitiful joke. "Better than Thad, that's for sure. With him gone, and the wedding cancelled, things can go back to normal. Dad returns to work, and Donna leaves him for breaking his promise to retire. Just the way I planned it."

"No one's told me the wedding was cancelled," Mabel said, although the bride's anger didn't bode well. "The last I knew, your father and Donna had had a bit of an argument, but it was probably just wedding-day jitters, and they've worked it all out."

"Nah, their disagreement is more than that. It's, it's, it's..." He paused to search for the right word. "You know. Existential. That's what it is. To be or not to be for their relationship. And it's gonna be 'not to be.' When I heard that nothing I'd said last night had worked, and Donna was with Father in the car and they were already on the way here, I used the nuclear option. Brilliant, wasn't it?"

He paused with a smug look on his face, apparently waiting for praise.

Mabel had no intention of giving him what he wanted. "I have no idea what you're talking about."

Grant shook his head judgmentally. "You'll never make it as a businessman...woman...person...whatever. Gotta take risks, go for the jugular, clean kill."

"It's your father's happiness you're talking about killing, isn't it?"

"Exactly. Maybe you could understand my brilliance, after all. See, I called Father and had him put it on speakerphone, and then I, oh, so casually, let slip the one thing I knew that Donna could never forgive Dad for." He lowered his voice confidentially. "Sometimes you need luck to get what you want, although you need to be smart enough to know how to use it when it comes your way. If it weren't for dear Paige, Father and Donna would have been in separate cars. But they weren't, so all I had to do was add my genius words. They worked just as I knew they would. I could hear how angry Donna was before Father hung up on me. He's probably mad at me now, but he'll get over it and thank me for it later."

Mabel wasn't so sure about that. And it made her wonder where Grant had been calling his father from. Ken had thought Grant had been with his father all morning, but apparently he hadn't been staying at Stan's house or he'd have been in the car with the couple on the way to the farm. Given how drunk he was, it seemed likely he'd been drinking for quite a while, and he probably wouldn't have done that in front of his father, who needed his best man to be sober.

If Grant had been alone for the last couple of hours, he didn't have an alibi for the time of Rainey's death. The two men had fought the day before, and they could have arranged a rematch that ended in the reporter's death. Or, assuming the two deaths were related, Rainey might have tried to confront Grant about his role in the murder of Thad and it had led to an altercation. Either way, Grant was a promising suspect for both murders. The only question was how he could have gotten to and from the farm unseen to meet with Rainey in the woods.

What if, before Grant had heard about the limo problem and used that as an opportunity to get the wedding cancelled, he'd come to the farm, intending to create some other mischief that would derail the event, leaving his car out of sight? And while he was sneaking around, he'd run into Rainey, and they'd had a bigger argument than they'd had the previous day, and it had escalated into violence. Or perhaps the reporter had found some evidence to confirm what the bride's children thought, that Grant had killed Thad, and then Rainey had been killed to silence him.

There had been plenty of time between Mabel's finding the body and now for Grant to have escaped after killing Rainey. He could have gone through Emily's yard so as not to be spotted by the larger number of people at Skinner Farm, then gotten himself drunk before returning and feigning ignorance of what had happened. For all Mabel knew, he wasn't even as drunk as he appeared. After all, judging by the way he was weaving whenever he tried to push away from the support of the SUV, he would have had difficulty driving even a mile without ending up in a ditch, and yet he'd made it to her somewhat isolated farm without wrecking his vehicle.

Was it really possible Grant had killed both men? There were two different modus operandi for the murders, each with a different cause of death, one premeditated and one possibly not, but they could still be related. Especially if the second one was to cover up the first one. Rainey had hinted often enough that he knew something about Thad's death that no one else did, but Mabel had thought he was just self-aggrandizing. What if he had actually known something and was trying to use it as leverage against Grant?

It was all just speculation, though, and she could make an equally strong case against Paige. She needed some more facts before she considered telling Detective O'Connor about her theories. In the meantime, she needed to keep Grant from causing any more trouble. But how? Even if some of his incapacity was faked, the smell of alcohol on his breath meant he was still too impaired to drive, so she couldn't just send him home alone. What she'd like to do—lock him away somewhere to sober up—wasn't wise, not with O'Connor nearby and looking for an excuse to arrest her. He wouldn't be able to resist charging her with kidnapping if he found out she'd stuck Grant somewhere to keep him out of trouble, even if it was in his best interest as well as everyone else's.

It looked like she was stuck with having Grant loose and free to roam her property, attend the wedding, and possibly continue to meddle in his father's life. The only good news was that if he had, indeed, killed either Rainey or Thad or both, then as long as he was on the farm, he'd be easy for Detective O'Connor to arrest if she could find the evidence to show that Grant was the culprit.

For now, the most important thing to do was to get the SUV's keys away from Grant. Preferably without making a scene that would upset the guests. Then she could continue the increasingly critical search for Paige, so she could talk to the bride. The cars of arriving guests were starting to clog up the driveway, suggesting it was getting close to when the wedding was due to start, and it still wasn't clear whether it was going to happen.

"Why don't we get you some coffee?" Mabel suggested to Grant. "I'll just have your car put somewhere safe, and then we can go on over to the patio."

Grant held out the keys, but judging by the sly expression on his face, he was going to start his keep-away game again. Instead of reaching for them, she just held her hand out underneath his, waiting for him to drop the keys into her outstretched palm.

"You're no fun," he said at last before releasing them.

Whether he was truly intoxicated or just pretending, Grant managed to miss her hand completely, and the keys fell to the ground.

"Oops," he said with an O'Connor-like giggle, before leaning back against the SUV again and covering his eyes with one hand. "Can you get them for me? I'm feeling a little dizzy."

Mabel quickly snatched them off the gravel driveway before Grant could change his mind. She looked over her shoulder to see if she could toss them to one of the valets, but they were all occupied, either parking a car or running over to get one of the two cars behind Grant's SUV.

The SUV could stay where it was for now, since she didn't need to keep the driveway open for the arrival of a limo. The vehicle would serve as an even larger barrier than the sign in front of it to keep guests from driving beyond the parking area. It would have to be moved later, but for now, it was more important to get Grant away from his car and stowed somewhere he couldn't cause any more trouble. She considered the farmhouse, but the bride and groom were in there, and she couldn't give him the chance to make things even worse between the couple. And she definitely didn't want Grant out with the guests in the lavender field. He'd probably be inspired by the angry music to stomp-dance among the plants, trampling them. Or he might wander over to the creek and become the second person to drown there. She couldn't even stow him on the front porch, since it would give him access to the collection of car keys stored there. She'd probably have to pay the valets double the agreed-upon rate to deal with Grant if he decided to play keep-away with all of the guests' keys.

It was tempting to see if the EMTs could gently restrain Grant in the ambulance like they would do with an out-of-control patient, but she doubted they'd agree. That left the barn for hiding Grant. She could stick him in the cart that had been left behind when the tractor was driven out to the driveway's entrance. But how was she going to get him all the way over there when he was all but unconscious? He was too heavy for her to drag, the tractor wasn't available, thanks to Paige, and pushing Grant around in a wheelbarrow would attract too much negative attention.

Hosting a wedding wasn't supposed to be this complicated. Or deadly.

* * * *

The answer to Mabel's dilemma drove up in a white electric car and stopped behind Grant's SUV. Charlie Durbin climbed out and tossed his keys to Terry on the way over to ask Mabel, "Is there anything I can do to help?"

Mabel had seldom seen Charlie wearing a suit before. Some men who usually dressed casually looked awkward in business attire, but he looked every bit as comfortable in his navy suit as he usually did in jeans and a sweatshirt. And every bit as appealing.

"Is it that late already?" Mabel asked, reminded of how little time there was until the wedding—or cancellation—and that she couldn't afford to spend any more of it admiring Charlie. She looked down in a panic at the jeans and t-shirt she'd thrown on in the morning, well before any guests arrived. She had a nice outfit in her closet, thanks to hours spent on online searching for something appropriate for the owner of the wedding site— dressy enough to be respectful, while also bland enough to mark her as not being one of the guests. She'd eventually settled on a medium-gray pants suit that she could wear with a variety of blouses and accessories at a number of events, but now it was starting to look like she might only wear it this once, since after this weekend, no one would want to risk having a gathering of any kind at Skinner Farm. And she might not even get to wear it at all if Grant and the bride's children got their wishes and the wedding was cancelled.

"It's okay," Charlie said, apparently reading her mind. He was good at that. "I'm early, so you've still got time to change."

"I need to do a few things before I can even think of changing." Mabel glared down at the ground in front of her where Grant had slid down to sit, leaning against the SUV's dirty front tire. He seemed to have fallen asleep, but she didn't care if he could hear her talking about him. "It's mostly the fault of Grant here that today has been so crazy. The bride is threatening to cancel the wedding and possibly even the relationship, and, of course, the wedding planner has disappeared again."

Charlie squatted next to Grant to inspect him. "I don't think he's going to be awake enough to cause you any more problems in the foreseeable future."

"That's a problem in its own right," Mabel said. "He's supposed to be the best man. Although I guess that won't matter if the wedding is cancelled."

"How about if I toss him into the back seat of his SUV and then move it over into the parking area, somewhere at the far edge, so he won't be disturbed, but we can still find him if you need him. The weather's nice enough that he won't be too hot if I open the windows."

"Good idea," Mabel said, handing over the keys. "Let Terry know what's happening. He's doing a great job with the parking, and he'll keep an eye out in case Grant wakes up."

"Terry's a good kid," Charlie agreed.

"I've been lucky to have his help." Mabel glanced toward the ambulance to make sure Detective O'Connor wasn't in sight. She needed to tell someone what had happened in the woods, and it was safe to tell Charlie. He wasn't the type to spread panic or rumors. "Terry's been handling more than just parking today. There's been another murder. Rainey, over on the path to Emily's house. Terry's been helping to keep people from panicking or rubbernecking."

"This has been one heck of a weekend." Charlie unlocked and opened the back door of Grant's car before picking up the incapacitated man and dumping him not too gently into the back seat. "How's Emily doing?"

"She doesn't know about Rainey yet, and she seems to be coping pretty well, even though the bride might be cancelling the wedding. She's calm, but I'm worried that the site of the second murder makes Emily a suspect, and O'Connor already thinks she killed Thad."

"There can't possibly be any real evidence against her."

"That doesn't seem to bother O'Connor," Mabel muttered.

"Is there anything I can do to help?"

Just his being nearby was a help. "You can remind me never to get married. I couldn't handle all of the chaos and people and fighting."

"I can't make that promise," Charlie said. "You deserve a wedding when you find the right guy."

"At least remind me to keep it tiny, then. No bridesmaids or best men or photographers or planners." Loud, angry drumbeats coming from the lavender field punctuated her list. "No musicians either. And definitely no guests."

"Rory might have something to say about the no-guests thing," Charlie said. "But for the record, I wouldn't mind a small wedding either. Not that I'm proposing, mind you. I can't even get you to be my date for today, so it's way too soon for anything more serious."

"You don't really want me for a date today," Mabel said. "I'm a mess. And I'm too stressed to be good company."

"You're the only company I want," he said. "Besides, you owe me for dealing with Grant."

"I do, don't I?" Mabel was feeling less and less overwhelmed the longer Charlie was nearby. "What if I don't have time to change my clothes? Are you sure you'd want to be seen with me?"

"Absolutely," he said. "I always want to be seen with you, no matter what."

"Then it's a date," Mabel said. "But first I've got to find Paige and talk to the bride to make sure the wedding is still going to happen, or else it'll just be you and me sitting out in the lavender field, watching the sun set."

"I can think of worse ways to spend an evening in June." Charlie looked over his shoulder at the now-snoring Grant before adding, "And I'd do them all for you."

CHAPTER TWENTY

Charlie drove Grant's SUV over to the parking area, and Mabel headed for the patio, in case Paige had finally put in an appearance there now that it was almost time for the ceremony. Neither Rory nor Emily had seen her, though, so Mabel decided to check the barn again. There was no reason for Paige to be in there, but unless she'd left the property completely or was hiding in the woods somewhere, that was the most likely place for her to be.

The bride's kids stopped Mabel before she could cross the driveway. Beryl wore a lavender, knee-length bridesmaid dress, and Harlan wore a matching purple tie with a casual suit. Their clothes were cheerful, but their expressions lacked the happiness they should have had at a wedding.

"Have you seen our mother?" Beryl asked anxiously. "She should be gathering with the bridesmaids so we can walk her out to the lavender field."

"I'm not exactly sure where Donna is," Mabel hedged. If Donna hadn't already decided to cancel, her kids would be only too happy to push her in that direction. It would be better if Beryl and Harlan didn't talk to their mother until she'd made her decision, but they would be harder to stash somewhere than the inebriated Grant had been. "Why don't you go on out to the lavender field and look for her out there, while I look in other places."

"She's not out with the guests," Harlan said. "I just looked there."

"Then how about having a seat on the patio while I search for her?" Mabel suggested. "I'm sure the caterer can get you a drink while you wait."

"We can search with you," Beryl said. "I wore sensible shoes, since it's an outdoor wedding, and I can't just sit and wait. We both need to make sure Mom doesn't do something foolish."

"Like get married?"

Harlan hurried to say, "No. We're not opposed to it anymore. We had a long talk with Mom last night, and she convinced us that she really wasn't crying yesterday. It was just her allergies."

Beryl nodded. "We didn't believe her at first, but then she reminded us about the time when I must have been about twelve or thirteen, and I was so proud of getting her some lavender sachets for her birthday, using my own money from my very first babysitting job. She insisted on using every last one of them, despite how they made her eyes get all puffy. She'd been so determined not to make me feel bad at the time that I completely forgot it had even happened."

"She really does love Stan," Harlan said, with only a trace of residual reluctance. "And he's not such a bad guy. He's done some nice things for us over the years, helping us out of financial jams and paying for our education. We always thought Mom had pressured him into it, but she said he'd suggested most of them on his own. It's just that he's not very good at showing his emotions or talking about them, so we never realized how much he cares about us. And about Mom, most of all."

They both sounded a little bit surprised still by what they'd learned about Stan, which made their new appreciation for him seem particularly convincing. "What if I told you Donna's thinking about cancelling the wedding?"

"She can't do that," Beryl said in a shocked tone. "I mean, she can, but it wouldn't be good. She was looking forward to the wedding when we left her last night. I bet that greedy little brat, Grant, did something to upset her."

"Or else Ken Linden did," Harlan added thoughtfully. "He's been in love with her forever. It must be painful for him, having to document her wedding to someone else."

"Ken's had plenty of time to accept that Mom doesn't care about him that way," Beryl said. "Besides, he has to know she wouldn't turn to him even if she broke up with Stan. She's never seen Ken as anything but a friend. No, my money is on Grant being the one who meddled."

"Either way," Harlan said, "we've really got to find her before she can do anything rash." He turned to Mabel to explain, "Normally, Mom wouldn't do anything that might inconvenience people the way canceling the wedding would, but Grant's one great talent is that he can accurately identify a person's weakness, and then he uses it to manipulate them. He knows how much of a people pleaser Mom is, so if he convinced her that cancelling the wedding was somehow good for the other people she cares about, she would do it."

"He probably used us against her," Beryl said. "He must have convinced her that the marriage would be bad for us somehow, and I'm afraid that the way we were trying to stop the wedding before last night only made it easier for him. We've got to make sure Mom doesn't do the wrong thing just to protect us, when we don't need protecting."

Mabel wanted to believe them, but she also knew she wasn't great at reading people. Were they telling the truth about wanting to help convince their mother to go ahead with the wedding, or was that just what Mabel wanted to believe? Was it safe to tell them where Donna was? Or would they use the opportunity to finish what Grant had started?

Ultimately, it wasn't really up to her to decide whether the couple should get married or whose advice they should hear. It had to be left to the parties most directly involved. At least with Grant out of commission, a rational decision could be made without his conniving interference. And if Donna decided to cancel the wedding, then so be it. The guests could still enjoy Emily's food before they left, giving Mabel a little more time to talk to the most likely suspects and figure out who had killed Thad and Rainey.

"Follow me," Mabel said at last. "Donna's inside the farmhouse with Stan."

When they reached the kitchen door, Mabel gestured for Beryl and Harlan to keep their distance. They took a step back, and Mabel opened the door just enough to look inside.

The wedding couple were both in the kitchen. Donna was sitting at the table amid the metal serving trays and stacks of paper napkins printed with the couple's names and the date. Donna faced the door, her eyes red and puffy, this time definitely from crying rather than allergies. She'd skipped the traditional veil, and wore a sleeveless, cream, ankle-length dress with an overlay of lace on the bodice and down her arms to below the elbows. Stan had on a dark-gray tuxedo, and for once, he wasn't hunched over his phone. He sat across from the bride, leaning forward to hold both of her hands in what looked like supplication. When he turned to see what the sound was behind him, Mabel caught the shine of what she thought were tears on his cheeks.

She was going to shut the door again and suggest the couple needed a little privacy, but the bride's children grabbed the door and rushed inside. They took up positions on either side of Donna and pulled her into a three-way hug. She seemed to appreciate it, even if the very idea of being surrounded like that made Mabel cringe. Stan released his hold on Donna's hands and sat back as if he was as uncomfortable with the display of affection as Mabel was.

"Oh, Mom," Beryl said. "You can't let Grant do this to you."

Donna sniffled and wiped at the tears on her face with one of the printed napkins. "Grant? It's not his fault. He just told me what his father had done. Stan is the one who wouldn't apologize or discuss it. He never wants to talk about anything. He hasn't even been willing to discuss how upset he is over Thad's death. It's Stan and his refusal to share his feelings that jeopardized our future together, not his son."

Both children looked over at Stan accusingly.

Stan looked like a deer in the headlights, unable to form any sort of response to their unspoken questions.

Mabel went over and gestured for Stan to get to his feet. "Why don't you wait in my office, while Donna and her kids talk? I think it would be better for everyone."

He nodded and followed her down the hallway. The door was open a distance just wide enough for a cat to slip through, and Pixie wasn't in any of her usual favorite spots in the office. She hadn't been on the kitchen windowsill either, so perhaps she'd gone upstairs to get away from all the commotion and angst on the first floor. Pixie believed in causing drama, not watching or listening to it.

Mabel wished she could have handed Stan off to Emily to reassure him that things were going to work out. She'd have known what to say. But she'd left the couple on their own, probably because she had other critical work to do to prepare for the reception, so Mabel would have to muddle along on her own.

"It's going to be okay," Mabel told the groom. "Beryl and Harlan have changed their minds about trying to stop the wedding. They want you two to get married. If anyone can reassure Donna, they can."

"They're right to be angry with me," Stan said, wandering around the home office to inspect the contents of the bookcase, all nonfiction, most about either small business or agriculture. He turned his back on the shelves to add, "What happened today is all my fault. Grant likes to act up to get my attention, and sometimes it hurts other people. I know I wasn't a great father. Never spent enough time with my family. Donna always tells me I took the adage that time is money a bit too literally and gave Grant money instead of my attention. I have to convince her that I can change, with both him and her."

"It's going to be difficult to spend more time with family now that the buyer for your business is dead."

"Not really," he said. "If I can't find a buyer in the next thirty days, I'm just closing everything down. I promised Donna just now that I wouldn't take longer than that to retire. Otherwise, she would definitely have called the wedding off, and that would be worse than abandoning my business."

"Are you sure?" Mabel couldn't imagine giving up her work just because someone made it a condition of having a relationship. Charlie had made it clear he wouldn't make that kind of demand—asking her to stay in West Slocum with him—and she hadn't realized until just now how much she appreciated that lack of pressure from him. "Won't you end up resenting Donna for making you retire? That can't be good for a marriage."

"You know, I sort of did blame her until today," he said. "Our wedding felt like a business deal, with me retiring in return for her cooperating with the estate planning I wanted. And I kept thinking it was a bad bargain, since she was benefiting from both things, the retirement and the estate plan, and I was only getting one thing out of the deal. I'm grateful now—well, almost grateful—to Grant for making me see how much I wanted this marriage for its own sake. It won't be all that hard to quit working now."

"How do you think Grant's going to take it when he finds out the wedding is still on?" Mabel asked. "Assuming it is."

"It is. We'd just about resolved everything right before you arrived, and her kids will deal with any loose ends if they are, as you say, in favor of the marriage now. Grant will just have to cope." Stan looked over toward the hallway that led back to the kitchen. "Where is he, anyway? I told him he had to show up for the wedding today, in his tux and on time, or I'd cut off his allowance."

"He's here," Mabel said, although he hadn't been in a tux. "Unfortunately, I think you're going to need a new best man. He's...indisposed."

"Drunk, you mean," Stan said. "Celebrating the trouble he caused."

Mabel nodded. "Sleeping it off in his car in a quiet spot in the parking area."

"Maybe Harlan will take over the role of best man," Stan said. "I'll go ask him."

"Good idea." Mabel tried to remember what a best man had to do besides show up and stand next to the groom. All she could think of was producing the rings and giving a toast at the reception. The latter would be easy enough, but she wasn't sure about the former. "What about the wedding rings? Did your son have them? I can get someone to check to see if they're in his pockets."

"That's not necessary. I kept the set in my safe until this morning, so nothing could happen to them. They're custom platinum rings, after all, and extremely valuable." He patted the front pocket of his pants. "They're right here now."

Mabel wondered if he thought his son would have pawned the rings if he'd had custody of them, and that was why he hadn't entrusted them to Grant this morning while they were searching for a tux. Bad father or not, she doubted Stan would admit his son had criminal tendencies that might have inclined him toward either theft or murder.

She was saved from further small talk by Donna calling Stan's name. "We're ready for you now."

That hadn't taken long, Mabel thought. She hoped it was a good sign.

She led Stan out of the office and down the hallway. The bride was smiling, and her daughter was fixing her makeup. Definitely good signs.

"Let's do it," Donna said.

"Let's," Stan agreed.

Mabel checked the time. The ceremony should have started about ten minutes ago, and the bride would need a few more minutes to fix her makeup and prepare herself. Stan needed some time, too, to go over the role of best man with Harlan.

Mabel headed for the door. "I'll go find the wedding planner so she can tell the guests there's been a slight delay and keep them from getting restless while you all get ready."

* * * *

The music out in the lavender field had gotten even louder and more aggressive, with the sound hitting Mabel almost like a physical blow as she opened the back door to go outside. She hesitated, and Pixie took advantage of the opening, racing out from under the kitchen table and through the doorway before Mabel could stop her. She'd been too startled to react in time, since Pixie never went outside, never even tried to escape, instead satisfying her curiosity about visitors by sitting in the windowsill and watching from a safe distance.

The cat sprinted toward the lavender field, and Mabel ran after her. Rory called out from behind the buffet table, "What's wrong?" and Mabel threw over her shoulder, "Pixie is crashing the wedding ceremony."

By the time she arrived at the corner of the lavender field, she'd lost track of the little orange cat, who should have been easy to spot against the green plants. And then Mabel happened to look at the lavender-clad white arch on the wedding stage that marked where the bride, groom, and officiant would stand. Pixie was up at the very peak, peering out at the guests as if they'd gathered to watch her. At a particularly discordant note from the band a short distance to Pixie's left, she flicked an irritated glance in their direction. The guests also seemed annoyed by the musical performance and had given up trying to talk to each other over the noise, instead silently glaring at the band.

If the music wasn't enough to scare Pixie back to the farmhouse, it was going to be a challenge to get her out of the arch. Mabel would need a ladder to reach her there, and in the meantime, there was a chance someone tall would try to be helpful and reach up to grab the cat. If they tried it, she'd just jump down and run farther away. Pixie liked people well enough, but only on her terms. It was a totally understandable attitude, Mabel thought, but inconvenient at the moment.

As Mabel stood there watching the cat, torn between needing to get Paige to get the wedding back on track, and needing to get Pixie back in the house where she'd be safe, Charlie joined her. He shouted over the band's noise, "Is there a problem with the stage?"

"That's about the only thing that's not a problem today," she shouted back. "But Pixie is up on top of the arch."

He looked toward the stage before concluding, "It's sturdy enough to hold her."

"I'm not worried about that. I'm worried about her being outside where she doesn't have any survival skills. I don't think I'll be able to grab her until after things settle down out here, and I might need to borrow a ladder even then. I can't leave her, but I've also got to find the wedding planner so she can deal with the 'quartet' she hired before all the guests leave to save their hearing."

"I know enough not to volunteer to find the wedding planner, from everything I've heard about her, but I don't mind keeping an eye on Pixie. If she gets down and I can't catch her, I'll follow her so she can't get lost. She can be my date until you can join me."

"I knew I could count on you." More than Charlie could count on her, Mabel thought, as she realized she still hadn't had a chance to change into her wedding-appropriate outfit. At least this way, in her jeans and old t-shirt, none of the guests would realize she was the farm's owner or that her frantic running around was an indication of problems. Assuming they even noticed her with their attention focused on the annoying "quartet."

CHAPTER TWENTY-ONE

Mabel raced back to the barn to search for Paige. It was really the only place she could have been hiding, although it seemed odd that she hadn't emerged as the time for the ceremony approached. Didn't she want to mingle with the guests, networking and basking in the praise she thought she was due? At the very least, she should have been curious about what had happened, when two o'clock came and went without the musicians playing the "Bridal Chorus."

Still, Mabel had to hope Paige had somehow missed her cue to emerge and was waiting inside the barn. Otherwise, Mabel would have to deal with the annoyed guests herself, and for all of Paige's faults, she was better at social interactions than Mabel was.

It took a moment for Mabel's eyesight to adjust to the dimmer light inside the barn after being outside in the bright spring sunshine. The space was emptier than usual, with the tractor out at the beginning of the driveway and the harvest still a month away. The tractor's cart, where she would have dumped the drunk Grant if Charlie hadn't had a better idea, was in the far corner, about six feet away from the back wall.

Mabel was on her way to check the bathroom door when she heard a rustling near the ceiling. She turned to see the tuxedo cat, Jonesy, leaping from the rafters onto the shelving along the back wall, where the garlic harvest was stored in the fall. He jumped to the ground and sneezed even as Mabel caught a particularly strong whiff of lavender perfume and echoed the cat's sneeze with her own.

Paige had to be nearby. The scent was stronger than the last time Mabel had checked the barn, before Rainey had been killed.

She knocked on the bathroom door and got no response. She checked the knob, and it was unlocked, so she opened it to confirm Paige wasn't inside. The room was empty, although there was a strong residual cloud of the woman's perfume, so she'd been in there recently.

Mabel closed the door and leaned her back against it. Jonesy was over near the cart, sniffing intently at the ground, not even stopping when he sneezed. At least someone was doing his job, looking for critters that didn't belong in the barn.

Had the wedding planner really abandoned her clients on the day of the wedding? Perhaps Grant had called her to say the event was cancelled, and she'd believed him and settled into the barn to wait for everyone to leave, without realizing she was the one who should be telling the guests there wouldn't be a wedding today after all.

Or—another explanation occurred to Mabel—had Paige been scared into running away by the arrival of the ambulance and police? Until now, Mabel had assumed Paige was simply hiding, but as far as she could tell, no one had seen the wedding planner since Terry saw her talking to the reporter. If Paige had killed Rainey, she might have left the farm before the body was found. Reluctant as Mabel was to seek out O'Connor, it might be time to let him know Paige was missing and might be implicated in Rainey's death.

Before she did that, though, Mabel wanted to be absolutely sure the wedding planner wasn't just hiding. "Paige, if you're in here, I need to know right now. Otherwise I'm getting the cops involved in looking for you." O'Connor probably wouldn't do anything, but Paige didn't know that, and no one ever wanted to take the risk of being hunted by the police.

There was a rustling sound over behind the cart, near where Jonesy had been sniffing for mice. Then there was a feline hiss followed by a human squeal, and Jonesy scrabbled up the shelving and into the rafters.

Paige's head popped up from behind the cart, then she darted around to the front. "Your cat just attacked me."

"I don't see any blood."

"He missed."

"Then he wasn't really trying to hurt you, just giving you a warning," Mabel said. "And if he had scratched you, it would have been your own fault. He's a feral animal, and you invaded his territory. If you'd been out with the guests, doing your job, you'd have been safe."

"I *can't* go out there," she whined.

"Why not?"

"People will yell at me." Paige's face brightened. "Unless you can tell them to be nice to me, because none of this is my fault. You could do that, couldn't you?"

"No. It's your job to deal with people, even when they're angry. *Especially* when they're angry." If Paige was afraid of irritated people, she had definitely chosen the wrong career. She'd be happier in a job more like the one Mabel had chosen, working at a computer from home, where there was minimal need to talk to anyone and the conversations were virtually never in person. "If it helps, Donna isn't angry about the limo any longer."

"What limo?"

"The one you didn't reserve."

"Oh, that one." Paige shrugged and fumbled with the side seams of her baggy dress until she found the openings to the hidden pockets and stuck her hands inside. "It wasn't that big of a deal. I'm more concerned about today's death. I could have weathered what happened yesterday, but I'm done now."

"Done with what?"

"My career. My life. Everything." She began to cry, pulling a wad of toilet paper out of a pocket to dab at her eyes. "It's not my fault, but I'm going to be blamed."

"How did you know there's been another death?"

"The ambulance, of course."

"It could just have been someone who was sick, not dead."

Paige sniffled. "That's what I was hoping until I saw that horrible detective who laughed at me the whole time I was trying to answer his questions yesterday. He wouldn't show up for a simple accident or illness."

"Do you know who died?" Mabel asked.

"Was it one of my clients?" Paige resumed crying. Between sobs, she said, "That's really going to make me look bad. I might have been able to explain away a guest's death, but not the bride or groom."

"It wasn't anyone in the wedding party." She wasn't supposed to share any details, but if Paige had killed Rainey, she already knew who the victim was, and if she hadn't killed him, then it couldn't hurt the investigation if she knew. And Mabel desperately wanted to see the wedding planner's reaction to the name. "It was the reporter, Andrew Rainey."

Paige frowned. "Why would anyone kill him?"

"A lot of reasons," Mabel said. "I saw you talking to him on the porch earlier. He wasn't bothering you, was he?"

"Of course not. I know how to handle annoying men, but he wasn't like that. He understood how important I was for the wedding, and he wanted to do a story on my line of work. He said he could learn so much about it from me."

"Did you agree to talk to him?"

Paige dried the last of her tears. "I wanted to, but he said the interview had to be today, and that was right before I decided to sit things out to show everyone how much they needed me, and I thought I had too much work to do."

"So, you didn't set up an appointment with him?"

Paige shook her head. "I thought about seeing if I could find him after I got bored, but then I heard the ambulance, and I peeked outside, and Ken was right there, coming back from the lavender field, all out of breath and in an obvious panic. I've never seen him out of control like that, and if he was that upset by whatever had required the ambulance, then it had to be bad. So, when he told me I should stay out of sight, I did. Until just now, when your cat attacked me."

She could be lying. Her only alibi witnesses were the barn cats, and they couldn't testify to Paige's whereabouts. Ken could establish a bit of an alibi for her, of course, but only for where he'd seen her *after* the ambulance arrived, not before.

So, Paige didn't have an alibi, and it didn't take much thought to come up with a motive. It sounded like Rainey had pulled the same trick on Paige as he'd done to both Mabel and Grant, holding out the prospect of a positive story when he'd really intended to write something else entirely. If Rainey and Paige had, in fact, met in the woods, he might have revealed what he was really interested in writing about, probably focusing on her incompetence as a wedding planner, or perhaps he'd claimed to have known something that implicated her in Thad's death. Either way, their rendezvous could easily have led to her lashing out and killing Rainey.

The scenario was entirely plausible, but Mabel was aware she might be doing the same thing as O'Connor, building a case against someone she disliked for personal reasons. Her two top suspects—Paige and Grant—were, a little too conveniently perhaps, her least favorite of all the people involved with the wedding. Disliking someone didn't automatically make them guilty, and liking someone didn't automatically make them innocent.

In any event, Mabel didn't have time to solve the murders right now. Her first priority was to get the bride and groom married, then she'd do some more snooping during the reception, before all the likely suspects left. Grant wasn't going anywhere anytime soon, not with his keys in the possession of the valets, who wouldn't let him leave drunk, and she could keep an eye on Paige to make sure she didn't disappear.

* * * *

"It's safe for you to leave the barn now," Mabel told Paige. "The police have the crime scene under control, so it's time for you to mingle with the guests. You can let them know that everything's fine, but there's just a slight delay while the bride finishes getting ready."

"I don't want to," Paige said in a tone as childish as her words. "Everyone out there hates me. Most of them are mad because I messed up a few little things, and the others think I didn't mess up enough."

"Who would want there to be more problems?"

"The groom's son, for one," Paige said. "I only had a few dealings with Grant, but he hit on me every single time. And he tried to bribe me to ruin the wedding."

"What did he want you to do?"

"He didn't say exactly. He just wanted me to make everyone so miserable that his father would decide getting married was more trouble than it's worth."

Mabel tried not to sound accusatory when she said, "An awful lot of things did go wrong."

"Well, it wasn't because of me," Paige said indignantly.

"You set the wedding in a field of plants the bride is allergic to," Mabel said incredulously. "Then you forgot to sign a contract with the limo company. And you hired a thrash band instead of a quartet."

"There are four members in the band, so that makes it a quartet," Paige said defiantly. "Besides, they're great. I've been enjoying them from in here."

Mabel resisted the urge to roll her eyes. The sound was probably better in the barn than out in the field, thanks to the distance and the muffling qualities of the walls. "Even if you like the band, it's more appropriate for a dance party than a wedding. And the allergies and lack of a limo were definitely your fault."

She dug her hands deeper in her pockets and shrugged. "So I made a few mistakes."

"Your disappearing into the barn when guests were about to arrive wasn't a mistake," Mabel said. "You did that on purpose."

"But I was going to come back out and save the day at the last minute," Paige said, as if she sincerely thought that was a reasonable thing to do. "I just wanted everyone to understand how much they needed me."

"There's still time to turn things around. The bride's in the farmhouse kitchen, preparing for the ceremony. If you don't want to deal with the guests, maybe you could help Donna."

"She isn't going to want my help," Paige said. "Not now."

Ken Linden had arrived, camera in hand, just in time to overhear Paige's excuse for not doing her job. "You're right that Donna doesn't want your help. She's all set. But you're needed out with the guests. Someone has to let them know that the bride will be coming down the aisle in another ten minutes or so."

"Why don't you do it?" Paige asked mulishly.

"I have other work to do," Ken said with more patience than Mabel would have had.

"Then Mabel can do it," Page said. "I'm going home. No one wants me here."

"No one's leaving until the police say so," Mabel said. "So you might as well make yourself useful."

"And if you don't," Ken said, "I'll make sure you never get to work on another wedding anywhere on the East Coast. I can do it too. I'm well-enough known on the circuit that no one will hire anyone I warn against."

"All right," Paige said, starting to leave. "You don't have to be mean about it. I'll go talk to the stupid guests."

She was walking so slowly out of the barn that, at that rate, she wouldn't arrive in the lavender field until after the wedding was over. Mabel looked at Ken, wondering which of them would be better able to get her moving. He must have been thinking the same thing, because he shrugged, said, "I'll take care of it," and took a step forward.

Just then, as Paige's shuffle brought her to the edge of the driveway, she suddenly hiked up her long, bulky dress and took off running in the wrong direction, toward the parking area instead of out with the guests.

Perhaps Mabel had been too hasty in thinking it was just her dislike of Paige that had made her seem like a prime suspect in one or both of the murders.

"Paige won't get far," she told Ken as she got out her phone. She hesitated a moment while deciding which contact to send a text to. She could tell Joe Hansen, and he'd tell O'Connor, but the detective wouldn't believe Mabel without something more than circumstantial evidence, and he probably wouldn't even bother to detain Paige. Fortunately, there was another option. The wedding planner couldn't leave if the valets wouldn't give her her keys.

She texted Terry: *Don't let Paige have her car keys, no matter what she says.*

* * * *

"That should do it," Mabel told Ken. "Was there something you needed me for?"

"I just came to let you know I checked on Donna and she says she's almost ready, so things are back on track with the wedding. She thought you'd want to know. I also let the caterer know the reception would probably be running about half an hour late, but she said that wouldn't be a problem."

"Emily is amazing," Mabel said. Behind her, she saw Jonesy jumping from one rafter to another that was directly above the cart, then peer down at it intently. He'd been fascinated by it earlier, too, and she'd thought it was because Paige was hiding there at the time, but maybe there was something else going on.

Mabel went over to look, and Ken followed. "When Donna told me Paige had chosen the caterer, I thought it would be a disaster, but I had a taste of Emily's quiche yesterday, and it was excellent. I'll be recommending her to my clients who haven't already hired a caterer."

"She'd appreciate that." At least one good thing had come out of this weekend. Emily's catering business might not be doomed after all, Mabel thought as she peered into the cart that reeked of perfume but otherwise contained nothing remarkable. Just a hoe and a long-handled dibber from the recent squash planting, plus a few stems of lavender blossoms that Paige must have surreptitiously picked and brought back with her when she'd hidden in the barn.

At one point early in the negotiations for use of the farm for the wedding, Paige had suggested that a florist wouldn't be necessary, because they could just use the flowers in the field to create bouquets. Mabel had had to explain that she was only renting the field as a backdrop, not selling the harvest. Other brides were scheduled to have photographs taken in the lavender, and eventually the flowers would be cut and dried for sale at the farmers' market.

Mabel bent down to look under the cart. She'd thought the matter of who owned the lavender was settled, but after seeing the flowers in the cart, it felt like just one more example of how no one had respected her boundaries this weekend. Paige had picked forbidden flowers, Rainey had pursued a story she'd told him to leave alone, and Wetzel had ignored professional decorum to be rude and childish.

Mabel wasn't the only one whose boundaries had been ignored. Ken had felt the urge to prove that real men ate quiche, and he couldn't wait for the rest of the wedding party before diving into Emily's buffet.

Wait. Mabel froze, staring at the barn floor under the cart. The buffet had been taped off by the police before anyone other than Thad and Wetzel had sampled anything. When had Ken had the chance to try the quiche? He'd been out in the lavender field most of the day, or he accompanied the bride when she'd needed to repair her makeup.

She needed to think, preferably somewhere quiet—or as quiet as possible, given Paige's choice of musicians—and alone. Mabel couldn't concentrate with a potential killer nearby.

She gave the rest of the area under the cart a final cursory glance, and when she found nothing that explained Jonesy's interest, she stood and turned to Ken. "If the wedding's about to start, I should go get changed." Then she remembered Paige's bolting for her car. It would seem suspicious if Mabel didn't follow up on the apparent admission of guilt. "After I talk to the police, of course. They need to know that Paige tried to run away and should be questioned about both murders."

"Isn't that who you texted? The police?"

"No," she said absently as her mind raced, trying to figure out if Ken might really have killed Thad and Rainey. "I told the valets not to give Paige her keys. The police can take their time dealing with her now."

When could Ken have checked out the buffet? He'd been almost as indispensable to the rehearsal and photographs as the bride was. The only time he'd been alone before Thad died was when Ken had been left to wait in the kitchen while Donna was in the bathroom and Mabel went upstairs to get some makeup remover. She'd been gone longer than she'd expected, trying to figure out where the items were. It had certainly been long enough for him to have gone outside and sampled the buffet. But could he have seen the plate marked for Thad, poisoned it, and then gotten back inside the kitchen without anyone noticing? If he'd killed Thad, it would explain the delay in forwarding the time-stamped pictures to O'Connor. If there was anything she knew, it was how to upload files, and it wouldn't have been that burdensome to send the images to the police. Unless Ken could have been planning to review them all first, making sure none of them implicated him, and then deleting the evidence.

Ken interrupted her thoughts. "Maybe I should be the one to talk to the police. I got the distinct impression yesterday that the detective doesn't trust you."

"He doesn't," she agreed, paying only partial attention to what Ken had said. If he had killed Thad, then he must have killed Rainey too. She'd been assuming the photographer had been out in the lavender field setting up for the videography when the reporter was killed, but Ken had been near the barn right after the ambulance arrived, looking upset, according to Paige. Had it been because he'd just killed Rainey, rather than because he'd heard the ambulance and run back from the lavender field as Paige had assumed? When Mabel saw him a short time later, he'd been carrying not just one, but two cameras. Could one of them have belonged to Rainey? She'd been thinking that if the camera was the murder weapon, the killer had likely taken it with him in case there was incriminating evidence on it, like fingerprints or DNA. But what if there had been incriminating pictures on it, too, and that was why the killer took it? Ken wouldn't even need to dispose of it, just add it to his own collection, because no one paid much attention to a photographer carrying multiple cameras and they wouldn't think to check it for Rainey's blood.

"What's the detective got against you?" Ken asked. "I heard you were something of a celebrity around here."

"That was my aunt," Mabel said, as she considered whether Rainey had really been foolish enough to confront a killer on his own. She still wasn't sure how much to believe the reporter's hints that he knew more about the first murder than the police did. He'd seemed so convinced that Emily would be arrested soon, but he hadn't said anything about the police getting it right, just that he expected an arrest. Assuming he did have some information the police hadn't uncovered, Rainey could have been hoping to write about how O'Connor arrested an innocent person, or perhaps he'd meant to intervene at the last minute, like a *Perry Mason*–style surprise witness, to announce they were arresting the wrong person, based on some information he had. Or perhaps he'd meant to let the police get it wrong while he blackmailed the real culprit. Whether he'd been bluffing or not, the bottom line remained that he had most likely been silenced for what he'd known—or pretended to know—about Thad's death.

Mabel added, "Everyone in town knew and loved Aunt Peggy. And not just because she grew the best garlic on the East Coast."

"I wasn't talking about her," Ken said. "I heard about how you identified two killers while the police were on the wrong track. People talk about that sort of thing much more than garlic."

"Not in this town," Mabel said. "People here are pretty serious about their garlic."

"But it's true, right? You were responsible for the arrest of two killers."

Mabel shrugged. "Someone had to do it, and I was the only one who cared."

"Who do you think killed Thad?" Ken asked. "And the reporter?"

"I don't know." His questions were making her uncomfortable. Were they just simple curiosity, or was he trying to find out if she suspected him? If she had to name someone right now as the most likely suspect, it would be Ken, but she also knew that it could be because she needed someone other than Emily to be guilty, and it would be so much easier if it was someone she didn't like. She was starting to feel a little sympathy for O'Connor and his focus on making a case based on his personal feelings about the suspect. She was afraid she'd fallen into that trap herself while considering Paige and Grant as suspects. It was easier to picture someone committing murder if that person had engaged in other bad behavior, like Paige's seeming sabotage of the wedding, Grant's selfish meddling in his father's marriage, and Ken's threat to kick a cat.

She needed a second opinion. And, much as she hated to admit it, that second opinion needed to come from Detective O'Connor. For all she knew, he'd already found Rainey's camera, with fingerprints belonging to someone other than Ken. Even if he hadn't uncovered strong evidence like that, he at least had the forensic resources that she didn't. He could test the camera hanging around Ken's neck to determine whether it belonged to Rainey.

"We really should go talk to the police," Mabel said, preparing to leave.

"On second thought, I think I'll skip the conversation with the police," Ken said, moving closer to sandwich her between him and the cart at her back. "And you won't be able to talk to them either."

He put a hand into his jacket to pull a small metal flask out of his inner chest pocket.

Even with the cap tightly secured, she could tell it didn't hold the alcohol it was designed for. The smell wasn't terrible or even as strong as Paige's perfume. That might change if she continued inhaling it, since it was clearly some sort of chemical solution. Toxic, too, if it had been what poisoned Thad.

"That stinks," she said, sliding to the side so she wouldn't feel trapped, but Ken moved with her, blocking her escape.

"I guess you've got a better sense of smell than poor Thad did," Ken said with a small laugh. "His smoking pretty much destroyed his senses of smell and taste. I'd been trying to figure out how to get him to eat something I'd poisoned when I heard him tell Paige how lovely and subdued her perfume was. If he couldn't tell how overwhelming it was, he wouldn't notice a little poison in his cheesecake."

Ken's invasion of Mabel's personal space was bad enough, but she was becoming even more uncomfortable with the realization of how isolated they were, with everyone out at the lavender field or in front of the house with the cars. No one could see inside the barn from those angles, and the loud music created a barrier against anyone hearing if she called for help. Even if someone walked along the driveway in front of the barn and glanced inside, they wouldn't be able to see anything clearly because of the dim lighting in the back corner.

Ken was bigger than she was, and despite being older, looked to be physically fit, probably from the relatively strenuous work of photographing outdoors. Wrestling with him to try to grab the flask of poison wasn't a good option. Perhaps if she delayed long enough, someone would come looking for them. Not Charlie, since she'd set him to watching over Pixie, trusting him not to leave the cat unsupervised. Of course, at the time, she hadn't expected to be cornered by a killer and desperate for help.

The bride should be ready for her walk down the tractor path soon, and she'd want Ken nearby, both as a photographer and for more moral support. If Mabel could just keep him talking until Donna came looking for him, there would be a chance to escape. Mabel doubted he would try to pour the contents of the flask down her throat with his friend watching.

"How long have you been planning to kill Thad?" Mabel asked.

"Not long," Ken said, putting the flask back in his pocket and visually searching the barn for something while still keeping an eye on Mabel. "That's not exactly true, I suppose. I wanted to kill him four and a half years ago, when my daughter told me she was pregnant and he was refusing to accept responsibility. He'd even threatened to take her son away from her if she tried to pursue a paternity claim, and he had the money to hire the lawyers who could make it happen. But Lara is strong, and while I'm not rich, I could afford to support her and my grandson. We all moved on."

It all started to make sense. Mabel recalled Stan saying something about a woman once claiming his business partner had fathered her child, but he'd sounded dismissive of the idea. She'd like to think Stan never knew who the woman was—his girlfriend's godchild—or he might have helped her against his bully of a partner.

"So, what changed?" she asked.

"Nothing." He stopped searching the barn to focus on Mabel, watching her reaction. "After all this time, Thad was his same old self. Whenever Donna and Stan couldn't overhear, he kept gloating about what he'd gotten away with, hinting that he'd forgotten just how pretty she was, and maybe he should try to get her back in his bed. He didn't mind kids, he said, as long as he didn't have to pay for them."

Mabel thought her face probably reflected some sympathy for Ken. She'd have been tempted to at least punch Thad, if not kill him, if she were in Ken's shoes. She would have understood if that was all Ken had done, lashing out in the heat of the moment, but that wasn't what had happened. He'd coldly waited to carry out his revenge, and had done it in a way that implicated Emily. Mabel couldn't understand the cold-blooded plotting, and her sympathy evaporated with the reminder of how Emily could have been blamed for the two deaths.

"I can see how Thad might have enraged you, and you weren't thinking straight at the time," Mabel said with less-than-complete honesty. "But poison isn't a spur-of-the-moment weapon. You must have been planning to kill him when you brought the flask full of poison."

"I didn't even know Thad was going to be here, except as a guest I could ignore during the wedding. Until he showed up yesterday for the rehearsal, I thought Grant was going to be the best man. I really didn't plan it ahead of time, but I won't deny I was glad I had what I needed close at hand. It was in my car trunk from a recent supply run that I hadn't gotten around to bringing into my studio, and all I had to do was pour it into the flask I always bring to weddings, just in case I need a little something to get through the reception." Ken retrieved the flask from his pocket and untwisted the cap to wave it in front of her nose. "Do you recognize it? The reporter did."

So, that was what Rainey had been hinting about. He'd smelled and identified the poison at the scene of the crime, and had even realized that it implicated Ken. Apparently Rainey hadn't shared the information with O'Connor or he wouldn't have continued to view Emily as the prime suspect.

"I have no idea what it is," she said. "But I'm guessing it implicates you, Rainey confronted you about it, and that's why you killed him."

"I can see now why the police detective is jealous of you," Ken said. "He'd never have figured that out. I'm not sure he'll ever realize that the chemicals in Thad's system add up to the developer to make prints. Even after he finds it in your body too. It helps that it doesn't take much of it to cause organ failure, according to all the warning labels, so he won't have a lot to work with."

"O'Connor may not be perfect," Mabel said, "but he's got access to good forensics teams. The only way you're getting away with the murders is if you go on the run. There's still time to do that now. I'll even text Terry to have your truck waiting for you."

"I don't believe you. Even if I did, I can't leave until Donna is married. She needs me."

"You're willing to risk getting caught just to take her wedding pictures?" Mabel asked incredulously.

"I won't get caught. O'Connor will never suspect me, and you won't be able to say anything." He waved the flask at her again. "You'll be dead, with the source of the poison in your hand. I'll find you when it's too late for help, and then I'll tell everyone about what a tragedy it was, but at least we know why it happened, since I caught your deathbed confession. You just couldn't live with the guilt after killing two people."

"But why would I kill Thad? Rainey's death was obviously intended to cover up the first murder, but I didn't have any reason to poison Thad."

Ken shrugged. "I'm sure O'Connor will come up with a reason that makes sense to him. Better than anything I could suggest."

Ken was probably right. It wouldn't take much to convince the detective that his least-favorite person was a killer. O'Connor's only regret would be that he wouldn't have the opportunity to gloat when Mabel was finally locked up the way he'd wanted.

* * * *

The band stopped playing suddenly. Someone must have let them know that the bride was almost ready, and they needed to prepare to play the "Bridal Chorus." Mabel shuddered at the thought of what the thrash band would do to it.

"The bride must be ready and wondering where you are," Mabel said. "If you agree to turn yourself in after the wedding, you can go take the pictures, and I won't say anything until after it's over."

He raised the flask to her face. "I can't take that risk."

"So, you'll just keep killing people?" Mabel said, twisting away. She couldn't escape him completely, but she could make it impossible to pour the contents of the flask into her mouth. She'd had to give Billie Jean's kittens some pills at one point, and she knew how difficult it could be to force a reluctant mouth to stay open. "Someone will figure it out eventually. My friends won't believe I killed myself. And you'll lose any sympathy you might get from the district attorney and jury. They'd understand you were just trying to protect your daughter from Thad. But you went too far after him. Rainey didn't deserve to die. He didn't hurt your daughter. Neither did I."

"It would hurt Lara if I went to jail," he said. "Rainey wanted me to confess to him so he'd have a scoop, and then he'd tell the police so I'd be arrested."

"What did I do?"

"Nothing yet, but from what I heard about you, I realized you were going to figure out what happened," he said. "But now you're going to be my get-out-of-jail-free card by taking responsibility for the murders."

"All to protect your daughter?" Mabel asked, continuing to squirm as he tried to keep her face steady. "Then when will it ever end? You kill one ex-boyfriend, and a new one will pop up, and Lara won't have learned to deal with them because you interfered. The problem is that there's always another Thad in the wings. And another reporter looking for a scoop."

Ken laughed. "I wasn't expecting anyone to suggest I hadn't killed enough people."

She should have known the words would come out wrong. They always did when she was talking about emotional matters instead of data. "That's not what I meant."

"I know, and I wish I didn't have to do this. I like you. We could have been friends."

"You don't have to do it," Mabel said. "It would be better for everyone, especially Lara and her son, if you turn yourself in to O'Connor. You can do it quietly, and none of the guests would even notice it happening. Your daughter and grandson wouldn't have to see you dragged away in handcuffs, and Donna could have her wedding without interruption."

"No. I have to be there for Donna. She depends on me." He sounded less certain now, as if he were trying to convince himself.

"She'll be fine," Mabel said. "She would even tell you that she wants you to be safe, and you'll be better if you run away, like I thought Paige was doing. Your plan to frame me won't work, and you'll be caught. People will notice if I'm missing during the wedding. My date will notice. You don't want him ruining Donna's wedding by stopping it to gather a search party, do you?"

"I'll have to risk it." Ken unclipped the strap from his camera—actually, Rainey's camera, she thought.

She realized Ken was planning to use the strap to tie her hands to make it easier for him to force the poison into her. When he reached for her wrist, she screamed instinctively, even though no one could hear her.

But someone did hear her—Jonesy, the tuxedo cat. From his perch up in the rafters above her, he started yowling as loudly as Pixie did to announce visitors. It surprised Mabel, since the barn cats were usually quiet and well-behaved.

It surprised Ken even more, and while he was looking up to see what was making the noise that even drowned out the thrash band, Mabel scrabbled behind her for one of the tools abandoned in the cart to use as a defensive weapon. Her fingers brushed against the dibber, but it wasn't long enough or heavy enough to do much damage, so she reached past it for the hoe. It had a hefty wood handle with a sharp metal head at the end. She didn't want to kill Ken with the pointed end, but she might be able to incapacitate him with the handle long enough to run outside and get help.

Jonesy stopped yowling and leaped down from the rafters to land on Ken's head, sinking in his claws briefly to balance himself there while Ken screamed in pain and outrage. Jonesy jumped down to the floor as Ken cursed and threatened to kick the cat into the next county, but it was too late for him to do anything, with Jonesy having booked it out of the barn.

The distraction gave Mabel the opportunity to latch on to the handle of the hoe. She swung it up and then down on the arm that was holding the flask.

Ken dropped the flask and took a step back, cradling his arm against his chest. While he was still disoriented, Mabel gave him a shove that knocked him over, and she quickly followed the path Jonesy had taken out of the barn.

As her eyes adjusted to the bright light outdoors, she caught sight of Pixie coming in her direction, bounding along the tractor path from the lavender field. She must have heard Jonesy's yowling and come running to investigate. Right behind her was Charlie, making good on his promise to keep Pixie in sight. Beyond them, out in the lavender field, the groom and best man were standing on the stage, looking toward the barn, while all the guests had turned to see why first the cat and then Charlie had left the lavender field so precipitously. Over on the patio, Donna and her bridesmaid daughter had emerged from the kitchen, probably planning to head for the lavender field, but they were startled into indecision by the little parade going in the wrong direction.

Mabel took it all in in a flash, and detoured to run to Charlie, throwing herself in his arms, grateful he didn't have the same need for personal space that she usually did. A near-death experience temporarily changed the usual rule against hugs.

Charlie wrapped his arms around her and pulled her even closer, while Pixie joined them to rub against both their ankles.

A moment later O'Connor came around the corner of the ambulance. "There you are, Skinner. My people have been looking for you. Are you sure Rainey had a camera? The forensics team can't find it."

"I'm sure he had a camera." Mabel turned in Charlie's arms without breaking free, and pointed at the barn, where Ken was standing in the opening, still cradling his arm against his chest and blinking against the sunshine. "It's in there, with Ken Linden's fingerprints all over it, because he's the one who killed Rainey. And Thad."

"Oh, hell." For once, O'Connor didn't giggle or refuse to accept the obvious fact that he'd been pursuing the wrong suspect. "Not again."

CHAPTER TWENTY-TWO

As Ken was being escorted over to the ambulance—apparently his arm was broken, and he'd have to be treated under police guard before getting locked up—his daughter came running from the lavender field. She came alone, presumably having found someone to watch her son while she checked on her father.

The bride intercepted Lara and pulled her into a hug. "I'm sorry," Donna said. "We'll get through this together."

Lara buried her face against her godmother's chest and mumbled, "It's all my fault. He must have done it for me."

"No," Donna said firmly, urging Lara over to the patio. "It's not anyone's fault except your father's. We all could have done things differently with Thad, but we didn't make Ken into a killer."

O'Connor dispatched a uniformed officer out to the lavender field to collect everyone's contact information, although it seemed unlikely the guests had seen or heard anything useful for the case against Ken. O'Connor was almost apologetic—at least compared to his usual aggressiveness—when he told Mabel he needed to take her statement.

Finally, he was willing to listen to her, but why did it have to be now, when it meant leaving the safe warmth of Charlie's arms? She desperately wanted to tell O'Connor she'd talk to him later, when she had time for him, like he'd done to her the previous day. She knew it was childish, and she didn't want to ruin the chance at a possible truce with him, but she was feeling the effects of adrenaline dissipating, and it was so tempting to just stay where she was and ignore the detective.

She let O'Connor sweat for a moment, until Charlie gave her a little squeeze and whispered in her ear, "Go take care of business. I'll get

Pixie inside, and then I'll be waiting for you. I can't go to the wedding without my plus-one."

Mabel nodded and stepped away from his safe warmth to follow O'Connor a couple of feet into the barn. In the back corner, the forensics team had already started marking things, from the hoe to the camera and the flask that had spilled much of its contents onto the floor, making it smell, as she now knew, like a developing room.

The detective asked her what had happened, and for once he didn't interrupt or laugh snidely as she explained what Ken had confessed to and how Jonesy had helped her escape.

It was about an hour later by the time O'Connor was finally satisfied with her story and walked Mabel out of the barn. The guests were milling around, no longer seated, but chatting in small groups, while the band was huddled together, passing around what looked like a larger version of Ken's flask. A uniformed officer stood in the tractor path near the last row of chairs, presumably to keep everyone from leaving.

Paige had returned from her attempt to run away, apparently emboldened by the fact that someone else had made a bigger mess of the wedding than she had. She marched up to O'Connor. "The guests are getting restless, and I've run out of ways to keep them from leaving. Are you going to tell them why they need to wait some more, or can we finally have the wedding now?"

O'Connor laughed, and it seemed genuine, as if he thought Paige was joking about having a wedding in the aftermath of two actual murders and an attempted one.

"It's not funny," Paige said. "I worked really hard for this wedding, and we're not going to let a serial killer ruin it. The mayor's ready to officiate, the bride and groom are anxious to say, 'I do,' and the band is warmed up. All we need is your go-ahead, so your officer won't be in the middle of the pictures of the bride going to meet the groom."

O'Connor blinked, clearly taken aback. Mabel was, too, unprepared for the wedding planner's sudden assertiveness. Paige might grow into her job, after all. It was hard to imagine her ever facing as many challenges as there had been this weekend, and it looked like she might have learned something from the experience.

"Sure," O'Connor said at last. "Go ahead. Just as long as everyone stays away from the barn. And the woods."

"No problem," Paige said and whirled around to head back to the lavender field. As she passed the patio, she sent a thumbs-up signal to the bride and Lara, who were standing there, still looking a little shell-shocked.

Mabel looked around for Charlie, but didn't see him. He was probably inside the farmhouse, making sure Pixie didn't escape again. And waiting for his plus-one.

She looked down at her jeans and old t-shirt, and accepted that there wouldn't be time to get changed now, not with Paige pushing for the wedding to finally go forward immediately before anything else could go wrong.

Mabel headed over to the patio to wait for Charlie. In the meantime, Lara had jogged toward the lavender field to operate the video camera, and Donna had gone inside the farmhouse to make her final preparations, leaving Rory and Emily seated at one of the small round tables. They both jumped up to give her a group hug. Mabel didn't have the energy to resist, and she knew they needed the reassurance that she was unhurt. She thought maybe she did too.

Finally, her friends let her go, and as they took a step back, Emily said, "Thank you."

"For what?" Mabel asked.

"For saving me from O'Connor." Her soft face hardened, the way it did whenever she talked about her soon-to-be-ex-husband. "But don't you ever take that kind of risk for me again."

"I didn't know I was in danger when I went inside the barn."

"Still, you've got to be more careful," Emily said.

"She's right," Rory said. "You've got responsibilities to the farm and your friends. We can't lose you."

"I know," Mabel said. "I didn't get a chance to tell you earlier, but I've decided to hire Terry to manage the farm. He'll need some supervision, so I'll be sticking around for a bit longer."

Rory and Emily both made happy noises until Mabel said, "No time for that right now. O'Connor just gave his permission for the wedding to proceed, and you need to get the buffet ready for the reception."

As the two women headed for the buffet table, Donna and her bridesmaid daughter came out of the farmhouse. Donna's smile as she passed was both sad and determined.

Charlie emerged from the kitchen a moment later. "I think Pixie is going to want to go outside some more in the future. She wasn't happy about being closed in the front room. Have you considered getting a leash for her?"

"It will have to wait until after the wedding," Mabel said. "Shall we go get our seats?"

He offered his arm in a formal gesture, which seemed totally ridiculous given how casually she was dressed. She probably had some dirt and bits of dried plants on her jeans, but he didn't seem to care. She linked her arm in his, and they hurried over to the lavender field, staying off the tractor path and out of the video of the procession.

They slipped into the back row before the bride reached the chairs. Mabel turned to look toward the stage. The groom's son had apparently sobered up enough to leave his SUV, but not enough to act as the best man, assuming his father would even allow it, so he was slumped in a front row chair, probably sulking and definitely not turning, like everyone else was, to watch the bride approach.

The rest of the bridesmaids hurried to meet Donna and her daughter, so there was a full complement to lead her along the rows of chairs. As they headed for the stage, they were accompanied by the band's surprisingly classic and not-too-loud version of the "Bridal Chorus." As soon as the bride caught sight of the groom waiting patiently—with no sign of his phone—Donna's smile turned genuine, untarnished, at least for the moment, by the events of the weekend.

The bride had just stepped onto the stage and taken her place beside Stan, while the mayor was clearing his throat, when Mabel caught an impression of rapid movement at ground level, coming up the aisle. A moment later, Pixie scrambled up to her former perch on top of the arch and settled in to watch the proceedings. A harness for outdoor adventures, along with upgraded locks and latches, definitely had to be acquired before any more events could be held at Skinner Farm.

A ripple of amusement went through the crowd at Pixie's antics. The chairs were set closely enough together that Mabel could feel Charlie's laughter through the arm that touched hers. She tuned out the words the mayor was saying and tried to just enjoy the moment, with Charlie at her side, the farm looking lovely, and no one expecting her to make any small talk. Moments like this made her understand at least a little of what her aunt had felt for the farm, and renewed Mabel's determination to keep it going.

It was going to take a lot of work to ensure that a disaster like this weekend's wedding or the new competition from other markets wouldn't send the farm into bankruptcy. A lot of time, too, while Terry settled into his first full-time job.

It struck her that she didn't mind the prospect of staying in West Slocum however long it took to make sure her aunt's farm would continue as she'd have wanted it to. Mabel had friends here now, more than she'd ever had back in Maine. She had the barn cats, who depended on her—and vice versa, she thought, as she made a mental note to give Jonesy some extra treats for helping her escape from Ken—and she couldn't take either her friends or the cats back to her much smaller property in Maine. She also had at least one enemy here, but O'Connor had almost seemed resigned to the situation when he'd interviewed her this time, rather than bitter and vengeful.

And then there was Charlie. She couldn't take him back to Maine with her, and while he clearly wanted her to stay in West Slocum, he hadn't pressured her. He would wait until she was ready to make a bigger commitment than just attending a wedding together, and she trusted him to accept her decision if she couldn't take that next step.

Rory was going to say *I told you so*, but she had been right that Mabel belonged in West Slocum. At least for the foreseeable future, while she supervised Terry and explored her relationship with Charlie.

It was time to sell her house in Maine and give up on the idea of returning to her old life.

The thought should have been a little scary, since change had always made her anxious. But her new life, at least when no one was trying to kill her, was surprisingly good. She'd come to enjoy living on Skinner Farm and hoped to see the property thrive. It shouldn't be all that difficult, she told herself. She had plenty of support, between her friends, her new farm manager, and Charlie. All she needed to do was stay away from dead bodies.

RECIPES

Cheesecake Bars

2/3 cup butter
2/3 cup brown sugar
2 cups flour
1 cup walnuts
2 cups sugar
16 oz. chevre (or cream cheese or a mix of the two)
2 eggs
4 tablespoons milk
2 tablespoons lemon juice
1 teaspoon vanilla

Crust: Cream butter and sugar. Add flour and mix well before stirring in nuts. It will have a somewhat crumbly texture, like strudel topping. Reserve 1 cup for topping, and press remainder into bottom and sides of greased 9"-x-13" pan. Bake 12 minutes at 350 degrees.

Filling: Cream sugar and cream cheese. Add remaining ingredients and beat well. Spread over the cooked crust. Sprinkle with reserved topping.

Bake 25 minutes at 350 degrees. Cool before cutting into 2" squares. May be made ahead and frozen.

Garlic Scape Pesto

1 cup garlic scapes, cut into 1" pieces
1/2 cup fresh basil leaves
1/3 cup pine nuts
1/2 cup extra-virgin olive oil
1/2 cup grated Parmesan cheese
1/2 teaspoon lemon juice
Salt and pepper, to taste

Scapes are the stems of garlic plants, often removed about a month before the heads are mature. They can often be found in farmers' markets in June. When preparing the scapes, treat them like fresh asparagus, discarding the bulb on top oand any sections that have become old and tough.

Process scapes and basil in a food processor until smooth, about 30 seconds. Add nuts and process until smooth, drizzling in the oil while processing. Fold in the remaining ingredients by hand. Makes 2 cups.

Serve over pasta, spread on French bread, or use as a condiment on burgers. Scapes are only available for a short period each year, but you can freeze the pesto in jelly jars to have it on hand year-round.

Apple Garlic Jelly

4 heads garlic
2 pounds cored and chopped apples (or crabapples); do not peel!
8 cups water
2 cups sugar

1 1/2 tablespoons lemon juice

Remove the outer wrapping of the garlic heads. The individual cloves don't need to be peeled, but they should be separated and crushed.

Combine garlic, apples, and water in a large pan and boil until everything is mushy, about thirty minutes. Pour into a cheesecloth-lined colander and leave it for three hours (or overnight) to drain completely. There should be 8 cups of liquid when finished.

Pour liquid into large, nonreactive pan and bring to a simmer over medium heat. Add sugar half a cup at a time, returning to a simmer after each addition before adding more. Once all the sugar has been incorporated, raise the heat to bring to a full boil. Cook until reduced to 2 cups, about an hour. It won't be a true jelly; more of a honey-like consistency. Remove from heat and stir in lemon juice. Chill before serving. Keep refrigerated up to two months or freeze in jelly jars for longer storage.

May be used as a glaze for pork or chicken, or as Emily uses it for her catering, drizzled on top of chevre (or cream cheese) smeared on savory (not-sweet) crackers.

Printed in the United States
by Baker & Taylor Publisher Services